GOSSIP FROM
THRUSH GREEN

GOSSIP FROM THRUSH GREEN

MISS READ

Illustrated by J. S. Goodall

Houghton Mifflin Company Boston

1982

First American Edition 1982

Library of Congress Cataloging in Publication Data

Read, Miss.
Gossip from Thrush Green.

I. Title.
PR6069.A42G6   1982   823'.914   82-11718
ISBN 0-395-32215-4   AACR2

Printed in the United States of America

V 10 9 8 7 6 5 4 3 2 1

To
Janet
With love and thanks

Contents

1 Afternoon Tea

I N far too many places in England today, the agreeable
habit of taking afternoon tea has vanished.
'Such a shocking waste of time,' says one.

'Much too fattening a meal with all that dreadful starch,'
says another.

'Quite unnecessary, if one has had lunch or proposes to eat
in the evening,' says a third.

All very true, no doubt, but what a lot of innocent pleasure
these strong-minded people are missing! The very ritual of
tea-making, warming the pot, making sure that the water is
just boiling, inhaling the fragrant steam, arranging the
tea-cosy to fit snugly around the precious container, all the
preliminaries lead up to the exquisite pleasure of sipping the
brew from thin porcelain, and helping oneself to hot buttered
scones and strawberry jam, a slice of feather-light sponge
cake or home-made shortbread.

Taking tea is a highly civilised pastime, and fortunately is
still in favour at Thrush Green, where it has been brought to a
fine art. It is common practice in that pleasant village to
invite friends to tea rather than lunch or dinner. As Winnie
Bailey, the doctor's widow, pointed out one day to her old
friend Ella Bembridge, people could set off from their homes
in the light, and return before dark, except for the really
miserable weeks of mid-winter when one would probably
prefer to stay at home anyway.

'Besides,' said Ella, who was fond of her food, 'when else

can you eat home-made gingerbread, all squishy with black treacle? Or dip into the pounds of jam on the larder shelves?'

'I suppose one could make a sponge pudding with jam at the bottom,' replied Winnie thoughtfully, 'but Jenny and I prefer fresh fruit.'

'Jenny looks as though a sponge pudding might do her good,' said Ella, naming Winnie's maid and friend. 'She seems to have lost a lot of weight recently. She's not *dieting*, I hope?'

Winnie profferred the dish of shortbread, and Ella, who was certainly not dieting, took a piece.

'I've noticed it myself,' confessed Winnie. 'I do hope she's not doing too much in the house. As you know, we've offered to look after Tullivers when Frank and Phil are away, and Jeremy will stay with us. So I'm determined that Jenny shall not overwork then.'

Tullivers was the attractive house next door to Winnie Bailey's. Built of the local Cotswold stone, it faced south, standing at right angles to her own home, and their gardens adjoined. Since the death of her doctor husband, Donald, she had been more thankful than ever for her good neighbours, the Hursts.

Frank Hurst was an editor, and his wife Phyllida a freelance writer. They had met when Phil was busy submitting work some years earlier. Her first husband had been killed in a motoring accident, and she had been left to bring up her young son Jeremy with very little money.

This second marriage had turned out to be a very happy one, and the inhabitants of Thrush Green thoroughly approved of the Hursts, who played their part in village life, supplying prizes for raffles, jumble for the many rummage sales, and consenting, with apparent cheerfulness, to sit on at least half a dozen local committees. Jeremy was a happy child, now in Miss Watson's class as Thrush Green village school, and due to start at his new school, in nearby Lulling, next September.

In April, Frank and his wife were off to America where he was to spend six weeks lecturing. It was too long a period to keep Jeremy from school, and Winnie had offered at once to look after him.

'It would give me enormous pleasure,' she assured the Hursts, 'and the boy is never any bother. Just the reverse in fact. It would be such a comfort to have a man about the place again.'

And so it was arranged.

On this particular February afternoon, when Winnie and Ella were enjoying their modest tea-party, the weather was as bleak and dreary as any that that wretched month can produce.

A few brave snowdrops had emerged under the shelter of Winnie's front hedge, and the winter jasmine on the wall still made a gallant show, but the trees remained gaunt and bare, and the prevailing colour everywhere, from heavy clouds above to the misty fields below, was a uniform grey.

'The winters get longer,' commented Ella, craning her neck to look out of the window, 'and the summers shorter. Dimity and Charles don't agree, but I'm going to keep a weather diary next year to prove my point.'

Charles Henstock was the rector of Thrush Green, and had married Dimity, Ella's lifelong friend, a few years earlier. They lived contentedly in the most hideous house on the green, a tall, badly-proportioned Victorian horror, covered in peeling stucco, whose ugliness was made more notice-able by the mellow beauty of the surrounding Cotswold architecture.

Most of the Thrush Green residents were resigned to this

monstrosity, but Edward Young, the local architect, who lived in the most splendid of Thrush Green's houses, always maintained that a glimpse of the Henstocks' rectory gave him acute pains in the stomach. His wife Joan, a cheerful down-to-earth person, dismissed this as quite unnecessary chi-chi, and hoped that he was not going to grow into one of those tiresome people who affect hyper-sensitivity in order to impress others.

This trenchant remark had the effect of restoring Edward's good humour, but he still stuck to his guns and was the first to attack the unknown and long-dead architect of Thrush Green's great mistake.

'Dimity,' went on Ella, 'was wondering if she could persuade Charles to move his study upstairs. It's so cold and dark at the moment, and they could easily turn that little bedroom over the kitchen into a nice snug place for the writing of sermons. Heaven alone knows, there are only about two rooms in that house which get any sun.'

'I gather he doesn't like the idea,' commented Winnie.

'Well, he's not being *too* obstinate, but suggests that they wait until after their holiday.'

'That should put it off nicely,' agreed Winnie, pouring her guest a second cup of Darjeeling tea. 'Now tell me the rest of the news.'

Ella frowned with concentration.

'Dotty is toying with the idea of adopting a little girl.'

Winnie put down the tea pot with a crash.

'She can't be! The way she lives? No adoption society would countenance it!'

Dotty Harmer, an elderly eccentric friend, beloved of both, lived some half a mile away in a dilapidated cottage, surrounded by a garden full of chickens, ducks, geese, goats and any stray animals in need of succour. Indoors lived several cats, kittens, dogs and puppies. Occasionally, a wounded bird convalesced in a large cage in the kitchen, and once an ailing stoat had occupied the hospital accommodation.

'He is rather smelly,' Dotty had admitted, 'but it's handy for giving him scraps when I'm cooking.' Even her closest friends had found hasty excuses for declining invitations to meals whilst the stoat was in residence. At the best of times

Dotty's food was suspect, and a local ailment, known as 'Dotty's Collywobbles' was quite common.

'I don't think Dotty has thought about that side of it. She told me that now that she was getting on it might be a good idea to train someone to take over from her, and look after the animals and the house.'

'The mind boggles,' said Winnie, 'at the thought of dear Dotty training *anyone*.'

'Well, she said it seemed a shame that she had no one to

leave things to when she died, and it really could provide a very nice life for someone.'

'I am shocked to the core,' confessed Winnie. 'But there, we all know Dotty. She's probably forgotten about it by now, and is full of some other hare-brained scheme.'

'Let's hope so,' said Ella beginning to collect her bag and gloves. 'And that reminds me that I must get back to collect my goat's milk from her. She promised to call in about five-thirty with it, and I want her to choose some wool for a scarf. I've dug out my old hand loom, and I warn you now, Winnie dear, that all my friends will be getting a handwoven scarf next Christmas.'

'You are so kind,' said Winnie faintly, trying to remember how many lumpy scratchy scarves, of Ella's making, still remained unworn upstairs. Sometimes she wondered if fragments of heather and thistle remained in the wool. It was impossible to pass them on to the local jumble sales for Ella would soon come across them again in such a small community, and Winnie was too kind-hearted to inflict them upon such distant organisations as Chest and Heart Societies. Their members had quite enough to put up with already, she felt.

'By the way,' said Ella, turning at the front door, 'are you going to Violet's coffee morning? It's in aid of Distressed Gentlefolk.'

'I should think those three Lovelock sisters would qualify for that themselves,' observed Winnie.

'Don't you believe it,' said Ella forthrightly. 'With that treasure house around them? One day they'll be burgled, and then they really will be *distressed*, though no doubt they're well insured. Justin Venables will have seen to that.'

She set off down the wet path, a square stumpy figure, planting her sensible brogues heavily, her handwoven scarf swinging over her ample chest.

Winnie watched her departing figure affectionately.

'Yes, I'll be there,' she called, and closed the door upon the bleak world outside.

The Misses Lovelock, Violet, Ada and Bertha lived in a fine old house in Lulling High Street, less than a mile downhill from Thrush Green.

Here the three maiden ladies had been born at the beginning of the century, and here, presumably, they would one day die, unless some particularly forceful doctor could persuade them to end their days in one of the local hospitals.

They had been left comfortably off by their father, which was as well, as the house was large and needed a great deal of heating and maintenance. Not that they spent much on these last two items, and prudent visitors went warmly clothed when invited to the house, and could not help noticing that walls and woodwork were much in need of fresh paint.

The amount spent on food was even more meagre. The sisters seemed able to survive on thin bread and butter, lettuce when in season, and the occasional egg. Guests were lucky indeed if meat appeared on the table, not that the Lovelocks were vegetarians, but simply because meat was expensive and needed fuel and time to cook it. Most of their friends consumed a substantial sandwich before dining with the Lovelocks, or faced an evening of stomach rumblings whilst sipping weak coffee.

The extraordinary thing was that the house was crammed with valuable furniture, and with glass cabinets stuffed with antique silver and priceless porcelain. All three sisters had an eye for such things, and were shrewd bargainers. They were also quite shameless in asking for any attractive object which caught their eye in other people's houses, and this effrontery had stood them in good stead as a number of exquisite pieces in their collection proved. There were several people in Thrush Green and Lulling who cursed their momentary weakness in giving way to a wheedling Miss Ada or Miss Violet as they fingered some treasure which had taken their fancy.

On this particular afternoon, while Winnie was tidying away the tea things and Ella was unlocking her front door, the three sisters were sorting out an assortment of articles already delivered for the bring and buy stall at the coming coffee morning.

'I wonder,' said Violet pensively, 'if we should buy this in, dear?'

'Buying things in' was another well-known way of acquiring some desirable object. It really meant having first pick, as it were, at the preview, and many a donor had looked in vain for some pretty knick-knack on the stall when one or more of the Misses Lovelock had had a hand in the preparations.

Violet now held up a small silver-plated butter dish in the form of a shell.

Ada scrutinised it shrewdly.

'I think Joan Young sent it. Better not. It's only plate anyway.'

Violet replaced it reluctantly.

'Would you say fifty pence for these dreadful tea-cosies?' asked Bertha.

'Mrs Venables crocheted those,' said Ada reprovingly, 'and you know how her poor hands are crippled with arthritis. At least seventy pence, Bertha, in the circumstances.'

Bertha wrote three tickets for that amount. Ada always knew best.

A circular biscuit tin bearing portraits of King George V and Queen Mary proved to be a treasure chest of buttons, buckles, beads and other trifles.

The three white heads met over the box. Six skinny claws rattled the contents. Six eyes grew bright with desire.

'And who sent this?' enquired Bertha, anxious not to offend again.

'Miss Watson from the school,' replied Violet. She withdrew a long piece of narrow black ribbon studded with jet. 'How pretty this would look as an edging to my black blouse!'

'It would look better as a trimming on my evening bag,' said Bertha. She took hold of the other end.

'Miss Watson,' said Ada dreamily, 'will not be able to come to the coffee morning. These things were left her among a lot of other trifles, she told me, by her aunt in Birmingham.'

'Well, then — ' said Violet.

'In that case — ' said Bertha. Both ladies were a little pink in the face.

'Put it on one side,' said Ada, 'and we'll think about buying it in later. I see there are some charming jet buttons here too. They may have come from the same garment. A pity to part them, don't you think?'

Scrabbling happily, the three sisters continued their search, while outside the lamps came on in the High Street of Lulling, throwing pools of light upon the wet pavements, and the damp figures of those homeward bound.

One of the figures, head bent, and moving slowly towards the hill which led to Thrush Green, was that of St Andrew's Sexton, Albert Piggott, who lived alone in a cottage facing the church and conveniently next door to The Two Pheasants, Thrush Green's only public house.

Albert was always morose, but this evening his gloom was

deeper than ever. Cursed with habitual indigestion which his diet of alcohol, meat pie and pickles did nothing to help, he had just been to collect a packet of pills from Lulling's chemist.

Doctor Lovell of Thrush Green, who had married Joan Young's sister and had served as a junior partner to Donald Bailey, was now the senior partner in the practice, and Albert Piggott was one of his oldest and most persistent patients. It was vain to try to get the irritable old man to change his ways. All that he could do was to vary his prescription now and again in the hope that Albert's tormented digestive tract would respond, at least temporarily, to new treatment.

'Plain bicarb. again, I don't doubt,' muttered Albert, slouching homeward. 'What I really needs is good hot meals.'

He thought wistfully of Nelly's cooking. Nelly, his wife, had left him − twice, to make it worse − and both times to share life with the oilman whose flashy good looks and honeyed words had attracted her on his weekly rounds.

Nelly now lived with her new partner on the south coast, and it was he who now enjoyed her superb steak and kidney puddings, succulent roasts, and well-spiced casseroles. The very thought of that chap's luck brought on Albert's indigestion.

Not that Albert lacked attention. In many ways, he was better off.

Nelly's cooking had tended to be rich, even by normal standards. She excelled with cheese sauces, fried potatoes, and creamy puddings. Her cakes were dark and moist with fruit, her sponge cakes were filled with butter icing, and more icing decorated the top. Doctor Lovell's pleas to her to provide plainer fare for her husband fell on deaf ears. Nelly was an artist. Butter, sugar and the best quality meat and dairy foods were her materials. She cooked, and Albert ate. Doctor Lovell hadn't a chance.

But since Nelly's departure, presumably for good this time, his daughter Molly had done her best to look after the old man.

She was married to a fine young fellow called Ben Curdle, and the couple lived nearby with their little boy George in a flat at the top of the Youngs' house. Ben was employed in Lulling, and Molly helped Joan in the house. The arrangement worked well, for Molly had been known to the Youngs for all their lives. They had rejoiced when Molly had finally succeeded in escaping, through marriage, from the clutches of her selfish old father. Now that she was back in Thrush Green they only hoped that she would not be so kind-hearted as to fall into the trap again.

Molly, wiser than Nelly, cooked with prudence for her father, leaving him light dishes of fish or eggs as recommended by the doctor. More often than not these offerings were given to the cat by Albert, in Molly's absence. He dismissed them as 'pappy stuff' and either went next door for his pie and beer, or used the unwashed frying pan to cook himself another meal of bacon and eggs.

At times Molly despaired. Ben took a realistic attitude to the problem.

'Lord knows he's old enough to know what's good for him. Let him go his own way. Don't upset yourself on his account. He never put himself out for you, did he?'

There was truth in this. Molly had enough to do with looking after Ben and George, and the housework. She loved being back in Thrush Green. The only snag was her obstinate old father. At times she wished that Nelly would return to look after him. Although she disliked her blowsy step-mother, at least Albert's cottage had been kept clean and he had been looked after.

Albert trudged up the hill, the rain slanting into his face from the north. Lights glowed from the cottage windows. A car swished by, splashing the old man's legs.

The bulk of St Andrew's church stood massively against the night sky.

'Best lock up while I'm on me feet,' thought Albert, changing course towards the building. The door was ajar, but no one was inside.

Albert stood in the dark aisle looking towards the three shadowy windows behind the altar. The familiar church smell compounded of damp and brass polish met his nostrils. Somewhere a scuffling and squeaking broke the silence.

'Dratted mice!' exclaimed Albert, kicking a pew end.

Silence fell again.

Albert withdrew, clanging the heavy door behind him. From beneath the door mat he extracted the enormous key. He locked the door, and stuffed the key into his pocket to take across to the house for the night.

Standing in the shelter of the porch he surveyed the view through the rain. His own cottage, directly opposite, was in darkness. The Two Pheasants was not yet open, although he could see the landlord moving about in the bar.

Beside the pub stood the village school, the playground now deserted and swept by gusts of rain. A light was on in the main schoolroom which meant that Betty Bell was busy clearing up the day's mess. There was a light too downstairs in the school house where Miss Watson, the head mistress, and Miss Fogerty, her assistant, were sitting snugly by the fire discussing school matters in the home they shared.

Almost hidden from Albert's view by the angle of the porch was the fine house which stood next door to the school.

Here lived Harold Shoosmith, a bachelor until his sixties, but now newly married, and very content. There were lights upstairs and down, and the porch light too was on.

Albert grunted disapprovingly.

'Waste of electric,' he said aloud. 'Money to burn, no doubt.'

He hauled his large watch from his pocket and squinted at the illuminated dial. Still a quarter of an hour to go before old Jones opened up. Might as well go home and hang up the key, and take a couple of these dratted pills.

Clutching his coat around him, Albert set off through the downpour.

2   Friends and Relations

AN hour or two later, as Albert Piggott sipped his beer
and warmed his legs by the fire at The Two Pheasants,
his daughter Molly tucked up young George, and
then went to the window to look out upon Thrush Green.

Rain spattered the glass. The sash window rattled in its
frame against the onslaught of the wind. The lights of the
pub were reflected in long puddles in the roadway, and the
leafless trees scattered drops as their branches were tossed this
way and that.

It was a beast of a night, thought Molly, but she loved
Thrush Green, whatever the weather. For the first few years
of her marriage she had accompanied Ben on his tour of
towns and villages with the small travelling fair which had
once been owned by his grandmother, the redoubtable Mrs.
Curdle, who had also brought up the boy. She now lay in St
Andrew's churchyard, her grave lovingly tended by her
grandson.

It grieved Ben to part with the famous fair, but it was the
only thing to do. Customs and fashions change. A small
family fair could not compete with bingo halls and television,
and in the end Ben had sold it, and had taken a job with a firm
of agricultural engineers. Molly's happiness was a joy to see,
and Ben was content.

Or was he? Molly pondered upon this question as she gazed
upon the dark wet world. Never by word or sign had he shown

any regret for the life he had given up, but Molly sometimes wondered if he missed the travelling, the change of scene, the renewing of friendships in the towns where the fair rested.

After all, he had known nothing else. His home, as a child, had been the small horse-drawn caravan which now stood, a permanent reminder of Mrs Curdle and that way of life, in the orchard of their present home. He had played his part in the running of the fair, willing to do whatever was necessary at any time of the day or night.

Surely, thought Molly, he must sometimes find his new mode of living irksome. To leave home at the same time, to learn to watch the clock, to put down his tools when a whistle blew and to return to Thrush Green at a regular hour. Did he find it dull? Did he ever hanker for the freedom he once had? Did he feel tied by so much routine? Was he truly happy?

A particularly vicious squall flung a sharp shower against the glass by her face, making the girl recoil.

Well, no point in worrying about it, she told herself. She was lucky to have such a good-tempered husband, and maybe he was just as happy as she was.

She left the window, looked at her sleeping son, and went to cook Ben's supper.

Over the way, at Tullivers, Frank and Phil Hurst also had a problem on that stormy night.

Robert, Frank's son by his first marriage, was farming in Wales. He rarely rang up, and still more rarely wrote a letter, although father and son were fond of each other, and Frank was proud of the way in which the youngster had tackled life in Wales, a tough hill farm and four boisterous children.

'I've got a proposition for you, Dad,' said the cheerful voice on the telephone. 'When do you set off on the lecture trip?'

Frank told him.

'And you'll be away all through May?'

'That's right. Back the first week in June, if all goes well.'

'It's like this. A friend of mine, just married, is coming up to his new job in an estate agent's, somewhere in your area, near Oxford. He's got to be out of his house in April, and I just wondered if you'd feel like letting him have Tullivers for a few weeks.'

'Hasn't he got anywhere to go this end?'

'Their place isn't ready, and won't be until the summer. I wouldn't ask, Dad, if it weren't for the fact he's been good to me in the past, and there's a baby on the way as well. He's a nice chap. Very musical. You'd like him.'

'I can't say yes or no until I've talked it over with Phil. In any case, I'd need some sort of references. And I really don't know if I'd like a stranger in the house – or have any idea what to charge him.'

'Well, he hasn't much cash, that I do know, but he'd want to pay his whack obviously.'

There was silence for a moment, broken at last by Frank.

'I'll have a word with Phil, and ring you tomorrow.'

'Oh good! It would help him enormously if he knew there was somewhere to go when he leaves here. Give him time to look around, and chivvy the workmen your end.'

There was a crackling sound and Frank replaced the receiver.

Phil looked at him enquiringly.

'What's the problem?'

Frank told her.

'I'm not keen on the idea,' she said eventually. 'We don't know him from Adam, and I don't want to have someone here who might turn out to be a nuisance to the neighbours.'

'I should turn it down flat,' agreed Frank 'if it weren't for Robert. He speaks well of him, says he's musical, known him

for some time evidently, and he's been a good friend to him in the past. I must say it is all rather complicated.'

'Well, say we must know more and would like to meet him and his wife,' suggested Phil. 'And if we have any doubts, we harden our hearts.'

And on this sensible note the problem was shelved for twenty-four hours.

The storm blew itself out during the night, and Thrush Green woke to a morning so sweet and pearly that spirits rose at once.

Even Willie Marchant, the gloomy postman, noticed the sunshine as he tacked purposefully on his bicycle back and forth across the hill from Lulling.

'Lovely morning, Willie,' said Ella, meeting him at her gate.

'Ah!' agreed the postman. As usual, a cigarette end was clamped to his lower lip. Was it pulling the skin, or did he essay a rare smile? Ella could not be certain.

The Reverend Charles Henstock met Willie as he returned from early service, and collected his post from him.

'This makes one think of Spring,' commented the rector, sniffing the air appreciatively.

'Long way to go yet,' said Willie, as he pedalled away on his rounds. He was never one to rouse false hopes, and whatever his secret pleasure in the change in the weather, he intended to show his usual dour countenance to those he met.

General optimism greeted him.

Joan Young pointed out the bulbs poking through in her shrubbery. Little Miss Fogerty, who took in the letters at the school house, said that a blackbird had begun to build in the hedge. Harold Shoosmith next door could be heard singing in a fine resonant baritone voice, and his new wife gave Willie such a ravishing smile when she opened the door that he almost forgot himself and smiled back.

The Thrush Green post delivered, Willie set off in a leisurely way along the narrow lane which led westward to Lulling Woods. Once out of sight of Thrush Green eyes, Willie propped his bicycle against a stone wall, put his canvas mail bag on the grass to keep out any dampness, and sat himself upon it, leaning back comfortably in the lee of the wall. Here the sun was warm, a lark soared above him, greeting the morning with the same rapture as his clients, and Willie took out a fresh cigarette.

It was a good spot, Willie admitted, looking at the distant smudge of Lulling Woods against the sky line. Definitely a smell of new grass growing, and that was a fresh mole hill over there, he noted. Tiny buds like beads studded the hawthorn twigs nearby, and an early bemused bumble bee staggered drunkenly at the edge of the track.

Willie blew a cloud of smoke, and stretched luxuriously. Not a bad life, he told himself, especially with the summer ahead. Could do a lot worse than be a postman on a fine morning.

The barking of a dog reminded him of his duties. Dotty Harmer's cottage, a quarter of a mile distant, was his next call. Obviously, she was up and about, as the barking dog proved. No doubt the old girl was feeding the hens and goats and all the rest of the menagerie she kept in that ramshackle place. Nutty as a fruit cake, thought Willie, rising stiffly from the crushed mail bag, but got some guts. You couldn't help liking the old trout, and when you think of what she put up with when her wicked old Dad was alive — well, you had to hand it to her.

Willie himself had been a pupil for a short time under the redoubtable Mr George Harmer, headmaster of Lulling Grammar School. The memory of that martinet, his rigid rules, and ferocious punishment if they were broken, was still fresh in the minds of those who had suffered at his hands, although the old man had lain in the churchyard for many years now, leaving his daughter to enjoy the company of all those animals which had been forbidden whilst he lived.

Good luck to her, thought Willie, clambering on to his bicycle again. She deserved a bit of pleasure in her old age.

As he had guessed, Dotty was in the chicken run. She was trying to throw a rope over a stout bough of the plum tree which leant over the run. For one moment of alarm, Willie wondered if she were contemplating suicide, but Dotty would be the last person to take an easy way out of anything.

'Ah, Willie! How you startled me! I'm having such a job with these Brussels sprouts.'

She pointed to five or six leggy plants which were attached to one end of the rope. All became plain.

'You want 'em hauled up? Give it here,' said Willie. With one deft throw he cast the other end over the plum branch and pulled. Up went the plants.

'How high?' asked Willie, his head level with the dangling sprouts.

Dotty surveyed them, frowning with concentration.

'Not *quite* as high as that, I think, Willie. You see, I want the hens to get some exercise in leaping up to reach the greenstuff. They lead rather a sedentary life, and I'm sure their circulation and general good health would be improved by a little more exercise.'

'Ah,' agreed Willie, lowering the plants a trifle.

'On the other hand,' went on Dotty, 'I don't want them *too low* — '

Willie gave a slight hitch. The plants rose three inches.

'Or, of course, that defeats the object. But I don't want them so high that they lose heart and *don't try* to jump. Or, of course, too high for them to jump in *safety*. I don't want any *injuries*. Hens have funny little ways.'

Not the only ones, thought Willie, patiently lowering and raising the sprouts before Dotty's penetrating gaze.

'Right!' shouted Dotty suddenly, hand raised as if about to stop traffic. 'I think that will do spendidly. What do you think?'

'That's about it, I reckon,' said Willie, tying a knot.

Dotty beamed upon him.

'Most kind of you, Willie dear. Now if you'll just come in the kitchen I'll let you have two letters I wrote last night.'

He followed her towards the back door, stepping over three

kittens who jumped out at him from the currant bushes and dodging a goat which was tethered to a clothes post on the way.

The kitchen was in its usual state of chaos. Willie was quite familiar with its muddle of bowls, saucepans, boxes, string bags, piles of newspapers and a hundred assorted objects overflowing from the table, shelves and chairs. A vast fish kettle, black with age, simmered on the stove, and from it, to Willie's surprise, came quite a pleasant odour of food cooking.

'Now where did I put them?' enquired Dotty, standing stock still among the muddle. 'Somewhere safe, I know.'

She shifted a pile of newspapers hopefully. Willie's eyes raked the dresser.

'They'd be on top, most like,' he suggested, 'seeing as you only wrote them last night.'

'Very astute of you,' said Dotty. She lifted the lid of a vegetable dish on the table, and there were the letters.

'Safe and sound,' said Dotty happily, pressing them into Willie's hand. 'And now I musn't keep you from the Queen's business. A thousand thanks for your help with the hens. I'm sure they will be much invigorated after a few jumping sessions.'

She picked up a slice of cake which was lying on the table beside a small brown puddle of unidentified liquid. Coffee perhaps, thought Willie, or tea? Or worse?

'What about a little snack?' suggested Dotty. 'You could eat it on your way.'

'I'd best not, much as I'd like to,' replied Willie gallantly. 'It'd take the edge off my appetite for breakfast, you see. Thank you all the same.'

'Quite, quite!' said Dotty, dropping it down again. This time it was right in the puddle, Willie noticed.

He escaped before Dotty could offer him anything else, and moved briskly down the path towards his bicycle.

The hens, as far as he could see, were ignoring the sprouts completely. You'd have thought they would have done the decent thing and had a look at them anyway, thought Willie resentfully, after all the trouble they had gone to.

He went on his way, in the golden sunshine, suitably depressed.

Little Miss Fogerty and her headmistress, Miss Watson, were breakfasting in the sunny kitchen of the school house. Each had a boiled egg, one slice of toast, and another of Ryvita and marmalade.

It was their standard breakfast on schooldays, light but nourishing, and leaving no greasy frying pan to be washed. On Saturdays and Sundays, when time was less limited, they occasionally cooked bacon and egg or bacon and tomato, and now and again a kipper apiece.

Dorothy Watson loved her food but had to be careful of gaining too much weight. Agnes Fogerty, who had lived in lodgings nearby for many years, had discovered an equal interest in cooking since coming to live with her friend, and enjoyed watching her eat the dishes which she made. Agnes's weight never varied, whatever she ate, and had remained about eight stone for years.

Miss Fogerty had never been so happy as she was now, living with Dorothy and next door to another old friend, Isobel Shoosmith, who had been at college with her years before. Although she had not realised it at the time, looking back she could see that her life at Mrs White's had been quite lonely. True, she had had a pleasant bed-sitting-room, and Mrs White had cooked for her and always been welcoming, but on some cold summer evenings, sitting in her Lloyd loom armchair by a gas fire, turned low for reasons of economy, Agnes had experienced some bleakness.

It was such a pleasure now to wake each morning in the knowledge that she was near to her friends, and had no need to make a journey, in all weathers, to the school. She was usually down first in the kitchen, happy to see to the kettle and the eggs and toast in readiness for Dorothy, who was still rather slow in her movements since breaking a hip.

It was that accident which had led to Agnes being asked to share the school house, and she looked forward to several years together before retirement age. What happened then, Miss Fogerty sometimes wondered? But time enough when that day loomed nearer, she decided, and meanwhile life was perfect.

Willie Marchant had brought two letters, one from the office obviously and one which looked as though it were from Dorothy's brother Ray. Miss Fogerty sipped her tea whilst her headmistress read her correspondence.

'Ray and Kathleen are proposing to have a week or ten days touring the Cotswolds next month,' she told Agnes, as she stuffed his letter back into the envelope.

'How nice,' said Agnes. 'Are they likely to call here?'

'A call I should like,' said Dorothy, with some emphasis, 'but Ray seems to be inviting himself and Kathleen to stay here for a night or two.'

'Oh!' said Agnes, somewhat taken aback. The school house had only two bedrooms. The one which had once been the spare room she now occupied permanently. Before then, she knew, Ray had sometimes spent the night there on his travels as a commercial salesman. Since Dorothy's accident however things had been a little strained. She had confidently expected to convalesce with her brother and his wife, but they had made no offer, indeed nothing but excuses. If it had not been for Agnes's willingness to help, poor Miss Watson would have been unaided in her weakness. It was quite plain to Miss Fogerty that she had not forgiven or forgotten.

'I could easily make up a bed in the sitting room,' offered Agnes, 'if you would like to have mine. Then they could have the twin beds in your room.'

'It won't be necessary, Agnes dear,' said Dorothy, in the firm tones of a headmistress. 'We are not going to put ourselves out for them. They have quite enough money to afford a hotel. They can try The Fleece if they must come and stay here. Frankly, it won't break my heart if we don't see them at all.'

'Oh Dorothy!' begged gentle little Miss Fogerty, 'don't talk like that! He is your own flesh and blood — your own brother!'

'No fault of mine,' said Dorothy, briskly, rolling up her napkin. 'I didn't choose him, you know, but I do choose my *friends*!'

She glanced at the clock.

'Better clear up, I suppose, or we shall be late for school. I really ought to look out some pictures for my history lesson this morning.'

'Then you go over to school, dear,' said Miss Fogerty, 'and I'll see to the breakfast things.'

'You spoil me,' said Miss Watson, limping towards the door.

And how pleasant it was to have someone to spoil, thought Agnes, running the tap. More often than not she did stay behind to do this little chore, but never did she resent it. Looking after others, children or adults, was little Miss Fogerty's chief source of pleasure.

Miss Watson, making her way carefully across the playground, thought fondly of her assistant. She was the soul of unselfishness, as her ready offer to vacate her bedroom had shown yet again. But Miss Watson was determined that Agnes should now come first. She had been a loyal colleague for many years, respected by parents and children alike, and since the accident had proved a trusted friend and companion.

All that stuff about blood being thicker than water, thought Miss Watson robustly, was a lot of eyewash! She had had more help and affection from dear old Agnes than ever Ray and Kathleen had shown her. It had to be faced, they were a selfish pair, and she had no intention of upsetting Agnes's comfort, or her own, to save them a few pennies.

'You can come and help me to carry some pictures, George dear,' she said to young Curdle who was skipping about the playground. It was by way of being a royal command.

She swept ahead to enter her domain, followed by one of her willing subjects.

3   Jenny Falls Ill

THAT halcyon spell of weather lasted exactly two days, and then bitter winds lashed the area and continued into March.

During this bleak period the problem of letting Tullivers to Robert's friend was resolved. Frank discovered that he knew the young man's father. He and Dick Thomas had worked together on a west country newspaper for some time. He had an idea he had even met this son, Jack, when he was a babe in arms.

Robert had got the local vicar to send a letter to his father vouching for the young man, which Frank found rather touching. Obviously, Robert wanted everything to go smoothly. Frank was impressed too by a letter from Jack Thomas, and by the fact that he had managed to get his land-lord to extend his stay until the end of April, which would mean just one month at Tullivers if Frank were willing to let.

The young couple came to lunch at Tullivers one boister-ous March day and seemed enchanted by all that they saw. They discussed dates and terms, and Frank promised an agreement in writing. He was obviously much taken with them.

Phil was more cautious.

'They seem a sensible pair,' was Frank's comment as the Thomases drove away.

'I hope so,' said Phil. 'She didn't seem to know much about cooking, I thought.'

'Never mind! She'll soon learn,' replied Frank indulgently.

'That's what I'm afraid of! With my kitchen equipment!' retorted Phil. 'Anyway, they both looked clean, and were polite. We forgot to ask him about his music, by the way. Does he play an instrument?'

'A guitar,' said Frank.

'Well, that sounds reasonably quiet,' conceded Phil. 'I shouldn't like dear Winnie and Jenny disturbed with drums and cymbals.'

'Oh, I'm sure they wouldn't be so thoughtless as to upset the neighbours,' said Frank reassuringly, 'but I will mention that when I write.'

'It might be as well,' agreed Phil. 'After all we don't really know them, and they may not realise that most of us go to bed around ten at Thrush Green.'

And so the matter was left.

Across the green, at the rectory, Ella was visiting Charles and Dimity Henstock. The question of the rector's holiday was being discussed, and Dimity, always anxious for the health and happiness of her husband, was doing her best to get him to make a decision.

Ella, forthright as ever, was giving vociferous support.

'Don't be such an fool, Charles. Of course, you need a holiday. Everyone does. You'll come back full of beans, and with some new ideas for sermons.'

Charles looked wounded.

'My dear Ella, you speak as though you hear the same sermon time and time again. I assure you – '

'Oh yes, yes!' said Ella testily, fishing out a battered tobacco tin and beginning to roll herself a cigarette. 'I know it sounded like that, but I didn't mean anything so rude. You manage very well,' she continued kindly.

She licked the cigarette paper noisily.

'And I can truthfully say,' she continued, 'that I have only heard that one about the Good Samaritan three times, and the one about arrogance twice. Mind you, as you well know, I don't go *every* Sunday, but still, it's not a bad record on your part, Charles dear.'

The rector's chubby face was creased with distress, but he remained silent. Dimity flew to his support.

'Those sermons, Ella, were *quite different*. Charles approached the subject from a fresh way each time, and in any case, those themes are universal, and can stand being repeated. But you have a point, dear, about returning refreshed from holiday, and I wish Charles would see it.'

'If it's money you need,' said Ella bluntly, 'I can let you have some.'

'We're quite accustomed to being short of money,' said Charles, with a smile. 'But thank you, Ella, for a kind offer. The difficulty is to find the time.'

'Well, what's wrong with nipping away for a week or so between Easter and Whitsun? I can quite see that you've got to fix a holiday in a slack period. Like farmers.'

'Like farmers?' echoed Charles, bemused.

'They have to go away after hay-making or after harvest, you surely know that? And they usually get married in October when the harvest's in, and they have some corn money for a honeymoon.'

'What a grasp you have of agricultural economy,' commented Charles, 'but now I come to think of it, I do seem to marry young farmers in the autumn.'

'I think Ella's suggestion of a May break is very good,' said Dimity, bringing the subject to heel again. 'Why not write to Edgar? Better still, ring him up one evening. Yorkshire would be lovely then, if he could spare the house.'

Charles looked from one determined woman to the other. He knew when he was beaten.

'I'll do something this week,' he promised. 'In any case, I have neglected Edgar sadly for the last few months. That living of his in Yorkshire keeps him very busy, and I really should be the one who writes. But where do the weeks go, Ella? Do you know?'

'They turn into months far too quickly,' said Ella, 'and that's because we're all getting old and can't pack as much into a month as we used to. I'm sure Edgar will understand. What do you propose to do? To have a straight swap of livings for a week or two?'

'Probably. I must say, we both love the dales, and Edgar and Hilda seem to enjoy the Cotswolds. It's just a case of arranging dates.'

'Which is where I came in,' said Ella, heaving herself to her feet. She ground out her cigarette end in the earth surrounding Dimity's choicest geranium plant on the window sill. Dimity caught her breath in dismay, but, as a true Christian, forbore to comment.

'And of course I'll feed the cat,' continued Ella, making for the door. 'Does she still live on pig's liver?'

'I'm afraid so,' replied Dimity. 'Such dreadful stuff to chop up.'

'No worse than tripe,' said Ella, and vanished.

It was towards the end of March that Winnie Bailey crossed from her house into the surgery which had been her husband's, and was now occupied by John Lovell, the senior partner in the practice, since Donald's death.

He was a quiet conscientious young man who had learnt a

great deal from Winnie's husband, and was liked by his Thrush Green patients.

He glanced up from his papers as Winnie entered, and went to fetch a chair.

'I saw that the waiting room was empty,' said Winnie. 'Are you just off on the rounds?'

'In a few minutes, but no great hurry. Any trouble, Winnie?'

'It's Jenny. She's been off her food for a week or so, and had a horrible cough. But you know Jenny. She won't give up, and says it's nothing. Do come and have a look at her, John dear.'

'I'll come now,' said the young man, picking up his stethoscope. 'There's a particularly vicious flu bug about. It may be that.'

Together they returned to the hall, and thence to the kitchen, where Jenny stood at the sink peeling potatoes. She was unusually pale, John Lovell noticed, but her eyes were inflamed, and her forehead, when he felt it with the palm of his hand, was very hot.

'Sit down,' he directed. Jenny obeyed, but cast an accusing look at Winnie.

'Mrs Bailey,' she croaked. 'There wasn't no need to bother the doctor.'

'Unbutton your blouse,' he directed, arranging his stethoscope, 'and open your mouth.'

Gagged with a thermometer, and immobilised with the stethoscope dabbed here and there on her chest, poor Jenny submitted to a thorough examination.

When it was over John Lovell pronounced sentence.

'Bed for you, and lots to drink. You've a fine old temperature and your lungs are congested.'

'But I'm doing the potatoes!' protested Jenny.

'I can finish those,' said Winnie. 'You must do as Doctor

Lovell tells you. Up you go, and I'll bring you a hot water bottle and some lemon barley water.'

'I'll go back to the surgery,' John told Winnie, 'and let you have some inhalant and pills.'

Jenny departed reluctantly, and Winnie looked at John.

'I don't think it's much more than an infection of the lungs, but it could be the first stage of something catching. I suppose she's had all the childish ailments?'

'I'm not sure. She was brought up in an orphanage, you know, until she came to her foster-parents here. She was about ten or twelve, I think. No doubt she had all the catching things at the orphanage, but I'll find out from her.'

John went to fetch the medicine, and Winnie put on the kettle for Jenny's bottle.

Later, with two pills inside her, a hot bottle at her feet, and the jug of inhalant steaming on the bedside table Jenny tried to remember if and when she had had whooping cough, scarlet fever, measles, chicken pox, and all the other horrid excitements of childhood.

'I can't honestly recall all of them,' she confessed. 'There was always something going the rounds at the orphanage with so many of us. I know I didn't get ringworm,' she added, with some pride.

'Anyway, don't worry,' said Winnie. 'Let me drape this towel over your head, and you get busy with the Friar's Balsam.'

'Is that what it is?' said Jenny, from beneath her tent. 'I thought it was some new mixture of Doctor Lovell's.'

'It's probably got a long and different name,' agreed Winnie, 'but I wouldn't mind betting it's basically dear old Friar's Balsam.'

'Well, *that* can't harm me,' agreed Jenny with relief, and bent to her task.

*

The next day was one of those windy blue and white March beauties when great clouds scudded eastward, and the sunshine lifted everyone's spirits at Thrush Green.

Everyone, except Albert Piggott.

He was wandering morosely round the churchyard, bill-hook in hand. If challenged, he would have said that he was busy cutting away the long grass which grew near the tomb-stones and the surrounding low wall. In fact, he was killing time until ten o'clock when the pub opened.

A small van drew up near him on the other side of the wall, and Percy Hodge, a local farmer, clambered out.

'Ah, Albert!' he began. 'D'you want a little job in the garden?' Occasionally, Albert 'obliged' locally with odd jobs, but latterly he had preferred his leisure to this extra drinking money. Still, Percy was an old friend . . .

'What sort of job?' he enquired cautiously. 'I don't mind telling you, Perce, I ain't the man I was since my operation.'

'Nothing too heavy,' Percy assured him. 'But I've been given a sack of seed potatoes, and I ought to get 'em in. My dear Gertie always put the spuds in. I miss her, that I do.'

Albert was embarrassed to see tears in the eyes of the widower. Mind you, he could sympathise. By and large, wives were kittle-kattle, more trouble than they were worth, but when it came to cooking or gardening they had their uses.

'I suppose I could give you a hand,' said Albert grudg-ingly. 'But I don't reckon I'm up to digging trenches for a hundredweight of spuds.'

'Oh, I'd be with you,' said Percy, blowing his nose, 'and of course there'd be a few for your garden, Albert. Or don't you bother to cook spuds, now your Nelly's gone?'

'Molly does some for me, now and again,' replied Albert,

secretly nettled by this reference to his truant wife. 'I don't go hungry, and that's a fact.'

'Your Nelly was a good cook, that I did know. Same as my dear Gertie. A lovely hand she had with puff pastry. I miss her sorely, you know.'

Albert grunted. Who would have thought old Perce would have been so sorry for himself? Other men had to make do without a wife to look after them. He began to move slowly away from the wall. With Perce at a loose end like this he'd have him there gossiping all day.

'When d'you want me to come up?' he asked, slashing at a dock.

'Tomorrow night suit you? About six, say? Or earlier.'

'Say five,' said Albert. 'Gets dark early still.'

A welcome sound fell upon his ears. It was the landlord of The Two Pheasants opening his doors.

Percy Hodge turned to see what was happening. Albert put down his hook on a handy tombstone and looked more alert than he had since he awoke.

'Come and have a pint, Albert,' invited Percy.

And Albert needed no second bidding.

Hard by, at the village school, little Miss Fogerty was enjoying the exhilarating morning.

The view from the large window of her terrapin classroom in the playground never failed to give her exquisite pleasure. For years she had taught in the north-east-facing infants' room in the old building, and had pined for sunlight.

Now, transposed to this modern addition, she looked across the valley towards Lulling Woods and relished the warmth of the morning sun through her sensible fawn cardigan.

How lucky she was to have such an understanding headmistress, she thought. Headmistress and good friend, she amended. Life had never been so rich as it was now, living at the school house, and teaching in this delightful room.

She glanced at the large wall clock, and returned to her duties. Time for the class lesson on money, she told herself. There was a great deal to be said for the old-fashioned method of teaching the class as a whole, now and again, and some of these young children seemed to find great difficulty in recognising coins of the realm.

She bent to extract a pile of small boxes from the low cupboard. Each contained what Miss Fogerty still thought of as the new decimal money in cardboard. Time was, when she taught for so many years in the old building, that those same tough little boxes held cardboard farthings, halfpennies, pennies, sixpences and shillings. There was still the ancient wall chart, rolled up at the back of the cupboard, which showed:

4 farthings make   1 penny
12 pennies make   1 shilling
20 shillings make   1 pound

Miss Fogerty remembered very clearly how difficult it had been to trace the real coins and cut them out of coloured paper to fix on to the chart. But it had lasted for years, and these children's parents had chanted the table hundreds of times. She felt a pang of nostalgia for times past.

There had been something so solidly *English* about farthings and shillings! And feet and inches, come to that. She hoped that she was progressive enough to face the fact that with the world shrinking so rapidly with all this air travel, and instant communication methods, a common monetary unit was bound to come some day. But really, thought Miss

Fogerty, putting a box briskly on each low table, it seemed so *alien* to be dealing in tens when twelve pence to the shilling still haunted the back of one's mind.

'My granny,' said young Peter in the front row, 'learnt me a new song last night.'

'Taught, dear,' replied Miss Fogerty automatically.

'Called 'Sing a song of sixpence'. Shall I sing it?'

'Later, dear. Now, all sit up straight, and listen to me.'

'What is *sixpence?*' asked Peter.

High time we got on with the lesson, thought Agnes Fogerty, and directed her class to open the boxes.

Next door, Harold Shoosmith and his wife Isobel were admiring some early daffodils in their garden. From the house came the whirr of the vacuum cleaner as Betty Bell, their helper, crashed happily about her work.

'One thing about our Betty,' observed Harold, 'she tackles everything with a will. Lord alone knows how many glasses she's smashed since she's worked here.'

'Not many since I came,' replied Isobel. 'You haven't noticed but I do the glasses now.'

'Ah! That accounts for the fact that I haven't had to buy any more for eighteen months! Marrying you was the best day's work I ever did.'

'Of course it was,' agreed Isobel matter-of-factly. 'How lucky for you that I took you on.'

A window opened above them and Betty's voice hailed them.

'*Telephone!*' she roared.

While Harold was engaged with his caller, Betty caught at her mistress's arm.

'Is it all right if I go a couple of minutes early? Dotty – I mean Miss Harmer – wants me to give her a hand moving out her dresser. Lost some letter or other down the back as ought to be answered today.'

'Of course you can go,' said Isobel. Betty Bell was in great demand, she well knew. Dotty Harmer had employed her long before Isobel, or even Harold when a bachelor, had appeared on the scene. As well as these duties, Betty also kept the village school clean. Isobel was wise enough to recognise that a certain amount of flexibility in Betty's employment was inevitable.

'I must say,' went on Betty, attacking a side table with a flailing duster, 'it's a sight easier working here than at Miss Harmer's. I mean it's clean to start with. And tidy. Always was, even when Mr Shoosmith lived here alone. You don't expect a man to keep himself decent really, let alone a house, but he was always nicely washed and that, and the house always smelt fresh.'

Isobel said gravely that she was pleased to hear it.

'But down Miss Harmer's it's a fair old pig's breakfast, I can tell you. Can't never find nothing, and the dusters is old bloomers of hers like as not. Washed, of course, but you can't get the same gloss on things with 'em like this nice one.'

Isobel felt unequal to coping with this conversation, and said she would go and see to lunch.

An hour later, Betty entered Dotty's kitchen to find her other employer sitting at the cluttered table studying a form.

'Oh, how nice of you to come, Betty! As a matter of fact I managed to reach this wretched letter by inserting a long knitting needle in the crack. It fell down, and I was able to get it by lying on the floor, and wriggling it out with a poker.'

Her wrinkled old face glowed with pride.

'Well, you won't want me then,' said Betty, swatting a fly on the table. 'Filthy things, flies.'

'Oh, do wait while I just fill it in,' said Dotty, 'and perhaps you would be kind enough to post it as you go past the box.'

'Sure I will,' said Betty, lunging with a handy newspaper at another fly. 'You've got some real nasty flies in here.'

'Poor things,' said Miss Harmer, putting down her pen. 'So persecuted. I often wonder if they are as dangerous to health as modern pundits suggest. My grandmother used to sing a charming little song to my baby brother when flies were *quite accepted*.'

She began to sing in a small cracked voice, while Betty watched her with mingled exasperation and amusement.

> Baby bye, there's a fly,
> Let us watch it you and I,
> There it crawls, up the walls,
> Yet it never falls.

I believe with those six legs
You and I could walk on eggs.
There he goes, on his toes,
Tickling baby's nose.

'Well,' said Betty, 'fancy letting it! Downright insanitary!'

Dotty tapped the neglected form with her pen.

'Now, how did it go on?

Round and round, on the ground,
On the ceiling he is found
Catch him? No, let him go,
Do not hurt him so.

Now you see his wings of silk
Dabbling in the baby's milk
Fie, oh fie, you foolish fly!
How will you get dry?

'Did you ever?' exclaimed Betty. 'I mean, flies in the *milk*!'

'Well, it only goes to show how kind-hearted the Victorians were. And really so much more sensible about disease. My brother grew into a splendid specimen of manhood, despite flies.'

Betty looked at the clock.

'Tell you what, Miss Harmer, I'll come back for that form this afternoon. It'll give you time to work it out, and anyway Willie don't collect till five o'clock.'

Besides that, she thought privately, there was her shopping to do, and heaven alone knew when that would get done if she stayed listening to old Dotty.

'Perhaps that would be best,' agreed Dotty, turning again to her task, while Betty made her escape.

4 Dimity Gets Her Way

AS the Hursts' departure for America drew nearer there was much speculation about the temporary residents who were going to stay at Tullivers.

'Well, for your sake, Winnie,' said Ella Bembridge, 'I hope they're a quiet lot. Don't want a posse of hippies, or a commune, or whatever the "in-thing" is.'

'Good heavens,' said Winnie reassuringly, 'Frank and Phil would never let the place to people like that! I have every confidence in their judgement. They both liked the young couple, I know, and Frank knew his father years ago.'

'That's not saying much,' said Ella, lighting a ragged cigarette. 'I know a lot of respectable people of my age with the most *extraordinary* children.'

'Jenny says Phil is putting away her best glass and china, which is only prudent, but she seems quite happy to leave everything else as it is. And if she's content, I don't think we need to worry.'

'And how is our Jenny now?'

'She's still got this wretched cough, but won't stay in bed. She's up in her room now, in her dressing gown, dusting the place. I'm getting John to look at her again today. She's still so flushed, I feel sure she's running a temperature.'

'Will she need to do anything at Tullivers?' asked Ella.

'Phil won't hear of it,' replied Winnie. 'She offered, you know, but now that these young people are coming, they can cope, and I intend to dust and tidy up before they arrive, to save Jenny's efforts.'

'You'll be lucky! You know Jenny. A glutton for work!'

She was about to go when Dimity and Charles entered.

'We did knock,' said the rector, 'but I expect you had something noisy working.'

Winnie looked blank.

'Like the vacuum cleaner, or the fridge, or the washing machine,' enlarged Charles.

'Or the mighty wurlitzer,' added Ella.

'No need to knock anyway,' said Winnie, returning to normal. 'Do sit down. We were just discussing our new neighbours-to-be.'

'I shall call as soon as they have settled in,' said Charles. 'It will be so nice if they turn out to be regular churchgoers.'

'He plays the guitar,' said Ella.

'I trust that does not preclude him from Christian worship,' commented Charles.

'I heard that they met at Oxford, but didn't finish their courses,' contributed Dimity.

'Perhaps they preferred to get out into the world and earn their livings,' was Ella's suggestion. 'Bully for them, I'd say.'

'Well, he's an estate agent now,' said Winnie. 'Or at least, he will be. He's joining a firm somewhere near Bicester, I believe, so Robert said. Frank mentioned it.'

'Dotty intends to supply them with goat's milk,' said Dimity.

'Do they like it?' asked Winnie.

'They will after Dotty's called on them,' forecast Dimity.

'Well, I'm sure they will be very welcome here,' said the rector. 'We must see that they have an enjoyable stay at Thrush Green.'

Later in the day, Doctor Lovell mounted the stairs to see Jenny. She had insisted on dressing, but lay on her bed, trying to read. Her flushed face, and hot forehead, bespoke a high temperature.

'Let's have a look at your chest,' said John Lovell, after studying the thermometer.

Jenny cautiously undid the top button of her blouse.

'I shall need more than that, Jenny,' observed the doctor. 'You needn't be shy with me.'

Jenny undid two more buttons with some reluctance, and John studied the exposed flesh.

'Ever had chicken-pox?'

'I can't remember,' said Jenny. 'We had all sorts up at the orphanage.'

'Well, you've got it now,' said John. 'So no stirring from this bed until I tell you. Keep on with the tablets, and I'll see you have a cooling lotion to dab on the spots.'

'But what about Mrs Bailey?' cried poor Jenny. 'Won't she catch it?'

'If she had any sense,' replied the doctor, 'she caught it years ago, and is immune. Now, into bed with you.'

Jenny's illness made a pleasurable source of discussion at The Two Pheasants that night.

'No joke getting them childish ailments when you're grown up,' said the landlord, twirling a glass cloth inside a tumbler. 'My old uncle caught the measles when he was nigh on seventy, and we all reckoned it carried him off.'

'Affects the eyes, measles does,' agreed Albert Piggott knowledgeably. 'Got to keep the light low, and lay off the reading. I met a chap in hospital when they whipped out my appendix – '

Meaning glances, and a few groans, were exchanged among the regular patrons. Were they going to go through that lot again from old Albert?

'And he'd had measles a few months before and had to have his spectacles changed after that. Proper weak, his eyes was. Watered horrible.'

'Mumps is worse,' contributed Willie Marchant. 'Can upset all your natural functions. Rob you of your manhood, they say.'

'Well, we don't want to hear about it in here,' said the landlord briskly. 'There's two ladies over there, so watch what you're saying.'

Willie Marchant did not appear abashed, and continued.

'But chicken-pox is nasty too. Mixed up with shingles, and that's a real killer, I'm told.'

'Only if it meets round your ribs,' Albert assured him. 'You can have spots all over, but if they meets round your middle you're a goner.'

At this moment, Percy Hodge entered, and was informed of Jenny's illness.

'Poor old girl,' commented Percy, looking genuinely upset. 'I got it when I was about twenty. Got proper fed up with people telling me not to scratch. As though you could stop! Well, she's got my sympathy, that's a fact.'

'One thing,' said one of the regulars, 'she's in the right place. Got the doctor on the premises, as you might say, and you couldn't have anyone better than Mrs Bailey to look after you.'

And with that, all agreed.

The next morning Winnie was surprised to open the front door to Percy Hodge. He was holding a basket with a dozen of the largest, brownest eggs that she had ever encountered.

'Thought Jenny might be able to manage an egg,' said Percy.

'Won't you come in?'

'Well, that's nice of you. How is she?' he asked, following Winnie down the hall and into the kitchen.

'She seems a little easier now that the rash has come out,' replied Winnie, unpacking the basket and placing the superb eggs carefully in a blue and white basin. 'Percy, I've never seen such beauties as these! I shall take them upstairs to show her later on. I'm sure she will be so grateful. What a kind thought of yours.'

Percy suddenly looked shy.

'Well, I've known Jenny since we was at Sunday School together. She's a good girl. I was sorry to hear she was poorly. Give her my regards, won't you?'

He accepted the empty basket, and retraced his steps to the front door.

'Of course, I will,' promised Winnie, and watched Percy cross the green towards the lane leading to his farm.

What a very kind gesture, thought Winnie, toiling up-stairs with the eggs, and Percy's message, for the invalid.

She suddenly remembered that Percy was a recent widower. Could it be. . . ?

But no, she chided herself, of course not. She must not put two and two together and make five.

'Just look what someone's sent you,' she said to the in-valid, holding out the blue and white bowl.

'Good heavens!' cried Jenny. 'We'd best have an omelette for lunch!'

It was a sparkling April morning when the Hursts drove off from Tullivers to Heathrow.

Harold Shoosmith had offered to drive them there, and Jeremy and Winnie Bailey accompanied them in the car to see them off.

Much to everyone's relief, Jeremy was cheerful and excited. Winnie Bailey was quite prepared to cope with some tears at parting, but was pleasantly surprised when the final kisses were exchanged without too much emotion all round.

'Not very long before we're back,' promised Phil, producing a small parcel for her son. 'Don't open it until you get back to Aunt Winnie's, darling.'

Jeremy waved vigorously to his departing parents and was quite willing to return to Harold's car, clutching the present.

It had been arranged beforehand that there would be no waiting about at the airport to see the aeroplane leave the ground.

'Lord knows how long it will be before we finally get away,' Frank had said to Winne. 'You know it is these days: "Regret to say there is a mechanical fault". That's a two-hour job while they solder on the wing. Then the tannoy goes again: "Regret there is an electical fault", and off you go for your forty-third cup of coffee while they unravel the wires for another hour. No, Winnie dear, you and Harold make tracks back to Trush Green with the boy, and then we shall be able to ring you to ask if you mind fetching us back until the next day.'

Luckily, Frank's prognostications were proved wrong, and their flight actually departed on the right day, and only a quarter of an hour behind schedule.

'What do you think it can be?' asked Jeremy shaking the parcel vigorously, when they were on their return journey. 'It doesn't rattle.'

'Try smelling it,' suggested Harold. 'Might be bath cubes.'

'*Bath cubes?*' said Jeremy with disgust. 'Why *bath cubes?*'

'Right shaped box. Long and thin.'

'It might be sweets,' said Winnie. 'Some rather gorgeous nougat comes in boxes that shape.'

Jeremy's small fingers pressed round the edge of the wrapping paper.

'Anyway, I'm not to open it until we get home,' he said at last, 'so put your foot down, Uncle Harold. I'm *busting* to see what's inside.'

He sat in the front passenger seat, parcel held against his stomach and babbled happily to Harold about car engines, motor boats, his kitten, what Miss Fogerty said about tadpoles and a host of other interesting topics upon which Harold commented briefly as he drove.

In the back, Winnie Bailey, much relieved at the good spirits of her charge, dozed gently, and did not wake until the car stopped at Thrush Green.

'Now I can open it, can't I?' begged Jeremy.

'Of course,' said Winnie and Harold together.

The child ripped away the paper, and disclosed a long red box. Inside, lying upon a cream velvet bed lay a beautiful wrist watch.

Jeremy's eyes opened wide with amazement.

'Look!' he whispered. 'And it's mine! Shall I put it on?'

'Why not?' replied Harold.

He helped the child to slide the expanding bracelet over his wrist. The three sat in silence while the child savoured his good fortune.

At length, he gave a great sigh of supreme satisfaction.

'I can't believe it's really mine,' he said, to Winnie. 'I'm so glad I've had chicken pox.'

'Chicken pox?' said Winnie, bemused.

'I can go straight up to Jenny and show her,' said the boy, getting out of the car, and making for the Baileys' gate without a backward glance.

'I must thank you on behalf of us both,' said Winnie to Harold with a smile.

*

Over at the rectory Charles and Dimity were poring over a letter from their old friend Edgar. There was nothing that he and Hilda would enjoy more than two weeks at Thrush Green in the near future.

He had already made tentative arrangements with obliging neighbouring clergymen who would undertake his duties while he was away, so that Charles and Dimity would be quite free. He suggested the first two weeks in May, with Easter behind them and Whitsun well ahead.

Charles thought of Ella's remark about farmers taking their break between haytime and harvest. How well it would fit in, these two weeks between the great church festivals!

'I must get in touch with Anthony Bull at Lulling, and see if dear old Jocelyn feels up to coming out of retirement at Nidden,' he told Dimity, naming the Lulling vicar, and a saintly eighty-year-old who occasionally held the fort for local clergymen in times of emergency.

'Of course they'll help,' said Dimity, 'and they know full well that you will be happy to do the same for them at any time.'

'I'll go and see them both today,' replied Charles, 'and we'll ring Edgar about tea time.'

'Make it after six, dear,' said Dimity. 'Yorkshire is a long way off, and the phone call will be so much cheaper.'

'How right you are,' agreed the rector. With his modest stipend, it was a blessing to have Dimity to remind him of the need for frugality.

He looked round his study when his wife had departed to the kitchen. Since his marriage, Dimity had done her best to mitigate the austerity of this sunless room where so much of his work was done.

She had put a rug down by the desk, to keep his feet from the inhospitable cold linoleum which covered the floor of the room. She had bought some shabby but thick curtains from a village jumble sale, to take the place of the cotton ones which had draped the study windows ever since he had taken up residence years ago.

There was always a small vase of flowers on the side table, at the moment complete with pheasant's eye narcissi and sprigs of young greenery from the garden. An electric fire had been installed, and although Charles himself never thought to switch it on, used as he was to a monastic chill in the room, Dimity would tiptoe in and rectify matters on icy mornings.

He was a fortunate man, he told himself, to have such a wonderfully unselfish wife, and one who had the gift of making a home in the straitened circumstances in which they lived.

He thought of her suggestion about transferring his things from his present room to the upstairs one above the kitchen. Frankly, he disliked the idea. The very thought of carrying all his books up the steep stairs, of getting new shelves built, of sorting out his archaic filing system, and of asking someone to help him to manhandle his desk and armchair and all the other heavy furniture which was needed in his work, appalled him.

And yet Dimity was quite right, of course. That room was certainly much lighter and warmer. They would not need the electric fire as they did here. In the end, he supposed, they would save money. But what an upheaval! Could he face it?

He looked again at the results of Dimity's labours on his behalf. How it would please her to have him safely ensconced in that pleasant back room! Surely, it was the least that one could do, to give way to one who was so unselfish and loving!

Charles leapt to his feet on impulse, and traversed the dark wind tunnel of a corridor to find Dimity in the comparative warmth of the kitchen at its end.

'My dear,' he cried, 'I've decided that your idea of moving the study upstairs is a wonderful one! As soon as we get back from Yorkshire we'll transfer everything, and meanwhile I'll think of someone to ask to make some shelves while we're away.'

Dimity left the onion she was chopping on the draining board and came to hug her husband.

'What a relief, Charles dear! It will be so much better for you, I know. You really are a good man.'

Her face was radiant.

'I ought to be a lot better,' replied Charles. 'One can only go on trying, I suppose.'

That afternoon, when Charles had mounted his bicycle to go down the hill to Lulling to visit the vicar, Dimity went across the road to see Ella at the cottage which she had shared for many years with her redoubtable friend.

She found her threading her ancient handloom on the table in the sitting room window.

'Hello, Dim,' she greeted her friend. 'Look at this for organisation! I'm getting ahead with my scarves for Christmas. Any particular colour you fancy?'

Dimity swiftly went over the plentiful supply of Ella's scarves which were already stocked in a drawer. Pink, fawn, yellow, grey — now, what *hadn't* she got?

'I think a pale blue would be lovely,' she said bravely. 'It goes with so many colours, doesn't it? Thank you, Ella.'

She sat herself on the well-worn sofa, and watched Ella's hands moving deftly at her task.

'I've brought some good news,' she began.

'Won the pools?'

'Alas, no. But Charles has agreed to move his study upstairs.'

'Well, it's about time too. I wonder he hasn't had double pneumonia working in that morgue of his. Want a hand shifting stuff?'

'Well, not at the moment, Ella dear. But perhaps later. We don't propose to do anything until we come back from our holiday.'

'Tell me more,' demanded Ella.

Dimity explained about Edgar and Hilda, and the hoped-for help of Lulling's vicar and old Jocelyn.

'Thrush Green will be empty for most of May then,' said Ella. 'What with the Hursts away, and you two gallivanting in Yorkshire.'

'Oh come!' protested Dimity, 'that's only four of us. And in any case, the new couple will be at Tullivers then. Think how nice it will be to have some fresh faces here.'

'Depends on the faces,' replied Ella. 'Frankly, I prefer old friends. For all we know, these two outsiders are going to cause more trouble than Thrush Green bargains for.'

And as it happened, Ella was to be proved right.

5   The Henstocks Set Off

THE last day of April closed in golden tranquillity. Warm and calm, from dawn until sunset, there had been promise of the summer to come.

The daffodils and early blossom in the Thrush Green gardens scarcely stirred all day, and the bees were already busy, their legs powdered with yellow pollen.

Joan Young, wandering about their small orchard, thought that she had never seen such drifts of daffodils there before. They surged around the wheels of Mrs Curdle's ancient caravan, and she remembered, with a sudden pang, that this would be the first year without Curdles' Fair to enliven May the first.

What must Ben be thinking? He never mentioned the fair in her presence, but she knew that Molly wondered if he grieved over the loss.

For that matter, all Thrush Green mourned the passing of their much-loved fair. Now old Mrs Curdle lay at rest across the green she knew so well, and this reminded Joan of something else.

She returned to the house and called upstairs to Molly.

'Help yourself to daffodils. There are masses just now, and if Ben wants some for his mother's grave, tell him to pick all he wants.'

Later that evening she saw Ben carrying a fine bouquet across to the courtyard. He had paid his tribute to his grandmother every May day since the old lady's death, and

Joan liked to think that his loyal affection was shared by all Mrs Curdle's friends at Thrush Green.

Much to the consternation of everyone, the question of Dotty adopting a child cropped up once more.

She broached the subject herself one morning when she called at the rectory.

'You know it's weeks now since I wrote to four or five reputable adoption societies, and still no result. Isn't it dilatory? Here I am, hale and hearty, and all prepared to share a good home with some child in need — male or female — and all I've had have been acknowledgements of my letters.'

'But, Dotty dear,' began Dimity, 'these things always take time.'

Charles, more bravely, spoke his mind.

'I think you should reconsider the whole question of adoption, Dotty. You may be hale and hearty, but you are getting on, and I don't think any adoption society would allow a child to settle with you. And naturally, a home that can offer *two* parents is going to be preferred.'

Dotty snorted impatiently.

'I have filled in a form or two, come to think of it, and of course I had to put my age and status on them. And a rather strange fellow came to see me.'

That, thought Dimity, would be enough to put anyone off. Dotty's kitchen alone would strike horror into the heart of anyone trying to find a home for a stray cat, let alone a young human being.

'Are you sure he was from one of the societies?' asked Charles. 'Some very odd people call at houses these days to see if they are worth burgling later.'

Dotty dismissed this alarmist suggestion.

'Oh, he showed me some papers and a card which guaranteed his claims. I rather forget which society he represented, but I gave him a cup of coffee. He left most of it,' she added. 'Rather a waste of Dulcie's good goat's milk, I thought, but dear old Flossie finished it up when he had gone.'

She patted the cocker spaniel at her feet with affection. Flossie's tail thumped appreciatively on the rectory floor.

'I feel obliged to say this,' said Charles. 'I am positive that this idea of yours – though well-meant, and typical of your generosity, Dotty my dear – is quite wrong, and I can't help feeling that no adoption society would find you a suitable person to bring up a child.'

'And why not?' demanded Dotty, turning pink with wrath. 'I should put the child's interest first every time. There is plenty of room in my cottage, and all those lovely animals to enjoy. And of course I intend to leave my possessions, such as they are, to the child when I die.'

The kind rector sighed, but stuck to his guns. As Dimity, and all his parishioners knew well, his gentle manner cloaked an inflexible will when it came to doing his duty.

'Give up the idea, Dotty. Why not invite a younger relative or friend to share the cottage and to help you with your charges. What about Connie? You enjoy her company.'

Connie was Dotty's niece, a cheerful single woman in her forties, who lived some sixty miles west of Thrush Green and occasionally called on her aunt.

'Connie has quite enough to do with her own small-holding,' replied Dotty. 'And now she has taken up breeding Shetland ponies, and could not possibly find time to move in with me – even if she had the inclination.'

She reflected for a moment.

'Of course, if I could buy that small paddock of Percy Hodge's, there might be an incentive for Connie to bring the ponies there. I must say I should enjoy their company.'

'And Connie's too, I trust.'

Dotty shrugged her thin shoulders.

'Oh, Connie's quite a reasonable gel. David brought her up very sensibly without too much money to spend, but I don't want *Connie*. And I'm quite sure Connie doesn't want *me*!'

She rose to her feet, hitched up her wrinkled stockings, and set off for the door, followed by the faithful Flossie.

'I'm quite sure all your advice is for the best, Charles,' she told him. 'But I know what I want, and I don't intend to give up my plans just yet. Have a good holiday in Yorkshire. I shall call on Edgar and Hilda when they have settled in, and bring them a goat's cheese which is already maturing nicely in the larder.'

And on this gruesome note she left them.

The possibility of some poor unfortunate child finding itself adopted by Dotty was an absorbing topic of conversation for the residents of Thrush Green and Lulling.

All agreed that the idea was typical of Dotty – generous but outrageous. However, the general feeling was summed up by Willie Bond, Willie Marchant's fellow postman.

'No one in his right mind's going to let the old girl have a child living in that pig sty. Stands to reason, these adoption people know what they're up to. She doesn't stand a snowball's chance in Hades.'

It gave his listeners some comfort.

Equally absorbing was the strange behaviour of Percy Hodge during the indisposition of Winnie Bailey's Jenny.

The present of eggs was followed by some lamb chops, a box of soap, a large tray of pansy seedlings which Winnie felt obliged to bed out in pouring rain, and several bunches of flowers.

Jenny was bewildered by these attentions, and somewhat scornful.

'What will people think? Silly old man! Making me look a fool.'

'Not at all,' replied Winnie. 'It's most thoughtful of him. I'm sure it's all done in a purely friendly spirit.'

'Well, I'm not so sure he isn't missing his Gertie's cooking,' said Jenny bluntly. 'Looking around for a housekeeper, I'd say. I'm half a mind to snub him soundly, cheeky old thing! As if I'd ever leave you!'

'Don't worry about it,' begged Winnie. 'Just accept the situation, and be polite to him. Time enough to worry if he pops the question.'

But despite her calm exterior, Winnie herself was a little perturbed. Jenny, she suspected, had summed up the position very neatly. If, of course, her feelings changed, marriage to Percy might be a very good thing for dear unselfish Jenny. He was a kindly fellow, affectionate and thoughtful. He had a sizeable farm and a pleasantly situated farmhouse which Jenny would enjoy cherishing. No, thought Winnie, of course she would not stand in Jenny's way if that was what she wanted one day in the future, but how she would miss her if that situation arose!

Comment at The Two Pheasants was less polite.

'No fool like an old fool,' quoted one of the customers.

'You'd think old Perce would count his blessings being a peaceful old widower,' said another sourly. It was well-known that his own marriage was fraught with acidity, acrimony and the results of too much alcohol.

Albert Piggott grunted his agreement. He knew about wives too.

'Not that Jenny wouldn't do well for herself,' he conceded. 'Percy's a warm man. Got a bit in the building society, and

some in the post office. He told me so himself one day. And
then his Gertie was a rare one for managing. I bet she left a
nice little nest-egg. No, if Jenny's got any sense she could do
worse than plump for old Percy.'

'What Jenny does is one thing,' announced the local
dustman, pushing across his glass for a refill. 'What I hates to
see is a chap of Percy's age making sheeps' eyes at a gal. Looks
a right fool he does, mincin' along with a ruddy bunch of
flowers in his hand. Don't seem to care what people say,
neither. I told him straight: "You be a bigger fool than you
look, Perce Hodge, and that's sayin' something!" But he only
smirked. Hopeless, that's what he is! Absolutely hopeless!'

'Ah! He's got it bad,' agreed Mr Jones, the landlord. 'But
there, that's love. Takes you unawares like. Now drink up,
please gentlemen! You can all see the clock!'

And the affair of Percy and Jenny had to be discussed later
in the night air of Thrush Green.

Jeremy, naturally, was an interested observer of Percy's attentions, and frequently enquired about them.

Winnie did her best to evade his questions, but he was a
persistent young man, and sometimes caught her off guard.

'What will you do if Jenny goes to live at the farm?' he
asked one evening, looking up from an ancient jigsaw puzzle
which Winnie had unearthed for his pleasure.

'I don't suppose she will go,' answered Winnie equably.
'Jenny seems very happy here.'

'But it may be the last chance she gets of getting married,'
pursued Jeremy. 'I mean, she's quite *old*. Do you think she'll
have any babies?'

'Was that the door bell?' asked Winnie, playing for time.

'No. You see, you have to be pretty young to have babies.
Paul told me all about having them last holiday.'

He searched among the box of pieces and held up a bit of blue sky triumphantly.

And how much, wondered Winnie, did Paul Young impart to his friend of this particular subject? And had Phil been informed?

'Do you think Jenny knows about babies?'

'I'm quite sure she does,' said Winnie hastily.

'Well, it all sounded pretty odd to me when Paul told me, but I was jolly glad to know what that button in your stomach was for at last.'

'Really?' said Winnie, much intrigued.

'Didn't you know? It blows up like a balloon, and when it pops, a baby is there.'

'Indeed?' observed Winnie politely.

'I'm surprised you didn't know,' said Jeremy severely. 'I should have thought Uncle Donald would have told you, him being a doctor. He must have seen it happen.'

'Probably,' said Winnie, 'but he was always very careful not to discuss his patients with me.'

'Ah! That's it, of course! But you will let Jenny know what happens, won't you? She might not be sure.'

'I am positive that Jenny knows all that is necessary,' said Winnie, 'and in any case, arrangements between Mr Hodge and Jenny are entirely their affair. It's something we should not discuss.'

Jeremy looked at her in mild surprise.

'But *everyone*, absolutely *everyone* is talking about it in Thrush Green!' he told her.

And that, thought Winnie, could well be believed.

'Time for supper,' she said briskly, and made her escape to the kitchen.

The day of the Henstocks' departure for Yorkshire dawned

bright and windy. Great clouds scudded across the sky before
an exhilarating south-wester.

Dimity and Charles packed their luggage into the car in
high spirits. The ancient Ford had been polished the day
before, and gleamed with unusual splendour.

Before they set off, Dimity called at Ella's to give her the
key and a number of agitated last-minute directions.

'There are six tins of evaporated milk in the larder, for the
cat, but there is one opened in the fridge which should be
finished up. And there's *plenty* of pig's liver in the freezer, Ella
dear, if you don't mind taking out a *small* packet the night
before you need it. I've left scissors as well as a knife and fork
with her plates, and perhaps — '

'My dear Dim,' said Ella, 'calm down! I know where
everything is, and that cat won't starve, believe me. Now,
you two go and have a real break, and forget all the duties
here. They'll be waiting for you when you get back — you
know that.'

'We really will relax,' promised Dimity. 'You can't imagine how we've been looking forward to it. You know the
house will be empty until Wednesday? Hilda and Edgar are
breaking their journey at Coventry to see a cousin in
hospital.'

'I'll keep my eye on things,' Ella assured her, ushering her
firmly down the garden path. 'Now off you go, and I'll see
you the minute you get back. Have a lovely time.'

She watched Dimity flutter across the road and enter the
gloomy portal of the Victorian rectory, then turned back to
tackle the daily crossword.

'Poor old Dim,' she said aloud, as she searched for a pencil.
'Do her a world of good to see the back of that dreary house.'

She little thought that her words would prove to be a
prophecy.

*

The bright breezy weather continued in the early days of May, much to the satisfaction of Thrush Green gardeners, zealous housewives who rushed to wash blankets, and Miss Fogerty and Miss Watson who had the inestimable relief of seeing their charges running off steam in the open air at playtimes.

'I think I really must find some new toys for the wet day cupboard,' observed Agnes to her headmistress. They were enjoying their morning coffee in Agnes's new classroom, and the infant mistress was surveying a pile of torn comics and incomplete jig-saw puzzles which were due to be deposited in the dustbin.

'They've done very well,' conceded Miss Watson, scrutinizing the top comic. 'I see this one is dated 1965. Pity dear old "Rainbow" is now defunct. Did you have it as a child, Agnes?'

'Alas, no! My father thought comics an unnecessary in-dulgence, but I sometimes saw "Rainbow" at a little friend's house. I particularly enjoyed Marzipan the Magician, and a little girl with two dogs.'

'Bluebell,' said Miss Watson. 'At least, I think it was. It's some time since I read the paper, but how I *loved* Mrs Bruin! I wonder why she always wore a white cap, and that same frock with a poached-egg pattern?'

'Easy to draw, perhaps,' suggested Agnes practically. 'Do you think I could transfer some of the boxes of beads to the wet-day box?'

'An excellent idea,' said Miss Watson. 'And remind me to look out some old "Geographical" magazines when we go home. Plenty there to amuse them. Such beautiful pictures — and if you like they could cut some out and start scrap books.'

'That's most generous of you,' said little Miss Fogerty, pink with pleasure at the thought of such riches. With such small joys are good infants' teachers made happy, which may explain why so many remain ever youthful.

Later that evening, Miss Watson routed out the magazines from the landing cupboard, and the two ladies were busy leafing through them when the telephone rang.

Miss Watson retired to the hall and was there for some time. Agnes was just wondering whether a splendid picture of an African family wearing only long ear-rings and a spike through the nose was quite suitable for her infants, when her headmistress returned. She was breathing rather heavily.

'That was Ray,' she said. 'They are just about to set off on this Cotswold tour they had to postpone because of that wretched dog of theirs.'

'Is it better?' asked Agnes.

'Unfortunately, yes! They propose to bring it with them —

which I consider a mistake, and told Ray so — but, as you know, they are quite besotted with the animal and fear that it might pine in kennels.'

'Won't it be difficult to find hotels willing to take a labrador? I mean, it's such a large dog.'

'It is indeed, and this one is completely untrained, as you know. That is why Ray asked if they could stay here for two or three nights.'

'Oh! Can we manage?'

'We *cannot*!' said Dorothy Watson firmly. 'I told him so last time he mooted the question, and I suppose he thinks that I may have changed my mind. Well, I haven't. I have invited them to tea on the day they arrive in Lulling, and the dog can stay in the car while they eat it.'

'But, Dorothy, it may be a cold afternoon,' pleaded Agnes. 'Perhaps it could stay in the kitchen?'

'Well, we'll see,' said Dorothy, relenting a little, in the face of her friend's agitation. 'But I make no rash promises.'

And with that little Miss Fogerty had to be content.

She spent the night comforting herself with the thought that dear Dorothy's bark was always worse than her bite, and with another thought, equally cheering, that blood was thicker than water, and even if The Fleece forbade animals, The Fuchsia Bush always allowed pets to accompany their owners at lunch or tea.

The last of Agnes Fogerty's hopes was somewhat dashed the next morning by Willie Bond, the fat postman who shared the Thrush Green post round with gaunt Willie Marchant.

'Heard the latest?' he enquired, passing over three manilla envelopes obviously from the Education Office, and a post-card from America which, no doubt, was from the Hursts.

'No, Willie. What is it?'

Agnes could hear the kettle boiling, and was anxious to return to her duties.

'They say the old Fuchsia Bush is packing up.'

'Never!' gasped Agnes. 'I can't believe it! It always seems so busy.'

'Well, there it is. Can't make it pay, seemingly, and them girls wants the earth for wages, no doubt, so it'll have to put up its shutters.'

'We shall all miss it,' said Agnes.

'Your kettle's boiling from the sound of things,' said Willie, making slowly for the gate. 'Be all over the floor by the time you gets there.'

'Yes, of course, of course!'

Agnes hurried down the hall and met Dorothy entering the kitchen. She told her the dread news.

Miss Watson took the blow with her usual calm demeanour.

'I've no doubt that story is greatly exaggerated, Agnes, and I shan't waste my time believing it until I have heard officially. Willie Bond was always a scaremonger, and I remember that he was always given to tall tales, even as a child.'

'But I wonder how he came by the story?' wondered Agnes, tapping her boiled egg.

'Time alone will tell,' responded her headmistress. 'Could you pass the butter, dear?'

6 A Turbulent Tea Party

AS Miss Watson had surmised, Willie Bond's tidings were grossly exaggerated, although, even in the modified version, the truth was quite upsetting enough to the inhabitants of Lulling and Thrush Green.

The Fuchsia Bush, it seemed, was going to be open from 10 a.m. until 2.30 p.m., catering as usual for exhausted shoppers needing morning coffee, and local businessmen and women needing a modest lunch. The premises would then close until 6.30 p.m. when it would offer dinner to those who required it. The time-honoured afternoon tea was now a thing of the past, and regret and acrimony were widely expressed.

'Never heard such nonsense,' said Ella Bembridge to Winnie Bailey. 'The Fuchsia Bush was always busiest at tea time, and they've got that marvellous girl in the kitchen who knocks up the best scones in the Cotswolds. Why, those alone bring in dozens of travellers between four and five every afternoon.'

'They say it's a staffing problem,' replied Winnie. 'Evidently they can get part-timers to come in the morning and to cope with the lunches, and more to appear in the evenings when the husbands are home to look after the children.'

'Well, it's a scandal,' replied Ella, blowing out a cloud of acrid smoke. 'It was just the place to meet after shopping or the dentist, and I must say their Darjeeling tea took some beating. As for trying to compete with The Fleece and The

Crown and Anchor for dinners, it's plain idiotic.'

'Well, Jenny tells me that she knows two women who are going to do the evening stint there, and everyone feels it might work, so we must just wait and see.'

Miss Watson, proved right yet again, was inclined to be indulgent about the lost tea time at The Fuchsia Bush. In any case, teachers were usually buttoning children's coats, and exhorting them to keep out of trouble on their homeward journeys, at the relevant opening time. As she remarked to little Miss Fogerty:

'It won't affect us greatly, dear, but I think it is very foolish of these tea shops to close at such a time. American tourists alone must miss experiencing a truly English tea with attentive waitresses in those pretty flowered smocks to serve them.'

Miss Fogerty, whose purse had seldom allowed her to indulge in even such a modest repast as tea at The Fuchsia Bush, agreed wholeheartedly. She disliked change.

The Misses Lovelock, whose Georgian house stood close to the premises, were the only ones who seemed to favour the project.

'We shall have a little peace on summer afternoons now,' said Bertha. 'Why, I've even seen coaches stop there and drop *hordes* of people – some of them *not* quite out of the top drawer – and of course quite a few wandered about while they waited to go in, and one day a most dreadful man, with a squint, pressed his face to our window and very much frightened us all.'

'Good job it was downstairs,' Ella had remarked. 'Upstairs you might have been in your corsets, or less.'

Bertha chose to ignore such coarseness. Really, at times one wondered about Ella's upbringing!

'No,' said Violet, hastening to Bertha's support, 'we shan't

mind The Fuchsia Bush closing for teas, whatever the rest of
Lulling is saying.'

'You'll just get the racket later in the day,' observed Ella,
stubbing out a cigarette in a priceless Meissen bon-bon dish
at her side. 'Be plenty of cars parking, I expect, when they
open in the evening.'

And, happy to have the last word for once, Ella departed.

The visit of Miss Watson's brother Ray and his wife occurred
about this time. Although little Miss Fogerty was glad to see
that Dorothy's sisterly feelings had prompted her to invite
Ray and Kathleen to tea after school, nevertheless she had
inner forebodings about their reception.

There was no doubt about it. The unfortunate coolness
which had arisen dated from Dorothy's enforced stay in
hospital with a broken hip some time before. Agnes, who had

been a devoted visitor, realised that Dorothy's assumption that she would be invited to convalesce at Ray's was misplaced, to say the least of it. Luckily, she had been in a position to offer immediate help, and took up residence at the school house to look after the invalid. Dorothy, ever grateful, had reciprocated by asking her old colleague to make her stay a permanent one, and very happily the arrangement had turned out.

But Ray and Kathleen would never, it seemed, be quite as dear to her headmistress. Agnes could only hope that the proposed tea party would pass off pleasantly, and that bygones would remain bygones.

It was a perfect early May afternoon. Agnes had taken her little brood for a walk along the track to Lulling Woods, passing Dotty Harmer's house, and waving to that lady as she tended a large and smoky bonfire of garden rubbish near the hedge.

The grass was dry enough for the children to sit on before they returned, and Agnes leant back against a dry stone wall out of the light wind and admired some early coltsfoot across the track, and some young ferns, curled like sea horses, against the Cotswold stone. The children seemed content to lie on their backs, chewing grass, and gazing at the sky above. It was a well-known fact that little Miss Fogerty had the happy knack of keeping children quiet and contented. The present scene would have proved this to any onlooker.

Agnes allowed her mind to dwell on the approaching confrontation. Dorothy had made a superb three-tier sponge cake, using five eggs and the best butter, and Agnes herself had cut cucumber sandwiches during the lunch break, and carefully wrapped them to keep fresh. Home-made scones with plum jam, and some delicious chocolate biscuits filled with marshmallow completed the meal provided. It was particularly unselfish of dear Dorothy to add the last ingredient to their afternoon tea, thought Agnes, as she adored marshmallows but was obliged to resist such temptation in the interest of watching her weight.

Agnes looked at her watch.

'Time to be going!' she called, and shepherded her charges back to Thrush Green.

The two ladies were back in the school house by a quarter to four. Dorothy had changed into a becoming blue jersey two-piece, and Agnes had put on her best silk blouse with her mother's cameo brooch at the neck.

The tea tray waited in the sitting room, and on a side table were all the festive dishes. Some golden daffodils scented the air, and the ladies waited expectantly. The visitors were due at four o'clock, but at ten past they had not appeared.

Dorothy began to get restive, wandering to the window to look down the road, and then back to the kitchen to make sure that the kettle was ready. Agnes viewed her growing impatience with some apprehension. Dear Dorothy was a stickler for punctuality.

'Isn't it extraordinary,' exclaimed her headmistress, 'how people never arrive on time? I mean, if I say between seven and seven-thirty, it's usually a quarter to eight before the bell rings. Why not seven-fifteen? Why not seven, for that matter?'

Agnes assumed that this was a rhetorical question and forbore to answer.

The little clock on the mantel piece struck a quarter past four, and Dorothy plumped up a cushion with unnecessary force.

'Of course, Ray never had any idea of time, nor Kathleen, come to that. Ray was even late for his own wedding, I remember. The whole congregation waiting for the bridegroom! You can imagine! One expects some delay before the bride appears but – '

She broke off suddenly.

'Here they are at last! And about time too. Would you switch on the kettle, Agnes dear, while I let them in?'

Polite kisses were exchanged in the hall, and Miss Watson led the way into the sitting room. No apologies were made for their late arrival, she noticed, although it was now twenty five minutes past the hour, but she decided to ignore the omission. As she had remarked to Agnes, time meant nothing to this pair.

'And how are you finding The Fleece?' she enquired.

'Rather run down,' said Ray. 'Under new management, I gather, and not very competent.'

At that moment, a ferocious barking broke out, and Agnes, coming in with the tea pot, very nearly dropped it in her alarm.

The two visitors had rushed to the window, so that Agnes put down the tea pot without being greeted.

'Oh, *poor* Harrison!' cried Kathleen. 'He's seen a horrid cat. So upsetting. We'd better bring him in, Ray.'

Ray began to make for the door.

'By all means go and calm the dog,' said Dorothy, with a touch of hauteur, 'but I think it would be wise to leave him outside while we enjoy our tea.'

'He always has tea with us,' said Ray. 'He usually has a saucer on the hearth rug. With plenty of milk, of course.'

'But not today,' replied Dorothy firmly, the complete headmistress. 'Now do say hello to dear Agnes who has been looking forward to seeing you so much.'

Reminded of their manners, Ray and Kathleen greeted her warmly, and did their best to ignore the persistent whining and yelping issuing from their car. But clearly their minds were elsewhere, and conversation had to be carried on at a high pitch to overcome the appalling din made by the unhappy animal.

'I take it that the management at The Fleece welcomes animals?' ventured little Miss Fogerty.

'I wouldn't say *welcomes*,' said Ray. 'Harrison is being allowed to sleep in his basket in one of the stables. No dogs in the hotel. That's the rule, we were told the minute we arrived.'

'Why "Harrison"?' asked Dorothy, passing the cucumber sandwiches. Kathleen looked momentarily pleased.

'Well, you see he is the image of the butcher who used to come round when we were first married. Isn't he, Ray?'

'Exactly. Same brown eyes, same expression — '

'Same black coat?' murmured Dorothy.

The visitors laughed politely.

'Almost,' agreed Kathleen, 'and certainly interested in *meat*.'

Agnes, who began to feel that the dog would be better ignored, if such a happy situation should ever be possible with the ear-splitting cacophany engulfing them, asked after Kathleen's health. At once, Ray's wife assumed a melancholy expression.

'I'm having some new treatment for my migraine attacks,' she told them, accepting a second cup of tea.

'It's terribly expensive, and I have to make two trips a week, but I think it may be doing me good.'

'I am so glad,' said kind Agnes.

'And I've been having attacks of vertigo,' volunteered Ray, with a hint of pride. 'Something to do with the middle ear. Very disconcerting.'

Agnes wondered if the dog's powerful voice could contribute to this discomfort, but thought it wiser to remain silent.

Not once, she noticed, with rare warmth, had they enquired after poor Dorothy's broken hip — a much more serious business, surely!

'But there,' continued Kathleen, with sad recognition, 'I suppose we can't expect to be as spry as we were twenty years ago.'

'Indeed no!' agreed Dorothy, rising to cut the splendid sponge. She walked across to Kathleen, plate in hand. Was her limp rather more pronounced than usual, Agnes wondered? A little stiff from sitting perhaps, she decided.

'And how is the leg?' enquired Ray, somewhat tardily.

'I do my best to ignore it,' replied Dorothy. 'No one wants to hear about the troubles of the elderly.'

Kathleen greeted this pointed remark with a swiftly indrawn breath, and a meaning glance at her husband. He, man-like, pretended to be engrossed with his tea cup.

'And where are you proposing to go tomorrow?' asked Agnes hastily.

Before Ray could answer, Kathleen spoke.

'It's amazing how quickly people get over these hip operations these days. Why, a young curate we know was actually *dancing* six months after he fell from his bicycle.'

'He was fortunate,' said Dorothy.

'Oh, I don't know,' said Kathleen, shouting above the racket from the imprisoned dog. 'I'm sure it's a matter of attitude of mind. He *intended* to get better, just as quickly as possible. I think some people enjoy being invalids.'

Agnes noted with alarm that a pink flush was suffusing Dorothy's face, a sure sign of temper, and really, thought her loyal assistant, she had every right to be cross under the circumstances.

'I don't,' said Dorothy shortly.

'Of course not,' agreed Ray. 'It was exactly what I said to

Kathleen when she was so worried about you in hospital.'

'Indeed?' replied his sister icily.

'Kathleen was a martyr to her migraine at the time, as you know, otherwise we should have invited you to stay with us when you were discharged. But we knew you wanted to get home and pick up your normal life again. I said so at the time, didn't I, Kathleen?'

'You did indeed, dear,' said Kathleen, dabbing her mouth with a spotless linen napkin and leaving lipstick as well as jam upon it.

Before any civilised reply could be made, there was a rapping at the front door. Agnes, glad to escape, hurried to open it, and was confronted by Dotty Harmer with Flossie on a lead. A battered metal milk can dangled from the other hand.

Without being invited, Dotty pushed past Agnes and entered the sitting room. She was in a state of considerable agitation, and burst into speech.

'Oh, Dorothy my dear, there is a poor dog *absolutely stifling to death* in a car outside. No window left open, and it is in a terrible state of anxiety. Aren't people thoughtless? Really they need a horse-whipping, and my father would have administered it, I assure you, if he had come across such fiends! Someone calling at The Two Pheasants, I suppose, or at the Shoosmiths.'

'The dog belongs to my brother here,' said Dorothy, with a hint of smugness in her tone. 'I'm sorry it upset you so, Dotty dear. I'm afraid it must have upset a great many people at Thrush Green during the past hour.'

Dotty was not the slightest bit abashed.

'I don't think I have had the pleasure of meeting you before,' she said, transferring Flossie's lead to her left hand and entangling it dangerously with the milk can, whilst proffering her right.

'My sister-in-law Kathleen. My brother Ray. My friend Miss Harmer,' intoned Dorothy.

Ray bowed slightly, Kathleen gave a frosty smile, and Dorothy waved at the tea tray.

'Let me give you some tea, Dotty. Do sit down.'

Outside, the barking changed to a high-pitched squealing, even more agitating than before. Ray began to make for the door.

'Excuse me, I'd better bring Harrison in,' he said. He was through the door before anyone could stop him.

'So kind of you, Dorothy, but I'm on my way to Ella's and mustn't delay.'

She began to make her way to the door. Flossie's lead was now hopelessly tangled around Dotty's wrinkled stockings.

At that moment, Ray's labrador, slavering at the mouth, burst into the room, gave a demented yelp, and rushed at Flossie.

The noise was indescribable. Flossie, the meekest of animals, screamed with alarm. Harrison charged into the table, knocking the sponge cake, chocolate biscuits, two tea cups, milk jug and a flurry of knives and teaspoons to the floor.

Dotty, pulled off balance, fell across Agnes's chair, driving her mother's cameo brooch painfully into her throat. Dorothy, ever quick-witted, sat down abruptly before her own precarious balance added to the confusion, and Kathleen, cowering in her chair, gave way to hysterics.

This scene of chaos confronted Ray when at last he regained the sitting room. With commendable promptitude he caught Harrison by the collar, and held him firmly, while Agnes and Dotty recovered their balance. The milk-can had rolled under Agnes's armchair and was dispersing a rivulet of goat's milk over the carpet.

'I apologise for this mess,' said Dotty. 'You must let me pay for any cleaning you have to have done. Goat's milk can be so very *pervasive*. I'd better return home and fetch some more for Ella. Luckily, Dulcie is giving a splendidly heavy yield, at the moment.'

Quite in command of herself, she smiled politely in the direction of the hysterical Kathleen, now throwing herself about alarmingly in her chair, waved to Ray, and took the shaken, but now well-behaved, Flossie into the hall. Agnes accompanied her, hoping that the blood on her throat from the brooch's wound would not stain her best silk blouse.

'Are you *sure* you would not like to rest for a little?' enquired Agnes. 'The dining room has a most comfortable armchair, if you would like a few minutes' peace.'

'Thank you, my dear, but I am quite all right. The air will refresh me.'

Agnes watched her walk to the gate, as spry as a sparrow, and none the worse it seemed for her tumble. She returned, full of foreboding, to the scene of battle.

'Who *is* that interfering old busybody?' Ray was asking, as she returned.

'A dear friend of mine,' replied Dorothy, 'and a true animal lover. I absolutely agree with her that it was *monstrous* of you to leave that dog shut in the car.'

Kathleen's hysterics were now slightly muted, but had turned to shattering hiccups.

'If you remember,' she began, and gave a mighty hiccup, 'you yourself refused to have poor Harrison indoors.'

'I should have thought that *even you* knew better than to leave the car hermetically sealed. Calling yourselves animal lovers,' said Dorothy, with withering scorn. 'And the poor thing so badly trained that it cannot be brought into a Christian household.'

She bent down to retrieve the best china from the floor, whilst Ray picked up teaspoons with one hand and dabbed at the goat's milk with the other holding his handkerchief.

'*Please*, Ray,' said Dorothy, 'leave the mess to Agnes and me. We don't want it made worse by the use of your handkerchief.'

Agnes felt that, provoked though she might well be, such a slur on the cleanliness of her brother's personal linen, was carrying things rather far.

'I will fetch some clean water and a cloth,' she said hastily, and made her escape.

A wild wailing noise followed her. Obviously, Kathleen was off again!

'I think,' Ray was saying, when she returned with her cleaning materials, 'that we had better be going.'

'I whole-heartedly agree,' said Dorothy, standing facing him.

'You have thoroughly upset poor Kathleen,' he went on, 'and you know how she suffers with migraine.'

'When it suits her,' responded Dorothy.

'Are you implying,' cried her incensed brother, 'that Kathleen *pretends* to have these dreadful attacks?'

A terrible hiccup arrested Kathleen's wailing. She was now on her feet, eyes blazing.

'How dare you say such things? You know I'm a martyr to migraine! Not that I've ever had the slightest sympathy from you. You are the wickedest, most callous, unfeeling – '

Another hiccup rendered her temporarily speechless. Ray took the opportunity to put his arm about his wife, and to shepherd her and the panting Harrison to the door.

'Come along, my dear. We'll go straight back to The Fleece, and you must lie down with one of your tablets.'

'But poor Harrison hasn't had his tea,' wailed Kathleen. 'You know he likes it on the hearth rug!'

'There is plenty for him,' observed Dorothy, 'wherever he looks on the carpet.'

It was Agnes who saw them to the door, and then into their car.

'I shall never come here again,' cried Kathleen, still hic-cuping violently.

'We are deeply wounded,' said Ray. 'I don't think I shall want to see Dorothy – sister though she is – for a very long time!'

They drove towards Lulling, Harrison still barking, and Agnes returned to break the dreadful news that Dorothy might never see the pair again.

'What a relief!' said her headmistress, 'with infinite satisfaction. 'Now, we'll just get this place to rights, and have a quiet evening with our knitting, Agnes dear.'

7   The Fire

A FTER such a devastating experience it was hardly surprising that little Miss Fogerty slept badly. Usually, she read for half an hour, and then was more than ready to plump up her pillows, put out the bedside light, and welcome deep sleep within ten minutes.

But on this occasion sleep evaded her. She went over, in her mind, all the terrible details of that catastrophic tea party. The noise of Kathleen's hysterical wailing still sounded in her ears. Ray's furious face, and Dorothy's tart retorts tormented her memory.

St Andrew's clock struck midnight, and she tossed back the bedclothes and went to survey Thrush Green by moonlight.

It was still and beautiful. No lights shone from the houses around the green, but the moonlight silvered the windows and dappled the young leaves of the chestnut avenue. Far away, along the lane to Nidden, an owl gave his wavering cry, and from the other direction came the distant sound of one of Lulling's rare goods trains chugging through the deserted station.

The air was cool from the open window and scented with the pheasant-eye narcissi which grew against the wall. Agnes took deep breaths, relishing the silence and the peaceful scene. Below her, and to her right, the empty playground stretched. In twelve hours' time it would be astir and strident with children running and shouting.

The thought made Agnes return to her bed. She must be fit to attend to her duties in the morning. At this rate she would have seven hours' sleep at the most. She must compose herself.

She smoothed her sheets, straightened her winceyette nightgown, and put her head, with its wispy grey plait, down to the welcoming pillow.

The party must be forgotten. She owed it to the children. Within ten minutes she was asleep.

At about the same time, a little farther along the road, Albert Piggott sat up in bed and rubbed his rumbling stomach.

Should he, or should he not, go downstairs, take one of his indigestion tablets and make a cup of tea? It was on occasions like this that he missed a wife. It would have been the simplest thing to have aroused Nelly with a sharp dig of the elbow and to recount to her the overwhelming pain which he was suffering — pain which could only be assuaged by recourse to medicine and a hot drink — and which was too severe to allow him to fetch those ameliorations himself.

However, Nelly was not in his bed, but presumably in that of the oil man who had supplanted him in his fickle wife's affections. If he wanted medical attention he would have to supply it himself.

Muttering to himself, he climbed out of bed, a thin unsavoury figure clad in pants and vest, for Albert scorned such effete practices as changing from dayclothes into night attire, and stumbled down the stairs. His little cat, as thin, but far cleaner, than his master, greeted him with a mew, and was pleasantly surprised to be given a saucer of milk when Albert took the bottle from the cupboard.

The kettle seemed to take an unconscionable time to boil, and Albert gazed out of the kitchen window to the bulk of the church across the way.

It was as bright as day now that the moon was high and nearly full. It shone upon the rows of tomb stones which now lined the stubby walls of the churchyard, and lit up the Gothic windows facing towards Lulling. Sharp black shadows fell across the dewy grass, and even Albert's meagre appreciation of natural beauty was stirred by the sight.

He made the tea, poured out a mugful and took it back to bed with the bottle of tablets.

Propped up against the greasy pillow he sipped noisily, relishing the comfort of the hot liquid flowing into his tormented stomach. Two tablets were washed down, as he surveyed the moonlit bedroom.

He became conscious of the smell of smoke. It was very faint, and he dismissed it as coming from the last embers of the bonfire he had seen Harold Shoosmith making that morning. Nothing to do with him, anyway, thought Albert, depositing his empty mug on the linoleum.

The pain was now lulled into submission. Albert belched comfortably, turned over, and fell asleep.

Below, in the kitchen, the cat licked the last delicious drops of Albert's bounty, washed his face, and then set out, through the open kitchen window, upon the business of the night.

An hour later, Harold Shoosmith smelt the smoke. Could his bonfire be responsible? Surely, it had been out by tea time when he had conscientiously stirred the remnants? Nevertheless, bonfires occasionally had the disconcerting habit of resuscitating themselves and, apart from the danger, it was a pity if the beauty of such a night was being fouled by smoke of his making.

In the adjoining bed, his wife Isobel slept peacefully. He slipped quietly from his own, and made his way to the

bathroom which overlooked the garden where the rogue
bonfire had been lit.

All was peaceful. He could see the empty incinerator quite
clearly in the light of the moon. Not even a wisp of smoke
curled from it, he noted with relief.

But where then was the fire? Had Miss Watson or the
landlord of The Two Pheasants been burning garden rubbish?
As far as he could see, their gardens were as clear as his own,
although some smoke began to drift across from some conflagration farther along the green towards the south, even as
he watched.

He ran, now seriously alarmed, into the spare bedroom
whose side window looked across to the church and rectory.

To his horror, he saw that the smoke was pouring from the
roof of the Henstocks' house, and before he could close the
window a cracking report rent the air, the ridge of the
vicarage roof dipped suddenly, and a great flame leapt into
the air illuminating billowing clouds of thick smoke.

He ran downstairs, and Isobel woke to hear him crying:

'The fire brigade! And quickly! Thrush Green rectory is
well ablaze!'

She heard the receiver slammed down, and within two
seconds Harold was dragging trousers over his pyjamas and
fighting his way into a pullover.

'I'll come and help,' said Isobel, reaching for her clothes.

Within five minutes a little knot of helpers was gathered at
the blaze. The sight was awe-inspiring. The collapse of part
of the roof had let in air which intensified the conflagration.
Flames were now shooting skyward, and the upstairs windows
showed a red glow. Smoke poured from the main bedroom
window, and there were terrifying reports as the glass cracked
in the heat.

Mr Jones, the landlord of The Two Pheasants was organising a chain of water carriers from the tap in his bar, and Albert Piggott, stomach pains forgotten, had trundled out an archaic fire-fighting contraption which had been kept in the vestry since the second world war and had never been used since the time when a small incendiary bomb had set light to the tassels of the bell ropes, and an adjacent pile of copies of Stainer's 'Crucifixion', in 1942.

This relic, when attached to a nearby hydrant well-hidden in nettles in the churchyard spouted water at a dozen spots along its perished length and saturated several onlookers.

'Get the darn thing out of the way!' yelled Harold Shoosmith. 'We'll have someone falling over it!'

He and several other men, including Edward Young, the architect, and Ben Curdle, were busy removing furniture, books and papers, and anything they could grab downstairs, before the inevitable happened and the whole top floor collapsed. These were being piled, well away from danger, by willing hands. Ella Bembridge, for once without a cigarette in her mouth, worked as stoutly as the men, and would have forced her way into the building to collect some of Dimity's treasures, if she had not been forbidden to do so by Harold, who had taken charge with all the ready authority of one who had spent his life organising others.

The welcome sound of the fire brigade's siren sent people scattering to allow its access across the grass to the blazing house. It was a joy to see the speed and economy of effort with which the hoses were turned on.

'This started some hours ago, by the look of things,' said the captain to Harold. 'I can't think how it went undetected for so long.'

Harold explained that the house was empty, and at that moment a second fire engine arrived from Nidden, and

started work at the side of the building where the flames
seemed thickest.

A terrible roaring sound began to emanate from the
doomed building, and the bystanders were ordered to get
well away. With a thunderous rumbling the top floor of the
rectory now collapsed. Sparks, smoke and flames poured into
the air, and the heat became intense. People began to cough
in the acrid air, and to rub eyes reddened with smoke and
tears.

Now, it was quite obvious, nothing more could be
rescued. The rector's modest possessions which were still
inside the house must be consumed by the fire. It was a
tragedy that few could bear to witness, and Winnie Bailey, in
dressing gown and wellingtons, led the redoubtable Ella

away to her own house across the green. It was the only time she had seen her old friend in tears.

At first light, the people of Thrush Green gazed appalled at the havoc left by the events of the past twelve hours. Blackened stones and the gaunt charred remains of beams smoked in the morning air. Dirty rivulets of water moved sluggishly towards the gutters at the roadside, and puddles surrounded the remains of the Henstocks' home.

A tarpaulin had been thrown over the pathetic remnants which had been snatched from the blaze, and Harold had arranged for them to be stored in his garage and garden shed out of the weather's harm.

'I think Ella has Charles's telephone number,' he told Edward as the two begrimed and exhausted men were returning to their homes. 'But what about Hilda and Edgar? Aren't they due today?'

'Good Lord! I believe they are,' agreed Edward. 'I'll see if Joan knows anything about them. But first things first, old man. Bath and then coffee. Then a couple of hours' sleep for me — and you too, I recommend.'

'You're right. No point in ringing Charles and Dimity until about eight or nine. It's a tragic business, and particularly wretched when they are having one of their few breaks. Shall I ring or will you?'

'Do you mind tackling it? I'm supposed to be on the 9.30 train to London tomorrow — I mean, this morning — for a meeting.'

'Of course, I'll do it. Poor old Charles, it will break his heart, I fear.'

Four hours later, he sat in his study and rang the Yorkshire number. As he listened to the bell ringing so far away he

wondered how on earth one could break such appalling news
to a friend.

He was amazed to find how tired he was after the night's
activities. Muscles he had never noticed before seemed to
have sprung into painful evidence. His eyes were still sore,
and the hairs on his arms were singed. As for his finger nails,
despite energetic use of the nail brush, he had not seen them
so grimy and broken since his schooldays.

Luckily, it was Charles who answered the telephone,
Harold had already rehearsed what he should do if Dimity
had lifted the receiver. Charles would have to be summoned.
This was the sort of thing the men must cope with, thought
Harold, true to his Victorian principles.

'Nice to hear you,' was the rector's opening remark.
'You're up early. Everything all right at your end?'

'I'm afraid not. Charles, I have to tell you some bad news.
Are you sitting down?'

'Sitting down?' came the bewildered reply.

'Because this is going to be a shock,' continued Harold
doggedly. 'There was a bad accident here last night.'

'No! Not anyone hurt! Not *killed*, Harold, don't say that!'

'Nothing like that. Perhaps *accident* was the wrong word.
The fact is, your house has been badly damaged by fire.'

There was a brief silence.

'Hello!' shouted Harold. 'You there, Charles?'

'Yes, yes. But I can't have heard right. The house damaged
by fire? How badly?'

'I hate to tell you — but it is completely gutted. I think it
is quite beyond repair, Charles, as you will see.'

'I can't take it in. I really can't,' said the poor rector. 'How
could it have happened? We switched off everything, I'm
sure, and we hadn't had a fire in the grate for days. Surely, no
one would be so wicked as to set fire to the place?'

'I'm sure it wasn't that,' said Harold. 'I just felt you should know that our spare room is waiting for you and Dimity when you return, and could you tell us where to get in touch with Hilda and Edgar?'

'Oh dear, oh dear,' wailed Charles. 'How perfectly dreadful! Of course, they were due to arrive today, and I've no idea how we can get in touch. They were breaking their journey down to have a day or two in the midlands. Wait now, they were going to visit a cousin in hospital. In Coventry, I think Edgar said. Beyond that, I know nothing, but we shall start for home – '

The rector's voice broke, and Harold distinctly heard a sniff before he resumed.

'We'll be back during the day, Harold, and our deepest thanks for offering us shelter tonight. What a terrible affair. I must go and break it to dear Dimity, and then we must clear up things here, and set off for Thrush Green without delay.'

'We shall look forward to seeing you,' said Harold.

'And Harold,' said Charles in a firmer tone, 'I very much appreciate your telling me the news so kindly. It couldn't have been easy. You have prepared us to face whatever awaits us there, quite wonderfully.'

He rang off, and Harold went to tell Isobel how well he had taken it, and to make another assault upon his finger nails.

Joan Young came over to the Shoosmiths' house as soon as Edward had departed from London.

'I thought I'd offer to track down Hilda and Edgar,' she said. 'In any case, they can stop with us until things get sorted out. If only we knew how to get hold of them!'

'I thought of ringing hospitals in Coventry and asking if

Mr and Mrs Maddox were expected,' said Harold.

'Well, yes,' agreed Joan doubtfully, 'but do hospitals usually ask the names of visitors? It's such a shot in the dark.'

'Perhaps they could relay a message to the wards asking if anyone was expecting a visit from them. Is that possible, do you think?'

'It sounds highly unlikely,' said Joan, 'but I'll go back and put out a few feelers.'

The voice from the first hospital was brisk and rather impatient. Joan envisaged its owner as rushing, bedpan in hand, upon an urgent errand.

She embarked upon her message.

'Yes, yes!' said the voice. 'But if you could tell me the *patient's* name, I can get a message back to you.'

Joan said weakly that she did not know who the Maddoxes were visiting.

'In that case, I don't think I can help you. Visitors come at two o'clock until four here. I could get them to give their names at the reception desk, but as we have two hundred beds in this building alone, it would be rather a task.'

Joan said that she quite understood, thanked her and rang off. Obviously, this was going to be the pattern of any further investigations she might make. She decided that the project was impossible, and went to find Molly Curdle to help her with the beds for the unsuspecting Maddoxes, now, presumably, making their way to Thrush Green in expectation of a few carefree days in the rectory, poor dears.

Most of the inhabitants of Thrush Green went about their daily affairs in a state of shock that morning. Very few had slept throughout the night, and most had been helping to rescue the Henstocks' property until dawn arose and the firemen had departed.

Only the children, it seemed, viewed the wreckage with excitement. Little Miss Fogerty and Miss Watson had been far too upset to face their usual boiled egg at breakfast, and had nibbled Ryvita and marmalade simply to fuel their energies to get through their school duties.

Dorothy had given a short talk to the school at morning prayers, and told them how necessary it was to be of exceptionally good behaviour as so many people had been upset by the truly dreadful events of the night.

She then composed a suitable prayer asking for comfort to be given to the rector and his wife, and offering thanks for the bravery of the firemen and helpers, and for the merciful lack of injury to any person involved.

Agnes was full of admiration for Dorothy's powers of extempore prayer, and led her infants across the playground still pondering upon this facet of her headmistress's varied ability.

It was young George Curdle who spoke first.

'But why did God let the fire happen?' he asked.

For once in her life, Agnes felt unable to answer.

As it happened, Dimity and Charles arrived first on the scene, having driven non-stop from Yorkshire. Hastily prepared sandwiches had sustained them as they drove, and they chugged up the hill from Lulling as St Andrew's clock struck three.

No one saw them arrive, and for that they were grateful. They halted the car on the edge of the battered and rutted grass which was still sprinkled with the ash and trodden cinders of last night's activities.

Dimity covered her face with her hands and her thin shoulders shook. Charles's face was stony as he gazed unwinking at the scene. He put his arm round his grieving wife, but was quite unable to speak. They sat there, silent in their distress, for five terrible minutes.

Then, sighing, Charles opened the car door and stepped into the desolation of what had once been Thrush Green rectory.

He stirred the damp black ashes of the study floor with his foot. He could scarcely see for the blur of tears behind his spectacles, but he bent to investigate a glint of metal among the dust.

Turning it over in his hand, he recognised it. It was the silver figure of Christ which had been mounted on the ivory cross behind his desk. It was distorted and blackened by the heat, but Charles knew immediately what it was. He slipped it into his pocket, and turned to help Dimity over a low sooty wall which was all that was left of her kitchen.

And it was at that moment that Ella came from her cottage, and Harold and Isobel from their house, to give them what comfort they could.

That evening, when Edward Young arrived home, he found Hilda and Edgar, as well as Dimity and Charles, in his sitting room, still trying to get over the shock of the disaster.

It was as well that Joan had not continued with her efforts to trace them through Coventry hospitals and nursing homes, for their cousin, as it happened, had been sent home at the weekend and they had visited him in his own bedroom, finding him well on the way to recovery.

There was so much to discuss between all the old friends that it was beginning to get dark before the Maddoxes retired to an early bed. They proposed to leave after lunch the next day.

Joan and Edward walked back with the Henstocks to Harold's house, and hoped that they would be able to sleep, and so be released from their unhappiness for a few hours' oblivion.

They walked on together, past the silent school and the public house, until they rounded the bulk of St Andrew's church and stood facing the ruins.

The acrid stench which had hung over Thrush Green all day, was almost unbearable here.

Joan looked with pity and distaste at the mess which had once been the rectory.

She caught a glimpse of Edward's face in the dying light.

'Edward!' she said accusingly. 'You're *pleased*! How can you be so *heartless*!'

Edward hastened to explain himself.

'My darling, three-quarters of me grieves for dear old Charles and Dim, just as much as you do. But the other quarter — the professional bit — is so relieved to see the end of that ghastly place that it can't help rejoicing in a perverse sort of way.'

Joan gazed at him with disgust, and then began to smile.

She took his arm, and they turned their backs upon the wreckage, and set off towards their home.

'I suppose you are already planning a new house, monster that you are,' she observed.

'How did you guess?' asked Edward.

8 At Young Mr Venables'

IT was hardly surprising that, with all this excitement at Thrush Green, the advent of Tullivers' temporary residents passed with very little comment.

They had arrived in a battered van. Young Jack Thomas and his wife Mary appeared to have only two suitcases, but a vast array of cardboard boxes which seemed to be full of electrical equipment of some sort. Winnie Bailey, watching shamelessly from her bedroom window, surveyed the writhing tangles of flex and plugs and supposed that they might have brought their own television set, or portable electric fires with them.

As she watched, a noisy motorcycle roared up and parked alongside the van. Two figures, clad in black leather, dismounted and took off their helmets. Both shook out long blonde hair, but Winnie thought that one might possibly be a male.

All four vanished into the house, and Winnie decided to let them remain undisturbed for an hour or so before calling to see if she could be of any help. Jeremy was due soon from school, and after tea he could accompany her.

The boy was excited at the idea of seeing the new occupants of his home.

'Do you think they'll mind some of the cupboards being locked? I mean, mummy said my toys would be safer if I left them in the landing cupboard locked away, but they might need it for clothes and things, mightn't they?'

'I'm sure there's plenty of cupboard space for their needs,' Winnie assured him, thinking of the paucity of their travelling cases.

She lifted the heavy knocker which old Admiral Trigg had fixed to the front door of Tullivers years ago. It was in the form of a dolphin, a suitably nautical object for the old sea-farer to approve, and weighed several pounds. The door itself shuddered as the knocker thudded back into place.

Jack Thomas opened the door and gave Winnie such a dazzling smile that she was won over at once. She had handed the key earlier to his wife Mary, so that this was her first encounter with the new householder.

'Hello, you must be Jeremy,' said Jack, 'and of course you are Mrs Bailey. Do come in.'

They stepped into the sitting room where Winnie was surprised to see that several chairs had vanished and the remaining furniture was pushed back against the walls. The centre of the room was bare except for a number of the large cupboard boxes which Winnie had observed.

'Where are the chairs?' asked Jeremy.

'Oh, we've put 'em in the dining room. We'll probably live in there while we're here. You see, we need this space for the gear.'

He waved vaguely towards the tangle of wires in the boxes.

'Now, is there anything you need?' asked Winnie, returning to firmer ground. 'Bread, milk, eggs? Have you found out how to work the cooker and the lights? Do let me know if I can help.'

'Very sweet of you,' he said, with another heart-melting smile. 'I think we've all we need. We're going down to Lulling for a meal tonight.'

'I hear The Fuchsia Bush and The Fleece put on quite a good dinner,' replied Winnie.

'Oh, we'll fetch fish and chips,' said Jack. 'Much cheaper and less fag anyway than a meal out. And no washing up when you eat them straight from the paper.'

'Very true,' agreed Winnie.

'Shall I call the others?'

'No, no, don't trouble them. I'm sure you've all got enough to do moving in. But do come over if you want anything. I'm in most of the time. I hope you'll enjoy your stay with us,' she added politely, making for the door.

'I wish we could have fish and chips for supper,' said Jeremy wistfully as they walked home. 'But they'll have to wash up their plates, won't they? They won't really eat it all out of the paper with their fingers, will they? Won't they make dirty marks on the furniture?'

'Oh, I shouldn't think so,' said Winnie untruthfully. The same thought had gone through her mind, she had to admit.

But greasy fingers or not, thought Winnie, entering her own immaculate home, that smile of Jack Thomas's would forgive him anything.

The next few days were sad and busy ones for Charles and Dimity. The salvaged articles from the fire were pitifully small, and every hour brought a new loss to sight. Luckily, they had the clothes which they had packed for their Yorkshire holiday, and Harold and Isobel were able to lend them some immediate necessities, but there was the bewildering business of insurance and other matters to see to, and these things worried poor Charles very much.

Harold was a tower of strength, but so many necessary papers and documents had been consumed in the fire, and the fact that the property belonged to the Church with all sorts of legal and technical complications, made him advise Charles to see his old friend Justin Venables, the Lulling solicitor.

Charles decided to walk down the hill to Twitter and Venables' office at the end of the town. His appointment was for four o'clock, and the May sunshine was at its warmest as he set off past the school and across the green.

He averted his eyes from the empty spot where once his beloved rectory had stood. As it happened, two large lorries were on the site loading the remains of the rubble. Once they departed there would only be the scorched grass and the blackened soil to mark the place of the rector's home. The Church officials had been kind and sympathetic. He would be taken care of, supplied with a resting place very shortly, and would be kept informed, at every step, of the decisions of his ecclesiastical masters.

He had been severely upset to find that the investigation into the cause of the fire proved conclusively that faulty wiring in the airing cupboard was to blame.

The immersion heater was housed in the lower part of this cupboard, and Charles could not forgive himself for not switching it off before they left the house. He said so to Harold.

'But, you see, Dimity said we must leave on the hot water because Betty Bell's cousin from Lulling Woods was coming in to do some spring-cleaning before Edgar and Hilda arrived. I fear I was greatly to blame. Of course, I confessed at once to the man who came about it.'

'Forget it,' advised Harold. 'That wiring should have been renewed years ago, and the Church is jolly lucky you two weren't burnt to cinders in your beds. Why, some of it is two-plug stuff, and some three, and you've got lead-covered wiring in your study and rubber stuff in the kitchen, and what looked like naked copper to me in that back kitchen of yours.'

'It is rather a hotch-potch,' agreed the rector. '*Was*, I

mean. But then, you see, bits were added over the years, and I suppose they used whatever was in fashion. I know we had some trouble when we put in the refrigerator. All the lights blew out once when we opened the door. And the kettle used to snap on a red light sometimes, which frightened me very much, though Dimity assured me that it was a safety device. I'm afraid,' concluded the rector sadly, 'that I don't really understand electricity.'

'You'd have needed Faraday himself to sort out the system in your house,' said Harold. 'Just be thankful you weren't there when it finally blew up.'

'It wasn't so much *blowing up* as *smouldering*, they tell me,' replied Charles. 'You see the heat caught the lining paper on the shelves and that set light to the linen, and then the wooden slats, and then the roof timbers. And once the air got in everything became so much fiercer. I really can't bear to think of it. But, as you say, Harold, we must thank God that no one was hurt.'

He tried to put his anxieties out of his mind as he went down the hill to Lulling. The town was looking beautiful in its spring finery. The Cotswold stone garden walls were hung with bright mats of mauve aubretia and yellow alyssum. Daisies starred the lawns, and everywhere the heady scent of hyacinths and narcissi hung in the warm air.

The lime trees lining Lulling High Street fluttered their young green leaves, and the ancient japonica which fanned across the Misses Lovelock's Georgian house was already bright with scarlet flowers. Outside The Fuchsia Bush two tubs of splendid pink tulips flanked the door, and every window in the street, it seemed, held a vase of fresh spring flowers.

The rector's spirits rose as he strode along relishing the beauty around him. As expected, he was stopped several times by friends who commiserated with him and cheered him with their concern and sympathy.

He felt almost jaunty by the time he reached the solicitors' office, but the gloom of the entrance hall, a study in ginger-coloured grained paintwork, had a sobering effect upon the good man.

A plump middle-aged lady showed him into Justin's office on the left-hand side of the hall, and he was greeted affectionately.

'Just let me set you a chair, padre,' said Justin. 'Not that one. Take this, it has a padded seat.'

He levered up a heavy chair with a high Jacobean-type back and a seat upholstered in leather which was so old and rubbed that it resembled suede. It was, as Charles found, surprisingly comfortable.

'Tea now, I think, Muriel,' said Justin to the plump lady.

'Yes, sir,' she said, so humbly that Charles would not have been surprised to see her genuflect, or at least pull her forelock had she had such a thing. Obviously, Justin was the master in this establishment.

'Well now, just tell me the trouble,' began Justin, when the door had closed.

Charles gave a remarkably concise account of his actions before and after the fire, and explained his position as a tenant of Church property.

Justin listened carefully, his fingertips pressed together. He watched his client over his half-glasses and thought how rare and pleasant it was to be face to face with an absolutely honest man.

A discreet knock at the door heralded the arrival of Muriel with the tea tray. It was lowered reverently upon a vacant space on Justin's desk.

The good rector, had he given any thought to the matter,

would have been grateful for a mug of ready poured out tea with perhaps a bowl of granulated sugar with a well-worn teaspoon stuck in it. He was much impressed with the elegant apparatus now before Justin.

Two delicate china cups stood upon a snowy linen traycloth. An embroidered satin tea cosy covered a silver teapot, and small cubes of sugar, accompanied by silver clawed sugar-tongs, rested in a matching bowl. Some excellent shortbread fingers were ranged alongside.

'Well!' exclaimed Charles happily, 'I really didn't expect such a beautiful tea! And what a handsome tea cosy!'

'It is rather nice, isn't it?' agreed Justin, surveying it as though he had just noticed it. 'One of the girls in the office ran it up one Christmas. And the tray cloth too, I believe. Very good with her fingers obviously. A slice of lemon, Charles, or milk?'

'Milk, please. Do you usually have time for tea? I hope you

haven't gone to all this trouble on my behalf.'

'From four to four-thirty is teatime,' replied Justin firmly. 'I only see old friends then whom I like to invite to share my tea tray. Try the shortbread. Muriel makes it for me weekly.'

The rector could not help thinking in what a civilised way Justin seemed to conduct his business. He had no doubt that just as much work got done in the leisurely framework of Justin's day as was accomplished by so many feverish young men rushing from one thing to another.

'Of course, we have always stayed open until six o'clock,' said Justin, submerging his lemon slice gently with his teaspoon. 'So many of our clients appreciate being able to call here after their work is over. One needs a cup of tea to refresh one towards the end of the day.'

'Very sensible,' agreed Charles, dusting shortbread crumbs as unobtrusively as possible from his clerical grey trousers.

Over the tea tray Justin dealt with the rector's anxieties, and assured him that all would be satisfactorily arranged with the insurance people, the Church authorities, and all other interested parties in this sad affair.

It was exactly twenty-eight minutes past four when he rose and shook his old friend's hand in farewell.

'By the way,' he said, on his way to open the door, 'I am retiring at the end of this year.'

'You can't be!' exclaimed Charles. 'Why, you know you are always referred to as "young Mr Venables"! Who will take over?'

'Young Mr Venables will be seventy next birthday,' smiled Justin, 'and the boys here are in their forties and fifties. Plenty of good fellows to carry on at Twitter and Venables, believe me.'

'I can't take it in,' confessed Charles. 'Of course, I shan't mention this until you give me permission to do so.'

'You have it now, my dear fellow. There's no secret about it. Now, I mustn't keep you.'

He opened the office door, and saw Charles out into the sunshine.

The rector retraced his steps in thoughtful mood, pondering on Justin's decision to retire. Seventy next birthday, he had said. Well, perhaps he was right to leave the somewhat gloomy office and to feel free to enjoy his fishing and his golf when the sun shone. Certainly, Justin had served the little town well, as had his father before him. No doubt the middle-aged boys would carry on the good work, but it wouldn't please his old clients.

A car drew alongside the kerb just as Charles was approaching the Misses Lovelocks' house. It was driven by the vicar of Lulling, the Reverend Anthony Bull, and his mellifluous voice floated across the warm air.

'Get in, Charles, if you are making for home. I'm off to Nidden.'

Charles was rather looking forward to walking home in the spring sunshine, but it would have been churlish to turn down this offer, and in any case, he always enjoyed Anthony Bull's company.

He was a tall handsome man with a fine head and expressive hands. As a single man he had fluttered many maiden hearts, and even now, happily married as he was to a rich wife, a steady supply of embroidered slippers, hand-knitted socks, and useful memo pads decorated with last year's Christmas cards, flowed into the vicarage from adoring members of his congregation.

'We only got back from a few days in Devon yesterday,' said the vicar, 'and were appalled to hear about your house. I

gather you are at Harold's for the time being, but if you want
to come to us, Charles, the vicarage has plenty of room, and
we should both be delighted to put you up.'

Charles thanked him sincerely. The vicarage was an elegant Queen Ann house, overlooking Lulling's extensive
green. It was common knowledge that Mrs Bull's wealth had
contributed to the comfort of their establishment. The
beautiful old house had flourished under her cosseting, and
Charles could not think of anywhere more lovely to shelter, if
the need arose. He tried to say as much to the generous vicar.

'You've heard the rumour, I expect,' said Anthony Bull,
'about the re-organisation of the parishes around here? It's a
case of spreading us rather more thinly on the ground, I
gather. Nothing definite yet, but I shouldn't be surprised to
hear that we are all going to play General Post before long.'

'Do you know,' said Charles, 'I haven't heard the game of
General Post mentioned since I was a child! Nor Turn the
Trencher, for that matter, nor Postman's Knock. Do you
think people still play those party games?'

'I should like to think so,' responded the vicar, drawing up
outside Harold's house on Thrush Green, 'but I fear they play
rather more sophisticated games these days, with perhaps
rather less innocent enjoyment.'

At that moment, Charles saw Dotty Harmer emerging
from Ella's, milk can in one hand, and Flossie's lead in the
other. He did not feel equal to coping with that lady, much as
he admired and respected her.

He hurriedly got out from the car.

'Thank you again, Anthony, for the lift, and your very
kind offer of help.'

The vicar waved and drove off towards Nidden. What a
beautiful glossy car it was, thought Charles, without a trace
of envy. It was fitting that such a fine fellow as dear Anthony

should travel in such style, and live in such a splendid house.

He opened Harold's gate, and walked with a thankful heart into his own temporary abode.

9 Trouble At Tullivers

IT was soon apparent to the inhabitants of Thrush Green that young Jack Thomas departed from Tullivers each morning at eight o'clock. The shabby van took the road north towards Woodstock, and presumably from there he went to the estate office where he was employed.

His wife Mary and the other two residents were not seen until much later in the morning. The more censorious of Thrush Green's housewives deplored the fact that only once had Mary been seen to shake the mats, and that was at eleven-thirty in the morning. As for the nameless pair with the motor bicycle, they seemed to be invisible most of the time, although Ella reported that she had seen them having coffee one morning in The Fuchsia Bush, and later had noticed their vehicle propped outside the Job Centre in Lulling High Street. Were they proposing to settle locally, people wondered?

About a week after the fire, the peace of Thrush Green was shattered between eleven and twelve one starlit night, by the raucous sound of pop music and the throbbing of drums. Occasionally an ear-splitting shriek broke the rhythm, and above it all was the wailing of a nasal voice which might have been a woman's or a banshee's.

The downstairs lights at Tullivers were still ablaze at that time, and the noise certainly came from that house. Ella Bembridge, some hundred yards or more away, was wakened by the din, and so were Isobel and Harold Shoosmith, equally far away.

'What the heck goes on?' muttered Harold, leaning out of his bedroom window. 'Thoughtless louts! They'll wake everyone at Youngs' place, and I should think poor old Robert Bassett will be blown out of his bed at this rate.'

Robert Bassett and his wife were the elderly parents of Joan Young. Their home, converted from stables in the Youngs' garden, was one of the nearest houses to Tullivers. He had been very ill, and it was natural that Harold should be concerned first with his old friend's position so close to this shocking noise.

'I shall go and ring them,' said Harold firmly. Isobel heard him padding downstairs to the telephone.

There was a long wait, and then he returned.

'So much darn racket going on they can't hear the bell,' he fumed. 'I've a good mind to ring the police.'

'Wait a bit,' urged his wife. 'It will only make more to-do if the police come. It may stop soon.'

'I doubt it,' said Harold grimly, but he shut the window, and got back into bed.

He was not the only one to telephone to Tullivers. Edward Young, outraged on his father-in-law's behalf, also failed to get through, and as he was just out of a hot bath, he did not feel inclined to traipse across to Tullivers to remonstrate in person.

Joan had been along to see her parents, and had found them quite cheerful and in bed. Philosophically, they had inserted the ear plugs which they always took with them when travelling, and they appeared less perturbed than their children.

Winnie Bailey had contented herself with viewing Jeremy's sleeping form and postponing complaints until morning. The cacophany ended about half past one. The lights went out at Tullivers. The residents at Thrush Green

heaved sighs of relief, swore retribution at some more reasonable hour, and fell thankfully asleep.

Only Winnie Bailey's Jenny remained wakeful, and she
was seriously considering the geographical advantages of
Percy Hodge's farm house, should she ever be invited to live
there. There was now no doubt that Percy was seeking a
second wife, and was being uncommonly attentive to her.

Jenny, brought up in an orphanage and later a drudge –
though a grateful one – to the two old people who had
taken her in, could not help feeling touched by Percy's
devotion. On the other hand, did she really want to marry
at all?

Life at Thrush Green with kind Winnie Bailey held all the
happiness that she needed. Never had she enjoyed such
luxury as her own small flat overlooking the green. Winnie's
companionship was doubly precious because she had never
known such warmth and generosity of spirit. And how good
she had been to her in this last illness! And then she loved the
house they shared. It was a joy to polish the lovely old
furniture, to set the kitchen to rights, to shine the windows,
the silver, the brass. The thought of leaving Winnie and the
fine old home which they shared was insupportable.

And yet – poor Percy! He certainly missed his Gertie, and
he was a fine fellow still. She would be cared for if she threw
in her lot with his, and did he not perhaps need her more
desperately than Winnie did? Jenny's warm heart was smit-
ten when she recalled the buttons missing from his jacket,
and the worn shirt collar that needed turning. What a
problem!

St Andrew's church clock chimed four, and Jenny heaved a
sigh. Best leave it all until later! She'd be fit for nothing if she
didn't get a few hours' sleep, and tomorrow she had planned
to turn out the larder.

She pulled up the bedclothes, punched her feather pillow into shape, and was asleep in five minutes.

Harold Shoosmith rang Tullivers at seven-thirty next morning to remonstrate with young Jack Thomas before he left for work. The young man was as profuse in his apologies as can be expected from someone at that hour, only partially dressed, and attempting to get his own breakfast. It wouldn't happen again. They would make sure that all the windows were shut, and the volume kept down, during future rehearsals.

Before Harold had time to enquire further, the telephone went dead. Other residents rang later in the day but did not get quite as civil a response as Harold had received.

Winnie Bailey decided to call in person during the evening when, she supposed, young Jack Thomas would be home and would have had a meal after his day's work.

She found him sitting in the kitchen with Mary. As the motorcycle was not propped up near the front door, its usual resting-place, she imagined that the other couple were out.

The Thomases looked very tired and young, and Winnie wondered if she were being unkind in complaining. But the thought of further troubled nights, the disturbance of her charge Jeremy, and all the other neighbours nearby, hardened her heart.

They listened somewhat listlessly to her complaint. Even Jack's usual dazzling smile seemed dimmed, and he passed a hand over his hair as if bemused. As well he might be, thought Winnie tartly, after such a late night!

'The fact is,' he said, when Winnie had finished speaking, 'Bill and Lottie are going through a bad patch, and we offered them shelter while we're here. I used to run this band, and Lottie was our vocalist. Bill's the drummer — well, tym-

panist altogether really. Cymbals, triangle, the lot. Quite
handy.'

'But can't he take it over? I mean, you seem to have a job of
your own which must be quite demanding. I should have
thought you needed your sleep as much as the rest of us.'

'Well, the job doesn't bring in much bread, you know.'

'Bread?'

'Dough. Money,' translated Mary. 'If we can get an engagement now and again, it would help all four of us.'

'I can quite see that,' said Winnie, 'and I am in favour of
earning extra money if you can. But not at the expense of
your neighbours' well-being.'

'Well, we have to practise,' said Mary. 'No one's going to
take us on, unless we're competent.'

'We honestly had no idea we were making so much noise,'
protested Jack. 'I promise you we'll take more care in future.
I can't say we'll stop entirely. We need the money, and Bill

and Lottie are even more hard up than we are. At least, I've got a steady wage coming in. They're skint.'

'They seem to have money for what they want,' commented Mary to her husband. She sounded very bitter, and Winnie suspected that she at least would be glad to see the back of her two fellow residents.

'Well, I'll say no more,' said Winnie, rising. 'But for pity's sake spare Thrush Green any more nights like the last one. We're used to peace and quiet here after ten o'clock at night.'

The four young people at Tullivers were definitely in their neighbours' bad books. Apart from those who had accosted them openly with their complaints, there were plenty who stopped to tell each other how severely they had been disturbed, and how reprehensible such thoughtless conduct was.

'But there you are,' said Ella to Dotty as they shared a pot of coffee. 'Young things these days do exactly as they like. No respect for the older generation. No discipline, as we had.'

'Well, I certainly got enough,' admitted Dotty. 'As you know, Father was a trifle strict with his family.'

Ella privately considered this gentle censure as the understatement of the year. Tales of old Mr Harmer's punishments towards refractory pupils and his own children were enough to make even Ella blanch. The boys of his family had left home as soon as they could. Only Dotty had remained to look after her widower father in his old age, and a pretty thin time she had had, according to local gossip.

'One thing, they won't be here much longer,' said Dotty comfortably.

It was echoed, with some relief by Miss Watson to her assistant.

'A *temporary* nuisance,' was her comment. 'I hear Mr Shoosmith and Mrs Bailey both complained the next morning, so I shall not bother to tell them how we feel about such behaviour. But if it happens again — ' Here Dorothy stopped, with such a fierce headmistressy look, that even little Miss Fogerty trembled for anyone at Tullivers transgressing again.

Mr Jones at The Two Pheasants gave his opinion that that lot at Tullivers must have been dragged up in the back streets of some modern Sodom or Gomorrha to behave so badly, and he didn't know what the Hursts would find — or wouldn't find — when they returned. Which, he added, couldn't be too soon for him, and his audience at the bar agreed heartily.

Albert Piggott, nursing his half-pint of beer in the corner gave a highly-coloured account of how he was awakened by the din, and a further discourse, with repellent details, of what it had done to his stomach in the middle of the night.

One listener, more squeamish than the rest, hastily changed the subject to the report of young Mr Venables' retirement, and this new topic engaged the attention of Mr Jones's clients until closing time.

'Never be the same without him,' asserted Percy Hodge. 'Had a lovely way with him in court. Look how he got old Dotty off the hook when she run down that Cooke boy!'

'*Miss Harmer*,' said the landlord reprovingly, 'never done it. That's why.'

'That's as maybe,' replied Percy, undeterred by Mr Jones's rebuke. 'The point is a young chap like Mr Venables is going to be missed in Lulling. He spoke up for me something wonderful when the cows got out and some fool fellow came off his motorbike among 'em. Luckily they wasn't hurt.'

'What about the fellow?' enquired a stranger from Nidden.

'Oh, he broke a thigh and something in his back, I believe,' said Percy vaguely. 'Nothing much. They took him off to hospital, so he was all right. But my poor cows was upset for days.'

The rector of Thrush Green had no hard feelings towards the young newcomers. Harold Shoosmith would have said, if asked, that Charles Henstock had no hard feelings against any one, which made him the unique and saintly creature that he was.

As it happened, the affairs of the noisy night had not disturbed him, or Dimity, at all. They had both been deep in the sleep of the thoroughly exhausted, having had few good nights since their own tragedy.

So the rector's first pastoral visit to Tullivers was undertaken in happy mood. He felt rather ashamed, as he walked across the springy turf, that he had not called before, but so many pressing things in connection with the fire had engaged him, that he had found little time for his duties.

As he crossed the grass, he admired the rooks, swirling and dipping around the tall trees towards Nod. Perhaps they were 'winding up the water' as the old country folk said, and there would be rain in the night after this calm and sunny evening.

He purposely kept his eyes averted from the empty space where once his house had stood. He could not bear to look upon the gap. Would the church build him another house there? The ground belonged to it, of course. Or would that plot be sold, perhaps, and another home found for him?

It was worrying not to know what might happen. Harold and Isobel were kindness itself, but he and Dimity could not stay indefinitely. As it happened, they were going tomorrow to see dear old Mrs Jenner along the Nidden road. He had heard that she had a flat to let. It would be conveniently placed for church and parish, and he felt sure that it would be approved as temporary accommodation.

By now he was at Tullivers' front door, and even the unobservant rector could not help noticing that the late Admiral Trigg's massive brass knocker, in the shape of a dolphin, was tarnished as though it had been weeks since its last polishing.

Jack Thomas opened the door and looked a little startled when he saw the parson's collar.

'Oh, do come in,' he said, hastily remembering his manners. 'Mr Hendrick, isn't it?'

'Henstock. Charles Henstock,' answered the rector. 'And I must apologise for being so tardy in making your acquaintance, but you know we've had a little trouble lately.'

'We heard. Jolly tough luck. Did you lose much?'

He opened the door of the sitting room and ushered in his visitor. Charles could not help wondering what had happened to the chintz-covered armchairs and sofa which normally furnished the room. Now only three or four upright dining chairs stood against the wall, whilst a collection of wires, a microphone, and various instruments littered the centre of the carpet.

Charles perched on one of the chairs to which he was waved. Jack Thomas reversed another and sat facing him, with his arms folded along the back. Charles felt a flurry of panic, as though he were about to be cross-examined. He took a grip on himself.

'My wife and I wondered if we could be of any help while you are with us,' he began.

'As a matter of fact, Mrs Bailey has been very – er – *motherly*, and helped us quite a bit.'

'Oh, I'm sure of that! We are with the Shoosmiths at the moment. So handy for the church.'

There was a pause.

'Perhaps you are church goers?' he went on gently. There was a curious smell in the house. Some herbs perhaps, used in cooking? He found it rather disquieting.

'Would you like to meet the others?' asked Jack abruptly. 'They're a bit tied up at the moment, but I could fetch them.'

'Dear me, no!' replied the rector. Tied up? What an odd expression! 'But perhaps you would tell them that I called and hope they would like to attend any of our church services. I took the liberty of bringing a list of the times.'

He put a slip of paper on a small table beside him. There were marks of wet glasses upon its once glossy surface, and Charles was perturbed to see that one corner of his list turned darkly damp.

'Thank you,' said Jack, turning upon the rector the smile which had so dazzled Winnie Bailey. 'I don't know about Bill and Lottie, but Mary and I used to go to church once. We were both christened, I know, and I was confirmed at school, the same week that I was vaccinated during a smallpox scare.'

Really, thought the rector, getting to his feet, he speaks as though he were doubly insured in the space of a few days!

However, he found himself smiling kindly upon the young man. There certainly was something very fresh and attractive about him, and he was remarkably frank about being a lapsed church goer.

'Well, give my regards to your wife and friends,' he said, opening the front door, 'and we'll hope to see you all again before long.'

Jack walked with him to the gate, gazing about him and breathing deeply.

'One thing, we're enjoying Thrush Green,' he told the rector. 'It really is a marvellous place to live.'

'We think that too,' replied Charles simply, and allowed

his eyes to stray to the ravaged plot which he had once called home.

For the first time since the dreadful event, he found he could look at it with less pain. Was it a case of Time-the-great-healer? Or simply that he was getting accustomed to that sad gap in the sky line? Or was it that he felt that one day a house would rise again where his own had fallen?

Whatever the reason, the good rector was grateful for this small blessing of relief, and hurried back to the Shoosmiths' with a lightened heart.

Much to the relief of Thrush Green's inhabitants, the cacophany from Tullivers was not repeated. True, rehearsals went on, but Jack Thomas had kept his word. Windows were closed, and the lights went out around midnight — quite late enough for the early-to-bed neighbours, but certainly an improvement on the first night's prolonged din until the small hours.

Occasionally, the musical equipment was packed into the van when Jack returned from his work at the estate office, and all four would drive off for the evening. Presumably, some engagements had been secured, and rumour was rife at The Two Pheasants about how much they would be paid.

'I'd pay to get *out* of the room if that Lottie girl got screeching,' commented one.

'Some likes that sort of racket,' said his neighbour. 'My two kids has it on all the time on the telly.'

'More fool you to let 'em.'

'They wouldn't get no more than twenty quid between 'em,' surmised another. 'Wouldn't go far between four, would it?'

'The landlord at The Star over Lulling Woods way, gave 'em ten quid apiece, I heard, for an evening there.'

'Then he wants his head seen to,' said Mr Jones firmly, and changed the subject.

But there was a change of feeling towards the young people now that some improvement had been made in their behaviour. Bill and Lottie were seen but rarely, but Mary and Jack were about the green and in the shops at Lulling, and were much more sociable.

Winnie Bailey, who knew that the girl was pregnant, invited her to coffee one morning and renewed her offers of help. She had the feeling that Mary did most of the housework, and the shopping and cooking. She suspected too that the girl resented the other couple's presence. They certainly did not seem to pull their weight in the running of the household, and the girl appeared tired, as well she might be, as her pregnancy advanced.

Winnie asked how Jack's house-hunting plans were progressing, and Mary showed signs of enthusiasm for the first time.

'There's a small house near the office — the end one of a terrace, which I think we'll be able to have in a month's time. It will mean staying at a hotel for a few days after the Hursts come back here, but we shan't mind that.'

'And Bill and Lottie?'

'With any luck, they will have found somewhere in the next week or two. Not that they're searching very hard,' she added.

'Can they go back to their parents?'

'They *can*, but they don't want to. The first thing is to get a job. They're always hard up. Well, who isn't? I know I'm always staggered at the amount of money we seem to get through each week. I hope we'll be able to budget more satisfactorily when we get our own place. At least we shan't have Bill and Lottie scrounging for a loan.'

'Things will certainly be simpler,' agreed Winnie diplomatically, refilling her guest's cup. 'There's nothing so exciting as one's first home.'

She looked about the familiar sitting room, crowded with the personal treasures of many years.

'This was my first home,' she told the girl, 'and my last, I hope.'

'If I'm as quarter as happy,' said Mary, 'I shall be quite content.'

MRS Jenner, who had a sizeable old farmhouse a mile along the road to Nidden from Thrush Green, was a cousin of Percy Hodge's.

Like Dotty Harmer, her contemporary, she had been the only daughter, and when her mother died she kept house, and occasionally did a little nursing for neighbours.

She had trained at one of the London teaching hospitals and had worked in the capital until her mother fell ill. She was a large strong woman, eminently kind and practical, and well thought of in Lulling and Thrush Green.

On the death of her father she had refurbished the empty bedrooms, and had two or three paying guests who were in need of home nursing. The service she gave was outstanding, and many a local family blessed Mrs Jenner for the help she gave with elderly or invalid relatives.

But when Mrs Jenner's seventieth birthday had come and gone, she took stock of her situation. She now found it increasingly difficult to care for her patients as she wished. Carrying heavy trays upstairs, turning mattresses as well as elderly bodies, and facing disturbed nights all took their toll, and though Mrs Jenner's heart was as willing as ever, her ageing limbs were beginning to protest. Reluctantly, she decided that she must give up her nursing.

The next step was to provide a small income for herself. The old farmhouse was her main asset, and after considerable planning she decided to turn the top floor into one good-sized flat to let, and to live on the ground floor.

Her last patient had left her in February, and the altera-
tions to the house were virtually complete by the time the fire
had ravaged Thrush Green rectory. After she had heard that
Charles and Dimity were settled temporarily at Harold's she
wrote to the rector and offered them the flat if it would be of
any help to them. They welcomed the suggestion. No one
could have a better landlady than Mrs Jenner, and the accommodation was conveniently placed for all the rector's parish
duties.

The top floor flat was light and spacious, the furniture was
of good solid country-made workmanship, but Mrs Jenner
obligingly offered to move some elsewhere if the rector
preferred some of his own pieces.

In truth, the farmhouse was infinitely more comfortable
than the rectory had ever been. Large windows overlooked
the sunny garden with fields beyond.

'Perce has those now,' said Mrs Jenner, naming Jenny's
admirer. 'His father and mine farmed this place together, and it
was split up when they died. I only need this garden, and I let
my few acres to Percy who can do with them. He's a good help
to me when it's needed. Keeps me in vegetables and milk, and
can turn his hand to anything to do with wood or metal.'

'He's a very skilled fellow, I know,' agreed the rector.

'Great shame about Gertie. He misses her sorely,' went on
their landlady. 'But there, you know all about that. Come
and see the kitchen.'

As she led them from one room to the next, Dimity
realised that she was going to be more comfortable in these
quarters than she had been anywhere in her married life. The
carpets and curtains were well-worn, but beautifully clean.
The armchairs were deep and snug, the windows gleamed,
the furniture was glossy with years of polishing. Above all, it
was warm.

Whatever the future held for her, Dimity became more and more certain as she followed Mrs Jenner about the old thick-walled house, that her new home whenever it materialised, was going to be as similar in light, warmth and comfort as it could possibly be to Mrs Jenner's house. It would be smaller, she supposed. Some of the new church houses were even bungalows, she believed. How wonderful to have a home which would be easy to keep warm and clean! She recalled, with an inward shudder, the bleak Victorian rectory — its wind-tunnel of a passage, leading from the north-facing front door to the back one, its vast Gothic windows which rattled in the wind, its high ceilings, its wintry bedrooms and the ever-damp cellars. She knew that Charles grieved for its loss. She did too, for that matter, for it had been her first home as a bride. Nevertheless, she realised, as never before, that the place had been ugly, cold, impractical and hideously expensive to run.

She gazed about Mrs Jenner's neat kitchen. A small stove gave out a steady warmth. A kettle purred upon it. The saucepans winked from the walls, and a row of fine geraniums basked in the sunshine on the window sill.

'You won't want to make up your minds just yet, I feel sure,' said Mrs Jenner. 'But let me know when you decide.'

Dimity's eyes met those of Charles.

'I think we've decided already,' said the rector, with a smile.

'Then we'll have a cup of tea,' said their new landlady, lifting the kettle.

The next morning Dimity crossed the green to visit her old friend Ella Bembridge and to tell her about their new temporary home.

She found her engrossed in the morning post. Willie

Marchant was wheeling his bicycle from one gate to another, and had acknowledged her presence with a casual wave as she passed.

'Anything exciting?' asked Dimity.

'Two bills, a catalogue about Shetland woollies and a very vulgar leaflet about some hideous pottery with an order form headed: PLEASE RUSH ME THE FOLLOWING. That's enough to put you off for a start, isn't it?'

Dimity agreed.

'Besides this awful pottery they do jewellery based on Viking designs. Cashing in on those telly programmes, I suppose, though anyone less lovable than the Vikings it would be hard to find, I imagine.'

'Well, I suppose you could call them *brave*,' said Dimity tentatively.

'Don't you start,' growled Ella. 'The more I saw and heard

about them, the greater grew my admiration for dear old King Alfred. *Great* he certainly was, coping with those dreadful chaps with names like throat-clearings.'

'I've got some good news,' said Dimity, feeling it was about time to leave the inflammable subject of the Vikings. She told her about Mrs Jenner's flat, and Ella grew equally enthusiastic.

'Well, you couldn't do better. I should settle there permanently if I were you.'

'That would be blissful, wouldn't it? But I daresay the church people have other plans for us.'

At that moment there was a knock at the door, and Winnie Bailey entered.

After greetings, she unfolded a snowy linen napkin to display a minute piece of knitting.

'Do you, by any chance, have a spare number twelve needle, Ella dear? Mine has vanished. Jenny and I have turned everything upside down, and it's nowhere to be seen, and I want to give these bootees to Mary Thomas before they go.'

'Do babies wear bootees now?' asked Ella. 'I thought they were brought up in grow-bags.'

'I think the term is something like "growies",' said Winnie vaguely, 'but I always imagined they had bootees on inside those things.'

'My little brother,' said Dimity, 'had a long flannel which was folded over his feet and secured with two enormous safety pins.'

'Well, these grow-bags are simply the modern equivalent,' explained Ella, 'and I'm sure I have another twelve needle somewhere, unless I used it to stake a drooping indoor hyacinth last winter.'

She set about rummaging in the drawer of a side table,

scattering knitting needles, crochet hooks, carpet needles, bodkins, safety pins, stitch-holders and a mixed assortment of other metal tools for handicrafts.

While she was thus engaged, Dimity told Winnie about their new plans.

'Yes, I did know,' admitted Winnie. 'Percy Hodge told me last night when he came to see Jenny.'

'I might have guessed,' said Dimity, 'that everyone in Thrush Green knows the news now.'

'Well, I didn't know, did I?' said Ella comfortingly, advancing with a bristling handful of knitting needles.

'There you are, Winnie. All twelves, and ranging from my Aunt Milly's bone ones to pseudo tortoiseshell via steel and modern plastic. Take your pick.'

Winnie studied the needles.

'And how is Jenny? Is she likely to marry Percy, do you think?'

'I'll take the steel ones, if I may, Ella. And about Jenny — well, I really don't know. She still looks washed-out to me, I'd like her to have a few days away. To my mind, she's worried over Percy too. I hardly like to dissuade her — she might think my motives were a trifle self-centred — and I don't feel like doing the opposite. She must make up her own mind. I'm strictly neutral. All I want is Jenny's well-being.'

'But she might find that with Percy,' cried Dimity earnestly, thinking of her own late marriage to her beloved Charles. 'I mean it really seems so *cruel* to turn down the love of a good man like kind Percy. Especially when he misses Gertie so much.'

Her two companions gazed upon her with mingled affection, amusement and exasperation.

'"When in doubt, don't", is my motto,' said Ella forthrightly. 'And as for *love*, well, you know what the Provincial Lady maintained. She reckoned that a sound bank balance and good teeth far outweighed it in value.'

'I can hardly put that forward to Jenny,' said Winnie, rolling the needles with the bootees into a white bundle.

'Well, just tell her to look before she leaps,' advised Ella, accompanying Winnie to the door.

'I can only speak from personal experience,' said Dimity, 'but I have never for one moment had regrets about my marriage.'

'Naturally,' agreed Ella, 'but then Charles is in a class of his own.'

'You are particularly fortunate,' said Winnie.

'As though I didn't know!' exclaimed Dimity.

One golden May day succeeded another. In the growing warmth of early summer Thrush Green shook out its leaves and flowers, to the delight of its inhabitants.

The school children spent every playtime out in the sunshine, much to the relief of Miss Watson and Miss Fogerty, and even Albert Piggot looked less morose, and had taken off two of his winter waistcoats and his disreputable muffler.

Farmers surveyed their promising hay fields, gardeners plied hoes and gardening forks and bustled about with packets of seeds, twine and knives sticking out of their pockets. Birds flashed to and fro, feeding young, or scrapping with others who approached too near their own particular territory. Activity was everywhere apparent.

Except, it seemed, at Tullivers.

There the garden grew more neglected. Harold Shoosmith, surveying it worriedly whenever he passed, wondered if he should offer to mow the grass and clip the hedges. It was Frank and Phyllida he was thinking about, not the present occupants whose laziness appalled him. As it happened, Jack Thomas emerged one evening with the Hursts' mower, and cut the lawns, and one Sunday he snipped away the longest of the sprouting twigs in the hedge.

Obviously, Mary was in no condition to garden, and the other pair were seldom seen. Winnie began to wonder if they were still living there, and asked Mary one day over the dividing hedge between their gardens.

To her surprise, the girl's face flushed with anger.

'We've sent them packing,' she said shortly.

'I'm sorry. I shouldn't have asked. I didn't mean to upset you.'

'You haven't. Actually I'm so relieved, I can't tell you. They never fitted in, you know.'

'It looked rather that way.'

'Jack's too kind-hearted. They told him this sob story just before we came here, and he was sorry for them and offered them shelter until they found a job.'

'And have they?'

Mary gave a snort of disgust.

'They haven't exactly tried. They made a great thing of going down to Lulling to the Job Centre, but as far as I could see, they had no intention of taking anything offered them. I think they thought that the group would make a bomb. But of course it hasn't. Anyway, it was agreed that we should split any fee four ways, so that no one had very much.'

She paused for a moment.

'Especially if you're on pot,' she added.

'Pot? Drugs, do you mean?'

'Cannabis, and a bit of cocaine. I don't think they've got to the hard stuff yet, but I bet they will pretty soon. The stink of

the stuff made me so ill. That's what finally decided Jack to
send them packing.'

'So I should hope,' said Winnie.

'The final straw,' said Mary, 'was pinching the housekeeping money last week. I thought it had been vanishing for
some time, a fiver here and there. You know how easy it is,
especially when four people use the purse.'

'What was your system?'

'Oh, whoever went shopping for meat or eggs or groceries
just took the purse. We all put in a fiver at the beginning,
and then had a share out at the end of each week, and
refurbished the funds again.'

'It sounds a good idea.'

'In theory, yes. In practice, particularly with half paying
out for drugs, it was hopeless. My gold bangle's gone too. I
may have lost it — the catch was loose — but I can't help
feeling they pinched it. Jack refused to believe me — he's
much more high-minded than I am. Anyway, I got some of
that powder you can scatter in cash boxes and so on. It stains a
thief's hands bright red. It certainly worked with Bill and
Lottie last Thursday. We caught them literally red-handed.
I've never seen Jack so furious. They were out within an
hour.'

'Where have they gone?'

'I don't know. They can go back to their parents, but of
course they don't want to. We had our last share out and
they pushed off with about three pounds apiece. The motor
bike's in good order. It's up to them now. Frankly, I hope I
never clap eyes on them again. They've thoroughly spoiled
our time here.'

'Put them out of your mind,' advised Winnie. 'It's over
and done with, and now you must look ahead to the baby and
take care of yourself and Jack.'

'You are quite right. We should be able to move into the new house next week, and we're both looking forward to making a fresh start.'

She looked about her at the sunny garden, murmurous with bees among the wallflowers.

'We shall miss Thrush Green. It would have been perfect if only we had been alone.'

'You won't be far away,' said Winnie cheerfully. 'You'll be able to visit us, I hope, and see Thrush Green in a more favourable light.'

'See Eden without its serpent? I'll look forward to that.'

That same day, after the school children had raced home, Miss Watson and Miss Fogerty enjoyed a well-deserved rest in the school house garden.

In common with the majority of Thrush Green residents, a modest tea was before them.

A tray with two cups and saucers, milk jug, teapot and a plate bearing half a dozen delicious lemon curd tartlets, made a brave sight.

The two friends were content to bask in the sun in silent companionship. An inquisitive blackbird made forays from the hedge, its bright eyes focused on the tea tray. Apart from its pattering claws upon the dead leaves, and the distant shouts of tardily departing children across the green, a blissful somnolence enwrapped them.

Agnes allowed her mind to drift from school matters to the more personal needs of her modest wardrobe. Should she buy another cotton frock, suitable for school, or should she get Miss Crookshank to make up the length of blue checked gingham she had prudently bought before material became so expensive?

The difficulty was that Miss Crookshank would probably

need quite a month to get the frock made, pleading pressure of business, her mother's illness and other excuses, all probably quite genuine, Miss Fogerty told herself, but the result would be that the fine spell would probably be over by the time the garment was completed.

And, of course, she must get a new pattern. That princess-style, button-through one which had done so well for so many years, had its drawbacks. Far too often the bottom button had burst off when showing the children how to be a really energetic galloping horse in the playground. And, on occasions, she had discovered that the bodice gaped, which was immodest to say the least. Perhaps something with a yoke? No zip, of course, and certainly not at the back. Far too difficult to reach.

There was a lot to be said for buying a frock readymade. She had seen some attractive ones in two of the Lulling shops, but the prices had been excessive, and it was really a shocking waste not to have the gingham made up. On the other hand, was the gingham perhaps too light in colour for school wear? One must remember how quickly clothes grew grubby in contact with such things as coloured chalks, modelling clay, charcoal sticks, paste and poster paints, not to mention innumerable infants' fingers clutching at one's raiment.

Agnes, juggling gently with this problem, was brought to earth by a squeak from her companion.

'Oh dear, I didn't mean to wake you,' began Dorothy.

'I wasn't asleep, dear, I assure you. Did something sting you?'

'No, no. I was about to get up to carry in the tray, and my leg gave a twinge. All over now. I think I must have been sitting awkwardly.'

'Should you see the doctor again?' asked Agnes, full of solicitude.

'No, I'm really quite fit. Well, as fit as I'm going to be, I suspect.'

'But surely,' protested Agnes, 'you will go on getting stronger? It isn't all that long ago -- '.

'It's well over a year,' said Dorothy. 'It may improve, of course, but I seem to have been at this stage for months now. It doesn't worry me, Agnes dear, because I just face the fact that I'm slower and can't walk as far as I did. On the whole, I can do all I want to do.'

'I sometimes think you do too much,' said Agnes loyally. 'You should let me help you more.'

Dorothy laughed.

'You spoil me as it is. Besides, you are quite a few years older than I am.'

Agnes nodded, and silence engulfed them again. A bold robin now came to reconnoitre, and the blackbird rushed at it, scolding furiously. The robin stood its ground.

'Agnes,' said Dorothy at last. 'Have you ever thought of retiring?'

'*Retiring?*' cried Agnes. 'Why, do you think I should? I mean, am I working as you would wish? Do I do my duties satisfactorily — ?'

Dorothy broke in upon this panic.

'Of course, you do *everything* quite beautifully, Agnes. I've yet to meet a better teacher, as you should know. No, I only passed the remark because retirement is rather in my mind at the moment.'

'You don't mean it!' gasped Agnes. 'Why, you are still in your fifties — and don't look it, I assure you! I thought you would want to stay at Thrush Green until you were sixty-five.'

Dorothy nodded absently, her eyes upon the robin.

'So did I. But since this fall, I've been thinking about

things. Everything is much more of an effort. I'm beginning to wonder if I should go at sixty. I could give a year's notice when I get to fifty-nine next birthday. That should be ample time for a new head to be found.'

Agnes's mind, so recently swinging indolently from readymade frocks to Miss Crookshank's versions, was now in a state of violent agitation. To think that dear Dorothy was even contemplating such a step! She had always looked upon her as so much younger and stronger than herself. After all, her own birthday would bring her to sixty-two, and she had quite resigned herself to the idea of staying until she was sixty-five. In any case, she hoped to put a little more in her Building Society account before she drew her pension. She had thought about returning to modest lodgings when the time came for Dorothy to give up the school house or even earlier. It was not a very exciting prospect, she knew, but she could hardly expect Dorothy to want her for the rest of her days, when the job they did together was over.

In her bewilderment, she scarcely took in all that Dorothy was saying.

'I should have thought about it long ago,' Dorothy was saying. 'Something really modest, a bungalow perhaps with a small garden and a view of the sea, of course. What do you think, Agnes?'

'I don't quite follow you, Dorothy,' said little Miss Fogerty unhappily. Everything was awhirl in her mind.

'If I decided to retire at sixty,' said her headmistress patiently, 'I should have to have a house. I was thinking aloud really — wondering about dear old Barton-on-sea. What do you think?'

'You've always loved it there,' said Agnes carefully.

'But would you love it too?'

Agnes turned bemused eyes upon her.

'Would I be there too?' she quavered.

Miss Watson gave one of her famous snorts.

'*Of course* you'd be there too! I hope you don't intend to desert me when we've both retired.'

'Oh, Dorothy!' began Agnes, appalled at the idea of treachery.

'Unless,' said Dorothy, suddenly and surprisingly unsure, 'you would rather not?'

'Rather not?' echoed Agnes. 'Just do let me get my breath, Dorothy dear, and I'll try to tell you how I feel.'

'I'll pour us both another cup while you're pondering,' said Miss Watson, lifting the teapot.

J UNE arrived, and Tullivers stood empty again awaiting the return of Phil and Frank Hurst.
   Jeremy grew more and more excited as the time drew
nearer, and Winnie shared his joy. She admitted to herself
that she was relieved at the departure of the young people
next door, and she and Jenny were glad to be putting things
to rights after their slapdash housekeeping.

It did not take long to get Tullivers looking ship-shape,
although there were one or two things which would need
more specialised attention than Winnie and Jenny could
give.

A coffee table was badly stained, and someone appeared to
have trodden tar or some equally viscous material into the
sitting room carpet. The latter defied all their combined
attempts to clean it. Obviously, the whole thing would need
to go to professional cleaners.

Upstairs, there was a cracked hand basin and a peculiar
stain down one wall in the back bedroom. But, at first sight,
Tullivers gave its usual peaceful sunny welcome.

'Well, we've done all we can,' said Winnie, shutting the
front door. 'I'll put some flowers inside on the day they arrive.
How good it will be to see them back!'

They went next door, and Jenny filled the kettle for
Winnie's tea tray. The children were already coming out of
school, and Jeremy would be looking forward to a slice of her
gingerbread.

'Leave that for a minute, Jenny,' said Winnie, 'and come and sit down.'

She led the way into the sitting room and she and Jenny sighed with pleasure at being at rest after all their activities next door.

'Now, Jenny,' began Winnie, 'I've something to put to you. Are you happy here?'

'Happy?' exclaimed Jenny. 'You know I am! Never been happier. It's like a dream come true.'

'Good,' said Winnie. 'And I'm equally happy, except for one thing.'

She looked across at Jenny's bewildered expression.

'And that's your health, Jenny. You have never really picked up after that wretched illness, and I'm going to see that you have a little holiday.'

'But I don't *need* a little holiday'! wailed Jenny. 'I shouldn't know what to do! Honest, I wouldn't.'

'Well, I should like a little break myself as soon as Jeremy's back at Tullivers, and I have made enquiries at a very quiet hotel in Torquay where I propose we go together. I shall stay for the weekend and leave you there for another week. The sea air will do you a world of good.'

'But what — ' began Jenny, when Jeremy burst in.

'I'm *starving*!' he cried.

'Hear that?' said Winnie rising. 'We'll talk about this later on, Jenny, but meanwhile we must get the tea ready. We can't have the Hursts coming back to a boy skeleton.'

And Jenny, her head awhirl with these holiday proposals, went to cut up the gingerbread.

On the same afternoon, at the Youngs' splendid house, Joan and Molly were busy taking down the long and heavy velvet curtains which had kept out the bleak winter draughts of Thrush Green, and were replacing them with light chintz ones for the summer.

'Do you know,' said Joan, 'that these windows are almost fifteen feet in height? I hope to goodness all these curtains last out our time. We should never be able to afford more.'

Molly, perched on a kitchen chair was doing her best to reach the hooks at the top, and deciding that she must fetch the step ladder after all.

'How many metres would you need, I wonder?'

'Heaven alone knows, and I don't intend to try and work it out at my age. I'd have to tell the shop people in yards, and let them do the sums.'

At that moment, Molly gave a little cry, swayed on her precarious chair and was caught by her alarmed mistress.

She helped the fainting girl to an armchair, and pressed her head down upon her knees. She was much agitated. Molly never ailed.

Should she send for her brother-in-law Doctor John Lovell? But then he would probably be out on his rounds at this time.

She crouched on the floor gazing anxiously at her patient. To her relief, she saw the colour returning to Molly's cheeks, and the girl sat up.

'Lean back,' advised Joan, 'and I'll get you a drink.'

She hastened into the kitchen and collected a glass of water and some brandy. What could be the matter?

'Only the water,' whispered Molly, 'that other stuff makes me sick.'

Joan watched her as she sipped.

'Have you felt faint before?'

'Once or twice. Nothing much. Let's get on with the curtains.'

'Not on your life! They can wait. You're going upstairs to lie down. I shan't be able to look Ben in the eye if he finds you ill.'

'You know what I reckon it is?' said Molly.

'Tell me.'

'A baby on the way. To tell the truth, I thought it might be, and this seems to settle it.'

'Well, I'm glad to hear it, Molly dear, and you're going to see Doctor Lovell first thing tomorrow. When do you think it's due?'

'If I've reckoned aright, it should be late in December.'

'A Christmas baby!' cried Joan. 'Now, isn't that good news? You were very naughty to clamber about on that chair. If only I'd known!'

'No harm done,' said Molly cheerfully, getting up. 'You know, I'd much rather carry on here than go upstairs.'

'You'll do as you're told for once,' said Joan firmly. 'Edward will give me a hand with these curtains when he comes home. What are husbands for, I'd like to know?'

The Hursts returned to an ecstatic welcome from Jeremy and a heartfelt one from all their old friends at Thrush Green.

At first, they forbore to tell them of the shortcomings of Tullivers' temporary residents, but as Harold Shoosmith told Isobel: 'It is only a matter of time before all is revealed — and that much embellished, I have no doubt.' He was to be proved right within a week.

But before these unwelcome comments were made, Winnie and Jennie had packed their bags and taken the train to Torquay.

Jenny's agitation at first hearing of the plan had gradually changed to pleasurable anticipation. This was increased when she recalled that an old childhood friend, another inmate of the orphanage, had married a draper in the town. It was true that they only wrote to each other at Christmas time, exchanging handkerchiefs or bath salts, but they shared potent memories of their early home and had a strong affection for each other.

Winnie was delighted to hear of this link, and an invitation to Harry and Bessie to have tea with them at the hotel on the Sunday was warmly accepted.

The hotel itself gave Jenny confidence at once. She had secretly feared that everything would be over-poweringly grand. Certainly all in sight was harmonious and beautifully kept, a virtue which appealed to house-proud Jenny immediately. But besides this, the hotel staff were welcoming, the service unobtrusive and efficient, and the windows overlooked a well-kept garden with the sparkling sea beyond. Jenny's spirits rose as she unpacked in the bedroom next to Winnie's, stopping to gaze at the view on each trip to the wardrobe. Who would have thought she would ever be in such a lovely place? And so far from Thrush Green too?

To her surprise she felt relief rather than sadness at the thought of the distance between her present bedroom and the one at home. Somehow it was good to get away from the old familiar view, the chestnut avenue, the children running to school, Mr Jones watering the hanging baskets outside The Two Pheasants.

Above all, she had to admit, it was a relief to get away from Percy Hodge. Perhaps now she could see things more clearly without his presence to upset her.

Ah well! Tomorrow she would see Bessie again, and her husband for the first time. It was good to be looking forward to new interests. She would forget Thrush Green for a while, and really make the most of this wonderful holiday.

*

The sunshine which enhanced Jenny's first view of Torquay bathed the entire country.

At Thrush Green, early roses graced the window sills of Miss Fogerty's classroom. Mr Jones's geraniums burst into exuberant bloom, and the sound of the lawn mower was heard in the land.

The meadow leading to Lulling Woods was ablaze with buttercups. Daisies starred Thrush Green itself, and mothers watched their toddlers clutching bunches in their fat hands. The wooden seats were warm to sit upon, and young and old, eyes closed against the dazzling light, dreamt and dozed in perfect bliss.

Even Albert Piggott appeared less malevolent and, bill hook in hand to show that he was mindful of his duties, sunned himself upon a flat tombstone by the churchyard wall.

Along the lane to Nod and Nidden the cow parsley frothed and shed its lacy flowers in the breeze. Dotty Harmer admired its fragile beauty as she took Flossie for her afternoon walk. To tell the truth, the spaniel would have much preferred to spend the afternoon lying in the plum tree's shade in Dotty's garden but, obliging as ever, accompanied her beloved mistress with every appearance of pleasure. She was grateful to her owner, and had not forgotten how she had been rescued by her and given such a loving home. What if the melting tar did squeeze between her claws in this unpleasant way? It was a small price to pay for the pleasure of sharing a walk with Dotty and making her happy.

The elder flowers were beginning to open, turning their creamy faces to the sun, and Dotty turned her mind to making elder-flower champagne if only she could remember where she put the recipe. Behind the kitchen clock? In the Coalport vegetable dish? In mother's secretaire? She would have a good look around when she returned home.

She came within sight of Thrush Green, shimmering in the heat. Perhaps it would be a good idea to call at Ella's. The recipe had come from her in the first place.

She crossed the green, a scraggy shabby figure topped by a frayed coolie straw hat, the object of mirth to two young mothers lolling on one of the seats. Flossie panted obediently behind her.

Ella was in her garden, sitting in a deck chair. Across her lap was draped a small sack, and across that lay some strands of raffia in gaudy colours. A large needle threaded with a piece of scarlet raffia was in Ella's hand, but it was not being used.

Ella was asleep, her mouth ajar, her head lodged sideways. Dotty surveyed her for a few moments, trying to decide if she should tiptoe away. However, the recipe was needed im-

mediately if she wanted to pick really fresh elder flowers.

She coughed discreetly, and Ella awoke.

'Golly!' exclaimed Ella, reverting in her bemused state to the ejaculations of her childhood. 'You made me jump!'

'I'm sorry about that, but the front door was wide open, so I just came through.'

'And quite right too,' said Ella. 'Pull up that other chair and relax. What weather! That's why I opened the front door. You get a nice breeze right through the house that way, though I don't suppose the police would approve.'

'Was that young officer a good speaker? I couldn't come to the W.I. last Wednesday. One of the hens was indisposed, and I felt I should be at hand, you know.'

'Quite,' said Ella, envisaging Dotty crouched in the hen run holding a flaccid claw in her own skinny hand. 'How is she now?'

'Oh, quite recovered, thank you. I was sorry to miss the talk. About safety precautions, wasn't it? Not that I ever think of locking the house, though I suppose one should.'

'He seemed to think that *opening* the door to strangers was even worse.'

'But why? After all, one is obliged to open the door to see if they really are strangers.'

'Evidently, they are inclined to knock you on the head,' replied Ella, 'and then take anything of value before you come round.'

'How very unpleasant! I can't say I get many strangers, do you?'

'The odd tramp now and again. I always fill their billycans with hot water as requested, and give 'em a slice of bread and cheese.'

'I must admit that I do too. My father was quite outspoken about tramps, and said some very *wounding* things to them, I thought. You know, about Satan finding mischief for idle hands to do, and able-bodied men always being able to find work if they really looked for it. They seldom called twice.'

'I must say, I try to protect myself from an inundation of tramps by warning them not to leave any of their cryptic signs on the gate post.'

'Do they do that?'

'So I'm told. You know — a circle means: "Here's a soft touch," or a cross means: "Look out! The old cat chucks water over you!" Something of the sort.'

'I must look out for those things. By the way, Ella, what are you making with that sack?'

Ella held up her handiwork.

'Peg bags. Always sell well at sales of work, and the raffia brightens them up, doesn't it?'

'Yes, indeed,' agreed Dotty doubtfully. 'But won't the colours run if the bag gets wet?'

'Why should it get wet?' protested Ella. 'You don't leave your peg bag out in the rain, do you?'

'Yes,' said Dotty.

Dotty would, thought Ella.

'But as it's a good stout bag made out of father's old Burberry years ago, it doesn't come to any harm, you see.'

Here Flossie, who had taken advantage of some shade under a lilac bush, yawned noisily and thumped her tail upon some defenceless forget-me-nots.

Dotty took the hint.

'Time we were off, Ella dear.'

'Won't you stay to tea?'

'No, thank you. Dulcie must be picketed elsewhere for the rest of the day. She's eating voraciously now she's pregnant, and I thought a short spell by the hazel bushes would enliven her diet. Goats really do appreciate variety. That's why I

never get cross when I find that the dear thing has pulled
something off the line for a snack. She's obviously short of
some particular mineral or vitamin.'

Flossie struggled to her feet and lumbered over to her
mistress.

'She feels the heat,' commented Ella, charitably ignoring
the havoc caused by the spaniel's progress through the flower
bed.

'Perfect weather,' she went on, 'to be on holiday. It will do
Winnie and Jenny a power of good by the sea.'

Ella accompanied Dotty through the cool hall and out into
the blaze of Thrush Green. She watched her old friend cross
the grass and turn into the walled lane of golden Cotswold
stone on her way to Lulling Woods and the most pampered
goat in the locality. It was not until next morning that Dotty
realised she had forgotten to ask for the recipe.

At Torquay, the Sunday tea party was a great success, and
Winnie departed for home on the Monday morning feeling
relieved that Jenny had such good friends in the neighbourhood.

Bessie and Harry lived over the shop, not far from the
harbour, and from their upstairs sitting room there was a
view of the sea which delighted Jenny.

She was invited to lunch on the Tuesday, and when Harry
had returned to his duties below, the two old friends settled
down to compare the course of their lives since leaving the
orphanage.

They sat comfortably on a little balcony overlooking the
steep street and the distant sea, their feet lodged in the
decorative ironwork and their heads in the shade of the
canopy above them.

Jenny sighed contentedly.

'Who'd have thought we should find ourselves so comfortable when we were at the orphanage?'

'We've both been lucky,' agreed Bessie. 'And Harry's the perfect husband. I wonder you didn't marry, Jenny. You were always a pretty girl.'

'Never had much chance,' replied Jenny. 'Ma and Pa took up all my time. Not that I grudged it, mark you. They was good to me, and I was glad to pay 'em back, but I didn't get out and about much.'

'But now they're gone,' persisted Bessie. 'Don't you ever think of it?'

In the silence that followed only the distant sea gulls cried. Jenny wondered if she should unburden herself to her old friend, and perhaps get her advice. On the other hand, her natural shyness made her reluctant.

But the sun warmed her legs. The sea air was exhilarating. Thrush Green and its gossipers were far away, and for once Jenny threw aside her caution.

'Well, as a matter of fact, Bessie, there is someone at the moment,' she confessed, and the tale of Percy's attentions, her own embarrassment and uncertainty, Winnie Bailey's kindness and her needs, all came tumbling out.

Bessie, eyes closed against the brilliance of the afternoon, listened attentively. In common with the rest of mankind, Bessie loved a story, and here was a romantic drama of real life – its heroine lying close beside her and, better still, asking for her advice.

'So there it is,' finished Jenny, feeling mightily relieved after such an outpouring, 'and I hope I'll know what to do by the time I get back. It's my belief Mrs Bailey got me away to give me a chance to sort out my feelings rather than improve my health.'

'It's a bit difficult to know where one ends and the other

begins,' said Bessie sagaciously. 'I had stye after stye on my eyelids when Harry was courting me, but as soon as I said "Yes" they vanished.'

'But what do you think? He's such a good chap and he does miss his Gertie terribly. She was a wonderful manager, and the best cook in Thrush Green some said. He'd lost without her, and his clothes are getting something dreadful – buttons off, cuffs frayed – you know how men get their things.'

Bessie sat forward and propped her chin on her fist. She gazed out to sea as she spoke slowly.

'It's like this, Jenny. I don't doubt he's in need of a wife, and I don't doubt he'll find one pretty soon, if he's the nice fellow you say. But it's *you* I'm thinking of. Do *you* want to live with this Percy for the rest of your days? Do *you* want to give up the life you've just found simply because Percy's clothes need mending? You've always been unselfish. I can remember that from when we were little kids, and you've spent all your time till now looking after Ma and Pa. I don't say Percy wouldn't be grateful, and would treat you right. I'm sure he would. But is it what you want?'

'If you put it like that,' said Jenny, 'I suppose I should never have thought of Percy in that way, if he hadn't come – well, I suppose you could say – *courting*.'

'I'll tell you something else, Jenny, which always helped me when I was trying to decide about a man. I was no flibbertigibbet, mind you, but I did have quite a few lads in my time, before I met Harry, and I used to say to myself when they started to get serious: 'Now, would it break my heart to see him with someone else?' And, d'you know, half the time I used to think it would be a relief if they *did* find someone! Then I knew my own feelings!'

Jenny laughed.

'What a sensible way of looking at it! I can't tell you how you've helped, Bessie, and I think I'll know my own mind before I go back to Thrush Green. It's just that I hate to think of Percy being hurt.'

'Nice men aren't hurt for long,' said Bessie robustly. 'They find someone else quite easily, believe me. Mark my words, if you turn down your Percy he'll be married within the year! I've seen it happen time and time again, and no hearts broken either.'

And then the subject of Percy was shelved, and for the next few hours the talk was of what happened to Mary Carter, and to Joan King, and to the two sisters who ran away and incurred the wrath of the Principal.

Later, Jenny walked back to the hotel through a rose and lavender sunset, and loitered in the garden before going to her room.

The air was fragrant with night-scented stock, mignonette, and the aromatic spiciness of the cypress trees.

For the first time for months, Jenny felt at peace. That old saying about a trouble shared being a trouble halved was perfectly true, she reminded herself as she went thankfully up to bed.

W INNIE returned to her empty house and, much to her surprise, found that she quite enjoyed having it to herself.

Jenny's presence was always a comfort to her, particularly after dark, and she certainly missed the chatter of Jeremy after his few weeks' stay. But now that high summer was here, and the scents and sounds of Thrush Green floated through the open windows, Winnie felt no hint of loneliness and found a certain quiet pleasure in having no interruptions to her train of thought as she moved about the house she had lived in for so long.

Perhaps, after all, she would not miss Jenny so desperately if Percy's suit were successful. It was a surprising thought, and one which gave Winnie some pleasure. It must mean that she was over the worst of the shock of her dear Donald's death. Time, it seemed, as everyone had kept telling her, did heal wounds. She had not really believed it, but now she wondered. At least, this new-found confidence was welcome, and if Jenny were to leave her then she could bear it with greater fortitude than she had thought possible.

Her happiness continued through the week. Jenny was due to come home at teatime on the Saturday, and Winnie had instructed her to take a taxi from Lulling Station, despite Jenny's protests about the expense.

'I'm not having you walk over a mile, and uphill at that, struggling with a suitcase and all the rest of the luggage. And suppose it rains? No, you must do as I say, Jenny.'

And Jenny had agreed.

But on Friday afternoon Percy Hodge had appeared on the doorstep with a bunch of Mrs Sinkin pinks as big as a cauliflower and had announced that he would be meeting the 4.10 train.

'But we've arranged for Jenny to come up by taxi,' explained Winnie, somewhat taken aback.

'I know that. But I'd particularly like to have a word with Jenny, and it's a pleasure to meet her off the train. No need for a taxi when I've got the car.'

Winnie could do no more than thank him, but the expression 'like to have a word with Jenny' sounded ominous. Was he going to propose marriage between Lulling Station and Thrush Green? And what would Jenny think when she found Percy waiting at the station? And suppose that Percy was a little late and Jenny had already taken the taxi? Oh dear, what a muddle!

By the time seven o'clock came Winnie was decidedly agitated, although she realised that Percy and Jenny's affairs were their own business. In the end, she decided to ring Jenny at Torquay, and to let her know that Percy was meeting the train, and to leave it at that. At least, the girl would be prepared.

As it happened, Jenny had spent her last evening with Bessie and Harry, but Winnie left a message with the girl at the switchboard and could only hope that Jenny would get it when she returned. In a way, it was a relief not to have to speak directly to Jenny. She might have wanted lengthy explanations.

Winnie went to bed, telling herself that she had had quite enough for one day, and the morrow must take care of itself.

The morrow, as it happened, brought Ella Bembridge to

the door at ten o'clock in the morning.

Winnie had been in her garden picking roses and inspecting the raspberry canes. It looked as though there would be a fine crop this year, but rain would be needed to plump up the berries. The sky was cloudless, as it had been now for a week or more, and despite the needs of the raspberry canes, Winnie could not find it in her heart to pray for a change in the weather.

'Another glorious day!' she greeted Ella.

'Not for the Lovelock girls!' replied Ella. As none of the three sisters would ever see seventy-five again Winnie could not help feeling that *girls* was not the exact word for her three aged friends.

'Not ill?' exclaimed Winnie.

'Burgled!' said Ella, sitting down heavily on a delicate Sheraton chair which creaked a protest.

'No! When? How? What have they lost?'

'The answers are: Yes. Yesterday. By a person or persons unknown. And they're not sure yet what has gone, but it's nearly all old silver.'

'Poor old darlings! It will break their hearts. They loved their bits of silver.'

'Well, they were told often enough to keep it in a cupboard or the bank, but you know them! They said they enjoyed seeing it about them.'

'And why not? What's the fun of having lovely things if you don't enjoy them? My mother was left a diamond bracelet by her grandmother, and it was so wickedly valuable that it never saw the light of day but was in the bank's vault. My mother often grieved for it, I know.'

'Best place for it,' said Ella sturdily. 'You remember what that police officer told us about keeping valuables out of sight?'

'Of course I remember. And as a matter of fact, I've even locked the front door when I've been shopping in Lulling recently. What's more, I forgot where I'd hidden the key, and had to wait for Jenny to let me in. I'm sure people weren't so dishonest in our young days. It does make life very difficult for everyone.'

'Well, I thought I'd let you know in case you were seeing the girls some time soon.'

'I'll ring them to see if I can help,' said Winnie, 'but quite what to do is the question, isn't it? Their silver must have been worth a fortune. I suppose they were insured?'

'Lord knows!' replied Ella, heaving herself from the protesting chair. 'By the way, d'you want gooseberries? Bumper crop I've got, so come and help yourself. The Lovelock girls were picking theirs when the thief got in evidently.'

'What a bold fellow! And yes, please, I'd love some gooseberries to bottle. Nothing nicer than hot gooseberry tart on a bleak December day. Can I come one day next week when Jenny's back?'

'Any time you like,' said Ella, and stumped out into the morning blaze.

It was Miss Violet Lovelock who spoke to Winnie on the telephone, and although she sounded upset, her account of the burglary was remarkably clear and detailed.

'It's the *effrontery* of the crime that has so shaken us,' she cried, in her high quivering voice. 'We were only in the garden, you know, all busy picking our beautiful golden gooseberries for bottling. The wretched fellow must have pushed open the front door and seen us at it through the hall window. It gives a clear view of the garden as you know.'

'But why should he open the door?'

'Well, dear, the milkman normally leaves óur bottles in that rather fine cache-pot by the doorstep, but in this hot weather Bertha said it might be wiser for him to put it just inside the front door, and she left a note to that effect in the cache-pot. The thief must have seen it.'

'Very likely.'

'The milkman has been so unpunctual lately. We never know when he will appear. He's courting May Miller at the draper's, and his van stands outside for *hours*. I wonder he's not had up for loitering with intent.'

'You can't have a van charged with loitering, Violet dear.'

'Well, anyway,' went on Miss Lovelock, 'this wretched fellow lifted a carrier bag from the hall stand, went into the dining room and put *everything* – simply *everything* – from the sideboard into it. He also took everything from the hall table too.'

'And no one saw him?'

'Well, dear, a man on the bus saw him, we gather. The thief must have stepped into a bus as soon as he emerged. Extremely fortunate for him when you consider the paucity of public transport these days. This man – who saw him, I mean – has given a description to the police. He noticed that the carrier bag *clanked*, but as it was a Debenham's bag – such a *respectable* firm – he simply supposed that he had been buying kitchenware of some description, saucepans and fish kettles and so on.'

'Do Debenham's sell kitchenware?'

'I'm not sure. Shops sell such odd things these days, though never what you want. Bertha is having such a job buying double satin baby ribbon to thread through her best nightgown. It seems to have vanished from the market.'

'What's the next move, Violet? Are the police being helpful?'

'Oh, very! Most sympathetic. The only thing is that we are having such difficulty in providing a correct list. I wake in the night and think: 'Now, did I mention the pseudo-Lamerie posset cup which although made in Birmingham in 1905 was solid silver and quite charming?' The young officer who is dealing with us is patience itself, and always ready for a cup of Earl Grey tea. Luckily, he doesn't take sugar.'

There speaks a true Lovelock, thought Winnie, frugal even in adversity.

She put down the telephone after further expressions of sympathy, and went about her domestic duties.

The news about Molly's coming baby was soon general knowledge at Thrush Green. Everyone, with the exception of the baby's grandfather-to-be, Albert Piggott, was delighted.

'Lot of fuss about nothing,' growled Albert when congratulated by his fellow-drinkers at The Two Pheasants. 'If you ask me there's too many people in the world already, without adding to 'em.'

'You'll have to look after yourself a bit more, Albert me boy,' said one sagely. 'Can't expect Molly to do as she usually does for you, with another on the way.'

'D'you think I ain't thought of that meself?' snapped Albert, and gazed gloomily into his empty glass.

Little Miss Fogerty decided to put aside the cardigan she was knitting for next winter and to buy some baby wool at once for a jacket for the new child.

She was somewhat agitated about the choice of colour for the finished garment.

'I like pink myself,' she told Miss Watson, as they cracked

their boiled eggs, 'and I've no doubt Molly is hoping for a girl this time. But if it is another boy, pink looks so *effeminate*, doesn't it? Perhaps blue would be safer. Girls look just as pretty in blue, don't you think?'

Miss Watson agreed somewhat absent-mindedly, and Agnes was instantly alert.

'Tell me, Dorothy, is your leg paining you?' Her own problems were forgotten at once.

Miss Watson sighed.

'To tell you the truth, Agnes, I had a most disturbed night with it.'

'Then we'll call in Doctor Lovell immediately.'

'No, no. I saw him not long ago, you remember, and he told me then that it was nothing to worry about. It was only *referred pain*, he said.'

'So what!' remarked little Miss Fogerty, quite militant on her friend's behalf. 'If it's pain, it's pain, and hurts! What's the difference between *legitimate* pain and this *referred* variety?'

'I quite agree,' confessed Miss Watson, wincing as she moved her chair. 'All very unsatisfactory, but is one in a position to argue? I think we'll wait a day or two, and see how it goes on. I may have slept in an awkward position, and put my pelvic girdle out a little.'

'Maybe,' agreed Agnes. 'That's the worst of bones. They're all joined on and, I must admit, in the most careless fashion at times. But I warn you, Dorothy, I shall have no hesitation in summoning the doctor if I see you are suffering.'

Miss Watson smiled at her good friend. On the rare occasions when she was roused she looked, as she did now, like a ferocious mouse.

'I've no doubt I shall be as fit as a flea tomorrow,' she assured Agnes.

But even fleas, she reminded herself, as she rose painfully from the table, must have their off days.

Dimity and Charles Henstock, now happily installed at Mrs Jenner's, met Dotty Harmer in the lane leading from Thrush Green to Nidden. They told her the news of Molly's expectations.

Dotty stood stock-still, looking bemused, while Flossie snuffled happily at Charles Henstock's legs, her plume of tail greatly agitated in her pleasure.

'Due in December? What a long time. Are you sure that's correct, Charles? I've forgotten the gestation period for humans. Goats, rabbits and cats I am perfectly sound on, but *babies* now . . .'

'I can assure you, Dotty, that December is correct,' said Dimity. 'Nine months, you know, is the time needed, and now it's June, so in six months' time the baby will arrive.'

'Yes, yes, I'm quite sure Molly would know. Such a competent little mother as she is. It's just that I had forgotten for the moment.'

'Come and have some tea in our new home,' suggested Charles. 'You've thought no more, by the way, about adopting a child of your own?'

'I can't say I've had any encouragement,' retorted Dotty. 'From the adoption societies — or from you, for that matter, if you recall, Charles dear. I've decided to give up the plan. With much regret, I may say.'

Charles heaved a sigh of relief.

'And, yes please, I should love a cup of tea with you at Mrs Jenner's.'

They began to retrace their steps. Flossie bounding ahead.

'Of course,' said Dotty conversationally, as they entered Mrs Jenner's gate, 'elephants carry their young for two years. I think that is what was confusing me. Poor things!' She added pityingly.

Charles and Dimity, following Dotty's scarecrow figure up the path, exchanged glances of shared joy.

What would they do without Dotty?

As Jenny's train rushed eastward from Torquay through the June countryside, she looked back upon her holiday with great contentment.

To have been by the sea would have been happiness enough. So seldom had she seen it that the wonder of its immensity and its changing moods, even viewed from the serenity of Meadfoot Beach, filled her with awe and excitement.

She remembered the thrill of paddling at the edge of the waves, watching them frilling round her ankles. She had not ventured to bathe, paddling was as much as she dared to do, but the sight of her feet, grotesquely distorted beneath the green water, filled her with joyous amusement.

The sea itself and the soft salty air had worked wonders for her spirits. Jenny began to realise how very run down she must have been, and would always be grateful to Winnie Bailey for recognising the state of affairs, and for dealing so briskly and generously with it.

Swaying gently to the rhythm of the train, Jenny watched the telegraph poles flicker past against the background of green woods and fields. She would never be able to repay Winnie's kindness. The holiday had been wonderful, and an added bonus had been the joy of meeting Bessie again. The warm contentment which now engulfed her was due as much to Bessie's friendship and advice as to the healing properties of Torquay's sea and air.

Yesterday evening Bessie had raised again the subject of Percy Hodge, guessing that Jenny must be feeling some tremors again at the thought of returning to Thrush Green and to facing her admirer once more.

She did not know, of course, that Percy was to meet Jenny's train. Winnie Bailey's guarded message still awaited Jenny's return to the hotel. But she thought it would do no harm to see if her old friend were more settled in her mind. She raised the matter delicately, and Jenny sighed.

'I remember what you told me about imagining someone else with your young man,' she said, 'and it worked, you know. If only some nice woman would take on Percy I think I'd be truly relieved. He does *need* someone so.'

'I'm glad to hear you say that,' replied Bessie. 'But it needn't be you who supplies it. After all, Jenny, if his lost buttons and frayed collars worry you, then you could always offer to do some mending for him, as an old friend. You don't have to *marry* the fellow, now do you?'

And Jenny had laughed and agreed.

How sensible Bessie was! Of course, that was the right way to deal with Percy's ardours. Perhaps if she had had as many admirers as Bessie had in her young days, she would not have worried so much about dear old Percy's attentions. It was the sheer unexpectedness of being wanted by someone which had so agitated her. Bessie was probably quite right to say that Percy would find someone else within the year. She hoped he would. He was a good man and deserved some comfort and companionship.

As for her own feelings, well – it was nice to have been courted. She would always be grateful to Percy for singling her out. But what a relief it would be to be freed from the necessity and embarrassment of thanking him for flowers, eggs, soap, plants and all the other kind presents which Percy had brought to the door!

She closed her eyes against the Wiltshire meadows flashing past, and gave a sigh of contentment. Now she knew what to do. Now she could face Percy at the station. Probably he would say very little and just pick up her case, and talk about the weather. Then there would be no need to say anything much, except to tell him about Torquay. That should last beautifully until they reached Thrush Green. There really would not be much time to discuss feelings, thought Jenny with relief, and in any case, Percy was not a demonstrative man. And who knows, with any luck, his passion — such as it was — might have cooled in her absence, and meeting the train might simply be the gesture of an old friend.

As would be her offer to do his mending, thought Jenny, if the occasion arose. Well, at least she was in command of her own affairs now, and could cope with whatever Percy offered.

She dozed a little as the sunlight roamed around the carriage. The train's brakes squealed and the rhythm altered. Jenny awoke to see familiar fields running alongside.

She lifted down her case and stood by the window, swaying in the movement of the rattling carriage. In the distance she could see a little knot of people, and one figure standing alone. It was Percy.

He ran along by the side of the train and wrenched open the door. Jenny smiled and handed down the case as the train squealed to a halt.

Perfectly in command of her feelings, she began to step down, but before her foot had reached the platform, she was lifted bodily by Percy and enveloped in a great bear hug.

'How I've missed you, my girl!' cried Percy.

And Jenny's heart sank.

13 Jenny Decides

WINNIE Bailey awaited Jenny's arrival eagerly, but with a certain amount of anxiety. Had she received her message about Percy? How would Percy greet her? Would she have come to any firm decisions about her future whilst at Torquay?

The train was due at Lulling Station soon after four o'clock. Winnie prepared a tea tray. Jenny would need some refreshment after her journey, and over it perhaps she would hear something of Jenny's plans, as well as an account of the holiday.

By a quarter to five Winnie was beginning to feel slightly worried. If Percy had driven Jenny straight through Lulling High Street and up the sharp hill to Thrush Green, they should have arrived by half past four at the latest. Of course, she told herself, the train might have been behind time, but the more disturbing possibility was that Percy had made a detour to find a quiet spot to make a proposal.

She surveyed the tea tray. There were two cups and saucers, some tomato sandwiches and home-made biscuits. It might be as well to put out another cup in case Percy was now a fiancé. Trying to control her agitation, Winnie went to find a third cup, and to check the kettle.

At that moment, she heard a car stop, and hurried to the window.

Jenny alighted, and Percy lifted out her case from the back seat. They held a short conversation, and Winnie thought that Jenny seemed rather put out. Percy's face expressed his habitual happy bemusement when in Jenny's company, and he seemed to want to carry the case to the door.

Jenny lifted it herself, said farewell to her suitor, and strode determinedly up the path. Percy waved, and got back into the driver's seat, as Winnie hurried to open the front door.

'Won't Percy come in?' she asked.

'He's got to get back,' said Jenny shortly, watching the car pull away from the kerb.

'Well, my dear, it's lovely to have you home, and I'm just making some tea, so come and sit down.'

'I can do with a cup,' said Jenny thankfully. 'Percy can be a bit of a trial at times.'

And Winnie, pouring boiling water in the teapot, felt a pang of blessed relief.

Over the tea-cups, Jenny gave an account of her surprising welcome at the station.

'I was fair taken aback, as you can imagine, and I told him pretty straight not to behave so silly. But, bless you, he don't seem to take much notice when he's set on something, and he drove round the back way – he *said* to dodge the traffic, but that was all my eye and Betty Martin – which is why I'm so late. He would stop in the old avenue, and there he went on about how he'd missed me, and now I was back we could think about getting married, until I could have hit him.'

'And what did *you* say, Jenny?'

'When I could get a word in edgeways, I said I was sorry but I wasn't planning to get married to anyone, and certainly not to him. But you might just as well talk to a brick wall as Percy Hodge. He didn't seem to take it in. In the end I got quite wild, and begged to be put down so as I could walk home to get a bit calmer. But he wouldn't have it.'

'A persistent fellow,' agreed Winnie, feeling more cheerful every minute.

'More tea, Jenny dear?'

Jenny passed her cup.

'It's thirsty work turning down chaps, I can tell you,' she said, 'especially when they're as pig-headed as Percy. Well, in the end he said he was off to Wales tomorrow morning to get some cattle, and he'd be away two or three days, so I could get used to the idea of being engaged, and he'd call when he got back.'

'Oh dear, Jenny! Are you sure what you want to do?'

'Mrs Bailey,' said Jenny earnestly, 'I've thought of all this ever since I've left here, and I'm positive I don't want to marry Percy. What's more, I don't want to leave you.'

Winnie felt tears of relief pricking her eyes.

'Well, it's wonderful news for me, of course, and I'm glad you know your own mind. But I shouldn't like you to throw away your future happiness out of loyalty to me. Percy's a good fellow, and would make a kind husband, I'm sure, and he's obviously devoted to you. It's a good thing you have these few days to think things over.'

'I don't need a few days,' said Jenny robustly. 'I know now, and I feel all the better for coming to a decision. When Percy comes back I'll make it quite clear to him.'

'But do be *kind*!' pleaded Winnie. 'He'll be so disappointed.'

'Bessie says she wouldn't mind betting he's happily married within a year,' said Jenny shrewdly. 'But it won't be to me! I'll just go and rinse the tea things.' She jumped to her feet.

'You won't,' said Winnie. 'You've had enough to cope with in the past hour. Tea things can wait.'

*

There was no doubt about it. Jenny's holiday had set her up again, and she attacked her work with renewed vigour. Winnie rejoiced in her return to health and good spirits.

She said nothing more to Jenny about Percy, nor did she breathe a word to anyone else in Thrush Green, but somehow or other it seemed to be general knowledge, by the end of a week, that Percy Hodge had received his marching orders from Jenny.

Comment at The Two Pheasants was now completely contrary to earlier views expressed. Far from thinking that Jenny might have done very well for herself as Percy's second wife, the general opinion seemed to be that she had shown very good sense in repelling his advances.

Some went even further.

'Take my word for it,' said one worthy, 'she found something better down in Devon. You can tell by the look of her. Fair come to life since going to Torquay. There's a man at the bottom of it, I shouldn't wonder.'

'Can't blame her. After all, old Perce has been no more'n a thin string of misery since his Gertie went. Jenny's got herself to think of, and she's well enough off as she is in Doctor Bailey's place.'

'Talk about a lot of women clacking,' cried the landlord, 'you chaps is worse than the lot! Putting two and two together and making half a dozen! Maybe Perce hasn't asked her yet.'

'He ain't been near the place since he called after he got back from Wales. Why, he was everlasting mincing along with ruddy great bunches of flowers and that before she went away. Now look at him! Ain't I right?' he appealed to his fellow drinkers.

There were confirmatory grunts of agreement. Albert Piggott had the last word.

'It's my belief they've both seen the light, mates. This marrying and giving in marriage, what is cracked up so, can be a terrible let-down. And I'll have another half-pint of bitter, please, seeing I'm a free man without a wife to nag me.'

It was soon after this that Harold and Isobel Shoosmith had a little party. Encouraged by the blissful spell of June weather, when the roses and pinks were at their most beguiling, and the sun was still above the horizon at nine at night, they invited some two dozen old friends to drop by to see them.

The Henstocks and the Hursts arrived together. Frank Hurst had known Harold for many years and had been introduced to Phyllida by him when she was trying desperately to earn her living as a free-lance writer and had first come to live at Thrush Green.

Agnes Fogerty was one of Isobel's oldest friends. They had met as girls at college, and it was a shared joy now to live next door to each other. Dorothy Watson, chic in navy-blue silk, accompanied her assistant. The Youngs, the Bassetts, Winnie Bailey, Ella Bembridge and Dotty Harmer were all at the party, as well as several Lulling friends, including Anthony Bull, Lulling's handsome vicar.

The evening was warm and windless, and the guests wandered about in the garden congratulating Harold and Isobel on their superbly mown lawns and weedless garden beds.

'All Harold's doing,' Isobel told them. 'I'm just the dead-header of roses and pansies — a very lowly assistant gardener.'

'Any news about your new home?' enquired Anthony Bull of Charles, as they stood together under a copper beech tree.

'I gather there is some debate about building a smaller

place on the old site, or finding a readymade establishment and selling the existing plot. I suppose that the land might command a good price, although I know very little about these things.'

'It is not very big,' observed Anthony. 'I wonder if it would fetch a good price. Doubtful, I should think. But tell me, are you comfortable at Mrs Jenner's?'

Charles's chubby face was lit with a smile.

'Incredibly comfortable! Dimity and I had no idea one could be so warm and happy. The windows face south, you know, and the light is wonderful. I never need to put on my desk light when I am writing. I can't get over the joy of it.'

'It's a house I've always admired,' said Anthony. 'Much the same age as our vicarage. Those eighteenth century builders knew what they were doing, didn't they?'

'Without a doubt,' agreed Charles. 'Without a doubt. Although I grieve for our poor departed home, I'm just beginning to realise that it was badly designed, and dear Dimity must have put up with most uncomfortable surroundings, without a word of complaint.'

'Ah! You married an angel, Charles, and I did too. We are fortunate fellows.'

Phyllida Hurst came up to them.

'Good news! The Thomases' baby arrived yesterday. A boy, and Jack sounded so pleased on the telephone. Wasn't it sweet of him to ring?'

'A charming young man, I thought,' said Charles. 'And of course he would let you know. After all, they were greatly obliged to you for letting them have Tullivers.'

Anthony Bull had walked away to have a word with Miss Watson and Miss Fogerty. Phil spoke rapidly.

'I've only just discovered that the other young couple must have been a sore disappointment to you all.'

'Really?' replied Charles, his face puckered with bewilderment. 'I hardly saw them, I must confess.'

'They were on drugs, you know.'

'The sort you smoke?'

'I gather so.'

'That must have been the peculiar smell I noticed when I called. I thought it was something cooking – herbs, I imagined, of some sort.'

'Well, that's one way of looking at it!'

'How did you find out? Did Jack Thomas tell you?'

'No. Jeremy did.'

'*Jeremy!*' exclaimed the rector, 'but how on earth – ?'

'One of the boys at school has an older sister who has been on the stuff. She knew that the Thomases' friends bought it, and told her brother who told Jeremy evidently. I gather she's given it up now, thank heaven. Foolish girl to start, of course.'

'Well, you have surprised me,' said Charles. 'I can only hope that the other two will follow her example. And I am delighted to hear about the baby. Do congratulate the Thomases for us, if you are in touch.'

His eye alighted on the three Lovelock sisters who were admiring two small silver dishes containing nuts.

'Ah, do excuse me, Phyllida. I must have a word with the Lovelock girls. I haven't seen them since the burglary.'

He hastened away. Phil noted the predatory gleam in Miss Violet's eye as she put back the little dish on the table.

Was she already replacing their lost collection wondered Phil? She hastily quashed the unworthy thought, and went to talk to Joan Young.

Later that evening Dorothy Watson and Agnes Fogerty rested in their sitting room and discussed the excitement of the party.

'I thought that Joan Young looked very well in that bottle green frock. A very pretty neckline.'

Dorothy had a great eye for dress, as Agnes knew, and took enormous interest in the clothes of others. Agnes herself was content to be clean and respectable, but ever enthralled to hear her friend's comments on others' appearance.

'And did you notice,' continued Dorothy, 'that Ada Lovelock's evening bag was freshly adorned with some jet edging which looked to me remarkably like the stuff I sent to be sold at her recent coffee morning? I have never known such greed as those Lovelock sisters show when it comes to gewgaws.'

'You can't call all their lovely things *gewgaws*,' protested Agnes. 'And in any case, you can't be sure that the trimming was the material you sent.'

'Agnes dear, I am quite sure,' said Dorothy firmly. 'I am

the first to admire your fair-mindedness, but you must not deceive yourself. That trimming was undoubtedly *appropriated*, one might say *purloined*, by the Lovelocks, well before the coffee morning.'

'That's as maybe,' agreed Agnes, 'but the poor souls have suffered terribly from the loss of all their beautiful things, and I do think that they might be forgiven for buying in that jet edging. They might easily be in a state of shock.'

'They've been in that particular state of shock ever since I've known them,' said Dorothy. 'However, they're much too old to change their ways now, so we won't waste time in censuring them. Agnes dear, I'm uncommonly thirsty. Do you think a glass of fresh orange juice would be a good idea for us?'

'Of course it would,' said Agnes, getting up at once. 'Keep your legs up, my dear, you have been standing quite long enough, while I get us both something.'

One day, thought Dorothy, watching her friend bustling towards the kitchen, I hope I shall be able to repay the kindness of that completely selfless soul. But will it ever be possible?

A few mornings later, Charles Henstock sat at his desk and gazed out at the sunlit garden. He was attempting to write next Sunday's sermon, always a difficult task, and not made any easier on this gorgeous June day by all the happy distractions outside the window.

A blue tit, with a mimosa yellow breast, clung to the coconut half which swung from a branch of the old plum tree. His antics were as delightful as they were graceful. A bully-boy of a blackbird bustled below, chasing all the other groundlings away from the crumbs which fell from the tit's energetic assault on the coconut.

Above, a tiny silver aeroplane ruled a fast-fading line across the blue sky, and over in Percy Hodge's field a red and white cow sat chewing the cud with the same vague bliss in its surroundings which now enveloped the good rector. And curled up in the chair beside him was their cat, which had settled down at Mrs Jenner's as happily as they had themselves.

Dimity had gone to Lulling to shop and Charles found his new abode very quiet. Dimity's parting words had been to the effect that he would have peace in which to compose his sermon.

He certainly had that, he thought, putting down his pen and propping his head on his hand. How pretty the young leaves looked on the plum tree! How beautifully fashioned was the wing of the fluttering tit! How vivid the beak of the blackbird!

This was a very pleasant place to live, and he thanked God humbly for leading him to such a haven after the tragedy of the fire. Where, eventually, would his home be, he wondered yet again? It was surely time that he heard something from the Church. Anthony Bull, who always seemed to be so much better informed about things, had said that the new rearrangements of the parishes may have held up Charles's particular problem, but it was all rather unsettling. One would like to know one's future.

The good rector sighed, and picked up his pen again. He must make a start at least before Dimity returned. A great black rook now alighted on the grass and began to sidle timidly towards a crust thrown out by Mrs Jenner. The small birds took no notice of this formidable figure in their midst.

The rector decided suddenly to turn his observant idling to good account. His sermon should be about the joy of living in the present, and of looking at the wonders around. Did not

Our Lord Himself tell his followers not to worry about the morrow, what they should eat, what they should put on?

Now inspired, Charles began to settle down to his writing and to sharing his own happiness with his beloved parishioners.

While he was busy scribbling, Molly Curdle was being driven in the local taxi to the County Hospital for an antenatal examination. Doctor Lovell felt certain that all was well, but decided that a check on his own findings would be a sensible precaution at the splendid new maternity wing.

Joan Young would have taken her but had promised to go to a Women's Institute meeting in the neighbouring county. This involved lunching with the as-yet-unknown president, delivering her talk, judging the monthly competition — almost as hazardous and thankless a task as judging a baby show — and then driving back some twenty-five miles. Arthur Tranter was taking her place.

He was a cheerful man, some years older than Molly, but they had both attended Thrush Green School, and knew each other fairly well.

She sat beside him in the taxi, and they chatted amicably of this and that. Molly was careful not to mention her condition and congratulated herself on her still trim figure. However, she need not have troubled to hide anything from the percipient Mr Tranter.

'Havin' the baby up the County then?' he remarked conversationally.

'Possibly,' said Molly.

'I'll take you up if you want me to,' offered he.

'I gets no end of young mums to take there from Lulling. Bit far though, I always think. Too far sometimes for some of 'em. I've brought three into this world in my time, so you don't need to worry.'

Molly remained silent.

'I always say they can name 'em after the old taxi. Maurice, say, or Austin – both good names. I had a Cadillac once, bought off of an American chap up the air base, but none of the mums would name their kids after that. Might be called Cad for short, see?'

He roared with laughter at his own joke, unaffected by Molly's disapproval. She was glad when they began to run through the suburbs of the county town. It was quite bad enough having to face a strange doctor without Arthur's coarse remarks.

'You'll want the ante-natal, love, won't you? I'll be waiting. I've got a flask of coffee and today's paper so don't worry if you're held up. You never can tell with hospitals, can you?'

'No, indeed,' agreed Molly tremulously. Now that they had actually stopped outside the door, fear gripped her, and distasteful as she found Arthur Tranter at least he was an old acquaintance and a link with all that was familiar at distant Thrush Green.

As if he guessed her thoughts, he leant out and patted her arm.

'Cheer up, duck. All be over in next to no time, and we'll step on it and get you home before you have time to turn round.'

She gave him a grateful smile, and went in to face the trial ahead.

14 After The Storm

THE beautiful spell of June weather broke with a violent thunderstorm one torrid night. Lightning flickered eerily for several hours before the thunder asserted itself, and the rain began to rattle on the parched earth. Gutters gurgled, rivulets rippled down the hill to Lulling, and water butts, which had stood empty for weeks, filled rapidly.

So violent was the storm about three o'clock that Harold and Isobel decided that a cup of tea would be a very good thing, and Harold went down to make it. As he waited for the kettle to boil, he surveyed the wet world of Thrush Green through the window.

Other people were awake too, it seemed. There was a dim light at Tullivers, and Harold guessed correctly that it had been put on to allay young Jeremy's fears. There was another light at Ella Bembridge's. No doubt, thought Harold, she is brewing tea, as I am.

No lights showed otherwise. Presumably the Youngs, the Bassetts, Winnie Bailey, Jenny and all the other good folk of Thrush Green, were either deep in slumber or riding out the storm in the darkness of their bedrooms.

Harold thought, not for the first time, how fortunate he had been to settle at Thrush Green. Thousands of miles away when he was in business, he had first heard of this tiny English village, the birthplace of Nathaniel Patten, a zealous missionary, whose work Harold admired deeply. It was

Harold who had been instrumental in raising funds to buy the fine statue of Thrush Green's most distinguished son. He could see it now, glinting as the lightning lit the view. It was good to think that such a good fellow was properly honoured, and Harold was proud of his part in the affair.

He had not bargained though for the generous welcome he had received from the inhabitants of his chosen village. That was a bonus. He had found several people, much of his own age and interests, in this little community who had now become firm friends. He thought with affection and gratitude of the Henstocks, the Baileys, the Hursts, and many others who had made his path here so pleasant. He was lucky to have such good neighbours and Betty Bell to minister to his domestic comfort.

But luckiest of all, he told himself, as he attended to the boiling kettle, was the stroke of good fortune which had come unwittingly through little Agnes Fogerty next door. Her friendship with Isobel, her old college connection, had given him his wife, and a happiness he had never dared to hope for at his age.

Balancing the tray with great care, Harold mounted the stairs, ignoring a crash of thunder which rattled all the window panes.

Isobel, as beautiful as ever, was sitting up in bed, serenely ignoring the violence which raged outside.

'A quarter past three,' she exclaimed, catching sight of the bedside clock. 'What a time to be drinking tea!'

'Anytime,' Harold told her, 'is time to be drinking tea.'

Some half mile to the west, out of sight of Thrush Green, Dotty Harmer was awakened by the din and lay worrying about her animal charges.

Would Dulcie, the goat, be alarmed by the storm? She was

of a nervous disposition, and goats were generally acknowledged to be sensitive to climatic conditions. The chickens and ducks were much more phlegmatic by nature, and were no doubt quite unperturbed in their roosts. As for the many cats, they always took events very philosophically, and dear old Flossie, apart from flinching at any particularly ferocious roll of thunder, seemed quite calm at the end of Dotty's bed.

No, it was dear Dulcie that was her chief worry. Possessed of enormous strength and sleeping in a somewhat battered shed, even by Dotty's standards, she might well crash her way out and do extensive damage to her own and her neighbours' gardens.

There was no help for it, Dotty told herself, but to get up and investigate. The rain lashed against the cottage windows, the wind howled, and the lightning was alarming, but Dotty knew where her duty lay, and clambered out of bed.

She went as she was, barefoot and in her nightgown, down the stairs, followed by the faithful Flossie. In the kitchen she thrust her feet into wellingtons and dragged on her old mackintosh.

As a token concession to the elements she also tied a scarf over her skimpy grey locks, took a torch, and set off to Dulcie's shed.

The onslaught of the rain quite took her breath away, but she battled down the path beneath the flailing branches of the old fruit trees, which scattered showers of water and leaves with every gust of wind.

She looked into the hens' house and, apart from some squawks from her disturbed charges, all seemed well. No sound came from the ducks' shelter, and Dotty decided to leave well alone.

She struggled on, and was suddenly aware of what hard work it was. Her legs seemed leaden. Her heart raced. Water ran down her face from the already sodden scarf, but she pressed on.

By the light of the torch she saw that Dulcie was sitting down. Her chain was slack and in good order, and she was licking a lump of rock salt with evident enjoyment.

'Dear thing,' said Dotty. 'Good Dulcie! Just ignore this dreadful noise, my dear. It will all be over by morning.'

Much relieved, she shut the door again. She trundled the glistening garden roller against it, for good measure, and decided that all would be safe until morning.

It was easier going back with the wind behind her, but Dotty was glad to get to the porch where Flossie, who had taken one look at the weather, had prudently waited for her mistress.

The kitchen was a haven, and Dotty was thankful to rest on the kitchen chair before taking off her wet clothes. Five cats looked at her from their various resting places, ranging from a stack of newspapers to a pile of Dotty's underclothes which were awaiting ironing.

When she could breathe again more easily, Dotty struggled out of her coat and boots. The hem of her nightgown was drenched, but she could not be bothered to change it.

She wondered if it would be worthwhile making a hot drink. She felt uncommonly exhausted. Perhaps she needed a tonic? Perhaps she should see Doctor Lovell? She had not felt her heart behaving in that odd jumpy way before.

She sat for a few more moments, savouring the warmth of the kitchen, the cats' presence, and pondering upon the possibility of visiting Doctor Lovell.

'Oh, drat doctors!' exclaimed Dotty at last, and wearily climbed the stairs.

*

Most of Thrush Green's inhabitants had been disturbed in the night, but the morning dawned still and grey.

A light mist veiled the distance, and the warm earth, thoroughly drenched by the night's heavy rain, caused a humidity which reminded Harold of his days in the tropics.

Betty Bell, arriving like a whirlwind from Lulling Woods, gave a vivid account of the devastation caused in that usually comatose hamlet.

'And my neighbour's nappies — well her *baby's* nappies, of course, but you know what I mean — was wrenched off of her line and went all which-ways. Why, one of 'em blew into the pig sty! Think of that!'

Harold, who was trying to read his post in the study, made suitable noises. Despite the fact that his wife now ran their house, Betty still sought him out as soon as she arrived, to keep him up to date with local affairs. It could be rather trying.

'And they do say that one of them poplars up the rec was struck. Felled to the ground, Willie Marchant told me, and all frizzled round the edges. When you think — it might have been you or me!'

'I doubt if we should have been standing in the recreation ground at two in the morning,' commented Harold, slitting open an unpleasant looking envelope with OHMS on the corner.

'I was going to pop in to see if Miss Harmer was O.K., but I was a bit behindhand after collecting some flowerpots and a bucket and that what had been blown into our hedge. Still, I'll look in on the way home.'

'That would be kind,' agreed Harold.

'Well, I'm glad nothing happened here,' said Betty. 'No tiles off, nor trees broken and that. I'd best get on. Anything particular you want done? Windows, say, or silver?'

'You'd better have a word with my wife,' said Harold.

'I'll do that,' replied Betty, and vanished.

Next door, Miss Fogerty found her charges unusually heavy-eyed. She had planned to teach them a charming little poem of Humbert Wolfe's, but gave up when she found them bemused from lack of sleep and a prey to sighs and yawns.

Always a realist, she faced the fact that such a delightful poem deserved full attention, and at the moment something less intellectually demanding was called for.

'Give out the modelling clay, George dear,' she told young Curdle. 'You can choose which you want to make. Either a basket full of different sorts of fruit, or a tea tray with cups and saucers, and something nice to eat on a big plate.'

'And sugar lumps in a bowl?' asked Anne Cooke.

'Of course. And don't forget the teaspoons.'

There was a marked improvement in interest as the boards and glistening wet balls of clay were distributed.

Miss Fogerty watched them attack their work, and smiled upon them.

Baskets of fruit and tea trays were always good for twenty minutes at least, thought Agnes with satisfaction.

Albert Piggott, not many yards from Thrush Green School, felt as lazy and out-of-sorts as the children. To his disgust, the storm had blown leaves and twigs into the church porch, ripped one or two notices to shreds, and soaked the heavy mat which was bad enough to shift when it was dry, let alone sodden with rain.

He set about his duties dourly, one eye on the door of The Two Pheasants.

His indigestion was even worse than usual this morning.

Perhaps fried food was not good for him, but what could a chap cook when his lawful wedded wife had took off with the oil man? He could not fiddle about with pastry and vegetables and mixing gravy and all the other nonsenses his Nelly had mucked about with.

He plied his broom lethargically. Waste of time, all this cleaning. Come tomorrow it would be as bad again.

There was a welcome rattle from the door of the public house. Jones was unlocking, and about time too! Maybe half a pint, and a slab of cold pork pie, would settle his stomach.

Albert propped his broom against a Zenana Mission poster which had escaped the full fury of the storm, and set off with more vigour than had been apparent all the morning.

'Well, Albert, what a night, eh?' the landlord greeted him. 'I feel a bit washed out this morning, and that's the truth.'

He spoke for all Thrush Green.

A few mornings later, Ella Bembridge was surprised to see Dotty Harmer approaching, carrying the milk can which she usually brought about tea time with Ella's regular order of goat's milk.

Her old friend looked wispier and greyer than ever, she thought, as she ushered her into the sitting room. Flossie followed like Dotty's shadow.

'You're early today,' she said, taking the milk can from Dotty's bony hand. 'My word, you're jolly cold. Dotty! Are you all right?'

'Perfectly,' replied Dotty, looking about her vaguely. 'I've just milked Dulcie, so I thought I would come straight up with your milk while it was fresh.'

'And very nice to see you,' replied Ella. 'But you usually give me the afternoon milk.'

Dotty did not answer. Ella thought that she looked more than usually dishevelled and extremely tired.

'Let me get you a drink,' she urged. 'Coffee? Tea? Orange squash?'

'Could I have a small whisky? Father calls it a sundowner.'

'Of course you can have a small whisky, but it's not exactly sundown, you know. It's hardly ten o'clock.'

'Such light evenings,' agreed Dotty. 'I shall shut up the hens when I get back. Which reminds me, I can't stay very long. Father had one of his little tantrums this morning, and didn't want me to come out.'

She sat nodding to herself, oblivious of Ella's shocked silence.

What on earth had hit poor Dotty? Her dreadful old father had been dead for twenty years! 'One of his little tantrums', as Dotty euphemistically described it, would have struck fear

into the stoutest heart when he lived, but he was now resting
with other Thrush Green worthies under Albert Piggott's
sketchy care.

'Dotty,' began Ella, 'you are not well. It's only ten o'clock
in the morning, and you know you haven't had a living parent
for years! I'm giving you coffee. I'm not sure if whisky would
be the right thing for you just now.'

'I certainly don't want *whisky*,' responded Dotty. 'If Father
smelt strong liquor on my breath he would be most upset.'

She looked down at Flossie.

'What's this dog doing here?' she enquired, 'You didn't
tell me you were getting one.'

By now, Ella was seriously alarmed. The poor soul's mind
was wandering, and what on earth did you do with such a
patient? John Lovell would be in his surgery now, but she
could not leave her. She decided to get to the telephone in the
hall where she would have a clear view of the front door if
Dotty attempted to escape.

'I'm going to put on the kettle, Dotty, so lean back and
have a rest. I must ring the butcher too, so don't worry if I'm
a minute or two.'

'Pray take your time,' said Dotty graciously. 'It stays light
until almost eleven o'clock, you know, so there's no hurry.'

She leant back obediently in the armchair, and closed her
eyes.

Ella, much agitated, hurried to summon help.

John Lovell came himself before starting on his rounds.

He was greeted by Ella with almost incoherent gratitude,
and by Dotty with considerable hauteur.

When Ella had taken in the coffee she had found Dotty fast
asleep, and snoring in an eminently genteel fashion. Ella,
much relieved, hoped that she would stay in this state until

the doctor called. She awoke as Ella went to the front door.

'I'd like to examine her on a bed, Ella,' he said. 'All right?'

'Of course,' she replied. 'Dotty dear, you don't mind if Doctor Lovell has a look at you?'

'I mind very much,' cried Dotty, her papery old cheeks flushing pink, 'but as he has been called — *not* at my request, I hope he understands — I shall let him examine me, but I trust that you will be present.' She seemed to be more her old self since her nap.

Ella and John Lovell exchanged glances.

'Of course Ella can stay,' said the doctor. 'Let's go up.'

He was wonderfully gentle with their old friend, Ella noticed. She could not help noticing too, with considerable alarm, how pathetically frail Dotty was. Her legs and arms were like sticks. Her rib bones could be clearly seen as well as the bones of her neck and shoulders.

Ella turned to look out of the window as the examination went on. Dotty bore all in silence, but sighed with relief when he said that she could get dressed again.

They left her to do so and descended the stairs.

'What is it?' asked Ella.

'You can have it in one word. Malnutrition. She's in a pretty bad way, Ella, and I'm getting her into the Cottage Hospital right away. Can I use your phone?'

'Carry on. I'm shattered, but not surprised. She eats next to nothing, and works far too hard with that menagerie of hers.'

She stopped suddenly, hand to mouth.

'We'll have to get someone to look after them. I'll take on the cats and the poultry, and dear old Flossie can stay here — but that darn goat is beyond me, I don't mind confessing.'

'Don't worry. We'll get something sorted out. But she must get some attention immediately.'

He went into the hall, and Ella slumped inelegantly on the sofa, feeling as if she had been sand-bagged.

Flossie lumbered across the room and put her heavy head on Ella's knee. Ella fondled her long golden ears.

'Flossie, my girl,' she told her, 'we're in a fine old pickle this morning.'

Surprisingly enough, Dotty submitted to all the plans made for her with unaccustomed docility. John Lovell gave the two friends and Flossie a lift back to Lulling Woods and left them there to pack a bag for Dotty while he continued on his rounds.

Ella had expected a spate of instructions about food for the animals, and her own domestic arrangements, but Dotty scarcely said a word. She gave Ella directions about where to find clean nightgowns, a sponge bag, soap and so on in a weak voice, but seemed content to let her do the work.

It was as if she had had quite enough of present problems and was already drifting into oblivion. Ella had never seen anyone in such a state of exhaustion, and was very much alarmed. It was a great relief when a car from the hospital arrived and she could get into it with the patient.

A cheerful nurse, whose face seemed vaguely familiar to Ella, took charge of Dotty, and said that Ella could see her at any time. This sounded ominous to Ella, who knew little about modern hospital methods. She had a confused idea that only those at the point of death were allowed visitors. Surely, one had to come between two and four, or six or seven, and then only with one other person at the bedside?

She kissed Dotty goodbye, and wandered out into Lulling High Street. Where on earth had she seen that nurse before?

It was odd to be at large in the town at almost twelve o'clock. She felt shaky, and the thought of the hill up to

Thrush Green was a little daunting. She made her way to The Fuchsia Bush to get a cup of coffee, and to rest.

She had not been inside since the new arrangements had been made. It had been redecorated in a hideous shade of plum red which clashed appallingly with the old mauve curtains and made the interior unpleasantly gloomy.

Two waitresses, who had been busy painting their nails, now broke off their conversation, and the taller one advanced reluctantly to Ella's table.

'Just a cup of coffee, please.'

'We don't do coffee after twelve.'

'It isn't twelve yet,' Ella pointed out.

'But it will be by the time I get the coffee,' replied the girl, huffing on her nails to dry the varnish.

Honest wrath began to give Ella back her usual strength.

'If I don't get coffee within three minutes,' she said flatly, 'I shall see the manager immediately.'

'Oh well!' replied the girl, flouncing off, and casting her eyes to heaven as she passed her friend.

The cheek, thought Ella, taking out her tobacco tin and beginning to roll a cigarette with shaking fingers! Bad enough closing this place at tea time and making it look like a third-rate brothel — whatever they looked like — without having chits of girls making a song and dance about fetching a cup of instant when requested.

In the old days there had been some very pleasant waitresses here, thought Ella, blowing out a cloud of acrid smoke.

Ah, that was it, of course! That nice nurse had worked here years ago. No wonder her face was familiar. Some relation of dear old Mrs Jenner's, if she remembered rightly.

The coffee arrived, with only a small amount slopped in the saucer. It was hot and refreshing, and by the time Ella had drunk half of it, she was feeling more herself.

She must buy some meat for Flossie on the way back, and go and collect her at Dotty's and see that the rest of the animals were safe until the evening. As for Dulcie, she must find someone to milk that wretched animal, but at the moment she could not think of anyone brave enough to tackle the brute.

She stubbed out her cigarette, left the exact money on the bill slip – no tip for that young woman today – and went out into the sunshine.

As much refreshed by her little skirmish as by the coffee, Ella set off briskly to tackle the hill, and all that lay before her at Thrush Green.

WHILE Dotty Harmer lay, unusually quiescent, in her bed in the women's ward of Lulling Cottage Hospital, and Ella puffed up the hill to Thrush Green trying to decide if it were better to collect Flossie immediately or after she had eaten an early lunch, her old friend Dimity Henstock was busy discussing household matters with Charles.

'We really must buy more bed linen, Charles. Everything in that line went, as you know, and the July sales will be starting quite soon. I could save quite a lot of money.'

'Well, my dear, you know best, of course, but the insurance people haven't paid out yet, and our bank account is as slender as ever, I fear.'

'I do know that. The thing is that we shall have so much to buy with it. Beds, for instance. I think it would be sensible to have two single beds in the spare room. We've only had the double one there which means larger sheets which are expensive to launder.'

'But only *two* sheets,' pointed out Charles, 'instead of four.'

'Now I come to think of it,' said Dimity, 'Ella has some of my single sheets that I used when I lived there. I left them with her, but I don't think she has used them. Perhaps I could find out.'

'But we can't take Ella's sheets!' protested Charles.

'Strictly speaking, they are mine. Of course, if they are in use I shall leave them for Ella, but it would save me buying quite so many new ones. We shall need new blankets and covers too, of course.'

'Can you get all you want with fifty pounds?' asked Charles, his chubby face puckered with anxiety.

'No, Charles, I'm afraid I couldn't. But I shall spend fifty pounds to the very best advantage, believe me.'

'I know that.'

'If only the insurance people would pay up! Couldn't you write to them, or get Justin Venables to prod them?'

'I really don't like to do that.'

'Well, it's getting rather desperate, you know, Charles. I know we are very happy and comfortable here with Mrs Jenner's things, but we must look ahead to when we have a place of our own.'

The rector sighed.

'We have indeed been blessed. If only we could have a house as warm and light as this, Dimity.'

'And as old and beautiful,' agreed his wife. 'Well, whatever it is it will be lovely to settle in again. I'll call on Ella this afternoon, and find out about the sheets.'

'You won't rob her of them, will you?' pleaded Charles.

'Good heavens! I knew dear old Ella long before I met you, Charles, and you can rest assured that neither of us is going to fall out over a few rather shabby sheets!'

And with that the good rector had to be content.

Dimity set off to walk the half mile or so from Mrs Jenner's to Thrush Green. It was a calm day — 'soft weather' as the Irish call it — and there were very few people about.

Dimity enjoyed the peace of it all. She walked slowly, relishing the sounds of the countryside heard so clearly in the still air. A cow lowed in one of Percy Hodge's distant fields on her left. In the high branches of a walnut tree on her right she heard the excited squeaking of what she guessed were some long-tailed tits searching busily for insects, and she stopped by a farm gate to listen to the rare summer sound of a cricket in the grass.

It was all so very soothing, and Dimity's anxieties grew less pressing now that she was in the fresh air and able to enjoy the slower tempo of life about her. She wished that their plans were more definite. Surely they should know by now if a house were planned for the old site, although she was beginning to hope that somewhere else might be found for them. It would be good to make a fresh start. Not that she would ever want to go far from her friends at Thrush Green, but she felt that she could not face the effort needed to supervise the plans for a new abode, nor the delays which were bound to arise.

If only some pleasant place, like Mrs Jenner's, within a mile or so, say, from their old home could be found, how perfect it would be! Both she and Charles were now getting over the first numbing shock of their loss, and were beginning to long for a place of their own. Dimity knew Charles too well to expect him to take any positive action in asserting his needs. He would be content to wait humbly for what the Church provided, secure in his belief that all would be for the best. Dimity, a little less quiescent, was beginning to wonder if some pressure might not be a good thing.

She strolled on, and soon came in sight of Thrush Green. A sturdy figure, leading a spaniel, emerged from the lane which led to Lulling Woods, and Dimity recognised her old friend.

She caught up with her as she crossed the grass towards the home they had once shared.

'I was just coming to see you,' she cried, bending down to pat Flossie. 'How's Dotty?'

And Ella told her the sorry tale.

'Well,' declared Dimity, with unusual firmness, 'it's a blessing in disguise, Ella. She's looked really ill for months now, and won't take any advice. I'm quite relieved to hear that she's being properly looked after for a change.'

'But that's only temporary, Dim, that's what worries me. I think in a way, this trying to adopt a child was her muddle-headed way of having companionship and a bit of help with the work. Honestly, I'm pretty tough, but after clearing up the worst of that kitchen of hers, I was whacked. It wants a complete turn-out from top to bottom, that house of Dotty's, but who is going to take on the responsibility?'

'Do you think the niece might come for a bit when Dotty comes out of hospital?'

'Connie? She might. But she's got a small-holding of her own, I believe. Mind you, they get on pretty well, and Connie's got a good head on her shoulders. I don't think she'd stand any of Dotty's bullying. By the way, did you come for anything special?'

Dimity explained about the bed linen.

'I shall be glad to know they're in use,' replied Ella. 'They've been stored on the top shelf of the airing cupboard ever since you got married. Do them good to see the light of day.'

'And you're sure you have enough? Charles is most anxious that we don't take anything away which might be useful.'

'My dear old Dim, I've all my own stuff, and when mother died I inherited hers, including some lovely heavy linen sheets with lace insertion. Perishing cold in the winter, but bliss on a hot summer's night, so have no fear on that score. And incidentally, I have a pair of her rugs up in the loft which I shall never use. Say if you want them when you move into the new place. Heard any more yet?'

Dimity told her how things stood, and how she was beginning to worry about the delay.

'It'll sort itself out,' said Ella, rising. 'Let's get those sheets down before we forget them. And do you want some blackcurrants? The bushes at the end of the garden are laden.'

'Yes, please. It's Charles's favourite fruit. Nothing so good as blackcurrant tart in the winter.'

'Unless it's dear old rhubarb,' said Ella. 'Can't think why people turn up their noses at rhubarb. Good for you all the way through, I reckon.'

They were upstairs retrieving Dimity's sheets when Ella looked at her watch.

'It's Dulcie I'm worried about. She's due to be milked

said Albert.
e had two
, milk, all
ubercular
tty's – I
behind

r. 'I
rse.
ve
m

ound anyone to do it. I'm
s?'

ty turned her mind to Ella's

, I suppose, but he's pretty busy.
ght know of someone. He comes
sting bits of knowledge on his parish

come down to tea,' said Ella, as her friend
ed the car to get the sheets home, let alone
ts.'

ayed the message and then broached the subject

lbert Piggott once had goats,' said Charles im-
ely. 'I'm sure I could persuade him to take on a little
like that. He would be delighted to help Dotty. I'm
e.'

Dimity could not feel quite as positive about Albert's
delight as her warm-hearted husband, but passed on the good
news to Ella.

'God bless Charles!' cried Ella. 'If anyone can persuade
Albert to take on extra work then he's the man to do it.'

Charles was as good as his word. He left the car outside Ella's
house and walked by the church to Albert's cottage.

He found his sexton standing at the sink, washing up some
crockery in water so murky and afloat with unsavoury flotsam
that Charles wondered if it would really be more sanitary to
leave the china unwashed.

Charles explained the purpose of his visit while Albert
prodded morosely at the congealed food in a pie dish. His
expression brightened considerably when goats were
mentioned.

'Now, they're animals with a bit of character,
'It was my dad, not me, sir, as kept goats. W
nannies and a billy. We was brought up on goats
the lot of us. My old mum swore you could get the t
from cows' milk. Lor' bless you, I can milk old Do
mean Miss Harmer's – Dulcie, with one hand tied
me.'

He waved the dripping dish mop confidently.

'It's uncommonly good of you, Albert,' said the rect
shall pay you myself while the arrangements last, of cou
And I'm quite sure that Miss Harmer would want you to h
any surplus milk. It would do your indigestion good, I'
sure.'

'I always enjoyed a mug of goats' milk,' said Albert. 'And
my cat'd help out.'

'Then that's settled then,' said Charles, getting to his feet.
He gazed thoughtfully at the bowl of filthy water in the sink.

'Is there any hot water in the kettle?' he asked.

'Plenty. Want a cup of tea?'

'No, thank you, Albert. I'm having tea with Miss
Bembridge who will be so grateful to you for coping night
and morning with Dulcie's bounty. No, I just thought that
some fresh hot water might make your present task easier. I
fear I interrupted your work.'

'They're clean enough by now, I reckon,' said Albert,
casting a perfunctory glance at his handiwork. 'They'll soon
be dirty again time I've used 'em. Housework's a thankless job at the best of times. Fit only for women, I always
say.'

Charles, thankful that no woman was present to take up
the cudgels, hastened out into the fresh air of Thrush Green.

The summer term proceeded with increasing activity, as

Sports Day, Open Day, a Leavers' Service and end of term examinations all took place during the last few weeks.

Dorothy and Agnes coped with their usual efficiency, but both confessed to being inordinately tired one summer evening.

'You have every excuse,' Agnes told her friend. 'After all, the responsibility of the school's running falls largely upon your shoulders, and you have to be ready at any time to meet parents and managers and people from the office whenever any problem crops up. As well as coping with your poor leg,' she added.

'I greatly fear,' replied Miss Watson, 'that it's old age as well. So often I have told friends that they can't expect to get through as much work as they did when they were twenty years younger. Now I realise that I ought to take my own advice, but somehow, Agnes, one never thinks of oneself as old.'

There was a note of dejection in her voice which aroused Agnes's immediate sympathy.

'You do too much, you know. I hesitate to put myself forward, Dorothy, but I would willingly take on some of your less important duties if it would help.'

'I know you would. You are a great support and comfort, but I really think that the time has come to make a decision about retirement. I'm fifty-nine in a fortnight's time, and I intend to let the office know unofficially, early next term, that I propose to go at the end of the next school year.'

'Whatever you decide to do will be right, I am sure,' said loyal little Miss Fogerty, 'but won't it be a terrible wrench?'

'It will be *whenever* I go,' said Dorothy. 'But I shall feel much happier if I can see the end in sight. Can you remember how much in advance one's official resignation has to go in?'

'Three months, I think.'

'Then I shall put mine in at the end of the spring term. Plenty of time for advertisements to go in. Thrush Green School should draw many applicants. It's a pleasant spot to live in, and an efficient school, although perhaps it's not my place to say so.'

'You are quite the right person to say so. And whoever takes on the job will have you to thank for a splendidly working and happy school.'

'Thank you, Agnes, but I don't forget my staff too. The one big problem now is where we shall live. Do you still favour Barton-on-Sea, or somewhere close by?'

'It sounds perfect.'

'Well, I propose that we both spend a few days there when we break up, and have a look at some of the properties the agents have sent. We can stay at that nice little boarding house, and take our time over things. Agreed?'

'Yes, indeed, Dorothy. I shall look forward to it.'

Miss Watson gave a sigh.

'It will be a comfort to start moving towards retirement. And best of all, Agnes dear, to know that you feel you can be happy there with me. We must go into ways and means one evening when we feel more energetic, but I think my savings should be enough to find us somewhere modestly comfortable.'

'I hope you will use mine too,' said Agnes. 'Now, can I get you anything? Something to drink? Something to read? Your knitting?'

'What about a game of "Scrabble"? Always so soothing, I think.'

And little Miss Fogerty hastened to get out the board.

To the surprise of all Thrush Green, Albert Piggott approached his new duties with comparative zest.

He was observed setting off soon after eight in the morning towards Dotty's and again about six in the evening. Ella's milk was delivered as usual, on his return at night, and Betty Bell's left in the cool larder at Dotty's for her to collect on her way home from her many duties at Thrush Green.

Dulcie, always a generous nanny with her milk, seemed to take to Albert, and he carried home a plentiful supply for himself and his cat. Both appeared to flourish on it, and although Albert was teased by his usual colleagues at The Two Pheasants because he took to asking for half a pint of bitter instead of a pint, he put up with their joking with unusual good temper.

'It's a durn sight better dealing with animals than that church and graveyard,' he told them. 'That Dulcie's got more sense than any of you lot here. We gets on a treat. Goats is intelligent animals. And that's more'n you can say for men.'

'You'll be getting fat,' someone said, 'swigging down milk.'

'It's my belief it's doin' me good,' declared Albert. 'Wonderful soothing to the stummick. I reckon I'll buy some regular from Miss Harmer when she gets back. Saves me cooking too. Doctor Lovell said himself as milk's a *whole food*, and he's nobody's fool.'

To Ella's delight, he also offered to feed the hens and ducks in the mornings to save her making two trips a day. Such a change of heart in such a curmudgeonly character made a fascinating topic for the inhabitants of Thrush Green, and all agreed that Charles Henstock never did a better day's work than calling on Albert for help.

Meanwhile, Dotty remained in hospital. Her recovery was

being very slow so that she had plenty of time to think things over.

She was a surprisingly good patient. When some of the nursing staff had discovered that Dotty was in the women's ward there had been misgivings. Dotty's eccentricity was only exceeded by her obstinancy, as was well known in Lulling. The reputation of her fearsome father was still remembered, and in fact one of the doctors attached to the hospital was a former pupil of his, and could tell blood-curdling accounts of his late headmaster's disciplinary methods.

But, in truth, Dotty was a realist, and quite prepared to endure cheerfully what had to be. She saw now, as she rested against her pillows, that she had been foolish to think that she could cope with her energetic way of life without properly fuelling the machine which was her ageing body.

She accepted the nurses' ministrations with grace and gratitude. She believed the doctor, who remembered her father, when he told her gravely of the risks she ran by neglecting herself. He made it clear to her why she had been suffering from dizziness, why her back had a perpetual ache, why her legs throbbed and her heart palpitated so alarmingly. She would have to alter her way of life, he told her. If she intended to keep so many animals then she must have help. There really should be somebody living in the house with her. Had she thought of giving up altogether, and going to live in an old people's home? He could recommend several, very comfortable places, and with a warden to keep an eye on things.

To Dotty, the prospect appeared bleak in the extreme. Not that she had anything against homes for old people, and in fact her regular visits to local alms houses had always been enjoyable, during her father's lifetime, when she was younger and took on such duties. And several of her friends lived in just such places as Doctor Stokes mentioned, and seemed remarkably happy with their little coffee parties and handiwork, and visits to the hairdresser and chiropodist obligingly laid on by more mobile friends.

But Dotty knew quite well that such a way of life would never do for her.

For one thing, she would be *tidied up*. The haphazard clutter of objects, beneath her own thatched roof, which constituted home for Dotty, would have to be sorted out, given away or just put on the bonfire. She did not think that she could face such upheaval.

And then the thought of living without any animals was quite insupportable. To Dotty, her animal friends were far more dear than her human ones. Like Walt Whitman she could easily 'turn and live with the animals, so placid and self-contained'. They demanded so little and gave so much in return. She appreciated, with the poet, that:

> They do not sweat and whine about their condition,
> They do not lie awake in the dark and weep for their
>   sins.

and that they faced life with the same robustness as she herself faced it. The idea of living in a home, no matter how warm, clean and cared for she might be, but without even one animal for company, could not be borne.

She came in the end to a compromise. As the animals died, she would not replace them. She could not betray them by giving them away unless it were possible to place them in as perfect a setting as their present one. Perhaps young Jeremy Hurst might like two of the rabbits? Or Joan Young's Paul? They would be well cared for there, she knew.

The chickens and ducks were elderly, and Mr Jones from

The Two Pheasants would dispatch them humanely when their time came, as he usually did. And she must resist the temptation to buy more pullets, or to put twelve lovely pearly eggs under a broody hen. How she would miss yellow chicks running around!

The cats had been spayed, luckily, so that there would be no more kittens, sad though the thought was. As for Dulcie and Flossie they must stay on, and for a very long time too, Dotty hoped. She had been amazed to hear how willingly Albert Piggott had coped with the milking. With luck, he might be persuaded to continue, and of course, once Dulcie was dry, there must be no more mating.

Well, it was all very sad, thought Dotty, and gave a great sigh. A little fair-haired probationer nurse hurried to her side.

'All right, Miss Harmer?'

'Yes, thank you, nurse. I was only making a few plans for the future. Rather exhausting.'

'Like a cup of tea?' asked the girl, offering the panacea for all ills.

'Do you know,' said Dotty, sitting up and straightening her bed jacket, 'that would be most acceptable. Only a little milk and no sugar, please.'

She was feeling better already.

Sunday Lunch at the Misses Lovelock's

ONE Sunday morning the Misses Lovelock fluttered along Lulling High Street to St John's church. This large and beautiful building stood in an open space south of the town, and its tall spire was a landmark for many miles around.

It was three times the size of St Andrew's at Thrush Green and was noted for its stained glass windows, dating from the sixteenth century. Throughout the summer, coach loads of tourists came to see the church and to take photographs, particularly of the fine east window above the altar.

In their younger days, the Misses Lovelock had taken their turn in manning the modest stall near the vestry where books and pamphlets, bookmarks and slides of the outstanding features of St John's were on sale. Invariably, after their visit, the tourists wandered across the green into the High Street and sought tea at The Fuchsia Bush.

It was this recollection which formed the theme of their conversation as they proceeded towards morning service.

'I really can't think that The Fuchsia Bush is any better off for closing at tea time. Why, only yesterday, Violet, I saw a coach stop, and the driver banging on the door. There were quite thirty people on board, and I'm sure they all looked the sort who would want sandwiches, scones and home-made cakes.'

'Some,' said Miss Violet, with a sniff, 'looked as though they would want fish and chips as well.'

'What I'm trying to say, dear,' pointed out Miss Ada, 'is that the Fuchsia Bush is turning away good money.'

'Well, they get it at night, I suppose, at dinner time.'

'I think not. I was talking to one of the staff at the fishmonger's and she says they are never more than half full. People are finding it too expensive, she said, and prefer to eat at home.'

'And very sensible too,' put in Miss Bertha. 'I only hope that The Fuchsia Bush will see the folly of its ways, and remember that it is there to *serve* people. And people want *tea* from four o'clock onward. And if they desire to partake of fish and chips then, why shouldn't they find it provided?'

She gave a stern look at Miss Violet who pretended not to see, but rearranged a dove-grey glove.

'Winnie Bailey was wondering if a petition might be a good idea, with lots of signatures, you know, to persuade the management to open again at tea time.'

Bertha bridled.

'I shall certainly not append my signature. I do not intend to kow-tow for the sake of a cup of tea which I can brew for myself rather better next door.'

'I was thinking of the visitors, Bertha,' ventured Violet.

At that moment, the chiming of the church bells changed to one steady tolling of the tenor bell.

'We must step lively,' said Bertha, quickening her pace. 'It looks as though our hall clock must be running slow.'

During the sermon, Violet allowed her gaze to dwell on the glowing glass of the famous window. To be sure, she had never been able to see with absolute clarity just what the pictures showed. She knew that the incidents depicted were the draught of fishes, Jairus's daughter, and the miracle of water turning into wine. The illustrated pamphlet told her so. The colours were really magnificent, but there were so many pieces of glass in each picture, and all so intricately interposed, with those squiggly worms of lead everywhere, that she had often wondered if that really was a net full of fishes (Herring, perhaps? Surely not in the Sea of Galilee?) or simply the lower part of the fishermen's robes. Not perhaps the most *practical* garment for a fisherman, when one came to consider it.

Thus musing, she let her eyes pass from the mystery of the windows to the frank and handsome face of dear Anthony Bull as he stood declaiming in his beautiful voice.

What an actor he would have made, thought Violet! Such a presence, such manly beauty, such clarity of diction! And he really gave very sound sermons, nothing too highbrow and yet not patronisingly simple, as though his congregation was composed of non-intellectuals. This morning's subject, for instance, on the theme of good fellowship and the need to consider the feelings of others in everyday life, was being very well expressed.

She only hoped that Bertha, who could be rather unnecessarily tart at times, was listening attentively. How lucky they were in Lulling to have such a fine vicar! He really deserved a larger and more knowledgeable congregation than this quarter-filled church. A *better house*, thought Violet, was how it would be put in theatrical circles. Certainly, such a star performer, she decided, admiring a graceful gesture of his hands, deserved a truly discriminating audience, and no doubt he would have one someday.

Meanwhile, it was to be hoped that he would remain the vicar of Lulling for many a long day, delighting them all with his outstanding looks, his kindly manner and the genuine goodness of his way of life.

Sunday lunch at the Lovelocks' was always cold. Violet had set the table before going to church. Starched linen, heavy silver and Waterford glass dressed the table with splendour. It was a pity that the meal set upon it was so sparse.

Six thin slices of corned beef were flanked on one side by a Coalport dish containing sliced cold potatoes, and on the other by equally gelid carrots. A beautiful little cut glass bowl contained beetroot in vinegar. Liquid refreshment to accompany this inspired course consisted of lemon barley water in a glass jug covered with a lace cloth beaded round the edge.

'A very good sermon this morning,' commented Bertha, chewing her corned beef carefully with her few remaining teeth.

'Such a pity there were not more to hear it,' agreed Violet. 'I was thinking so in church.'

'Well, we appreciate dear Anthony even if we are only a

few,' said Ada. 'I think we can pride ourselves on being discriminating here in Lulling. We are very lucky to have him.'

Bertha cut a ring of beetroot carefully in half.

'But for how long, I wonder?' she said.

Her two elderly sisters gazed at her with curiosity. Had Bertha heard a rumour? And if so, from whom? And why had they not been told?

Bertha attempted to assume an air of nonchalance under their scrutiny. She was not very successful.

'Oh, it was just a chance remark of Mrs. Bull's when I saw her at the draper's yesterday. She was buying some hat elastic.'

'Bertha, people don't buy *hat* elastic these days!' cried Violet.

'Well, no, but I imagine she needed it for her undergarments, and one wouldn't want to ask for *knicker* elastic in a public place.'

'*Knicker* or *hat*,' pronounced Ada, 'is beside the point. What did she say?'

'Oh, something about changes in the air, and Anthony much perturbed about decisions to be made.'

The two sisters looked disappointed.

'That could be anything from altering the site of the compost heap in the churchyard, to replacing those dreadfully shabby hassocks in the Lady Chapel,' said Ada.

'Or some little matter of church ritual,' added Violet, putting her knife and fork neatly across her empty plate.

'Maybe, maybe!' agreed Bertha airily. 'Well, time alone will tell.'

She rose and collected the plates. When she returned she was bearing a dish full of glossy black cherries.

'A present from dear Colonel Fisher yesterday evening,'

she said, 'when you were both in the garden. I thought I would keep them as a surprise for dessert today.'

'Do you remember how we used to hang them over our ears?' said Violet, picking up a pair. 'We used to pretend the black ones were jet ear-rings and the red ones were ruby.'

The three old faces glowed at the memory, Anthony Bull's affairs forgotten in the excitement of this delicious surprise.

'I remember it as if it were yesterday,' declared Ada. 'You were always the pretty one, Violet, with your fair hair. The red cherries suited you best.'

'We were all pretty children,' said Bertha firmly, 'though no one would think so to see us now. Still, we are clean and healthy, and I suppose that is something at our age.'

They enjoyed their cherries, removing the stones politely from their mouths, behind delicately curved bony hands.

Later they stacked the china and silver in the kitchen to attend to later, and went into the sunshine to rest.

The sun warmed their old bones and Bertha yawned.

Violet began to giggle.

'Do you know, Bertha dear, your tongue is as purple as a chow's!'

'Really? No doubt yours is too after eating black cherries.'

The three old ladies put out their tongues and surveyed each others. Laughter shook their thin frames, and for a brief moment they reverted to the three pretty little girls who had played in this same sunlit garden, wearing starched pinafores and cherry ear-rings, over seventy years earlier.

A week or two later, the problem of Dotty Harmer's convalescence arose. Ella Bembridge had offered to have her at her cottage, but Winnie Bailey, secretly fearing that Ella's home might not provide the peace which Dotty would need for a week or two, suggested to her old friend that the invalid might stay with her.

'The spare room is empty, as you know, Ella dear, and Jenny is longing to do a bit of spoiling. We are both in the rudest of health now, and it would be a real pleasure to have Dotty. You've done more than your share with Flossie and the other animals.'

Ella gave in with good grace.

'Well, to tell you the truth, I am rather behind with my weaving, and the garden's been neglected. Not that I mind much, first things first, you know, but if you're quite sure, I'm happy about it.'

It was arranged that Harold Shoosmith and Isobel would collect Dotty, and Flossie would be transferred to Winnie's to be reunited with her mistress.

And so, one August afternoon, Harold and Isobel set off in the car, which had been polished for the occasion, to fetch their old friend.

She still looked remarkably frail and her steps were faltering as she made her way to the car on the arm of matron – a high honour not lightly bestowed. But Dotty's spirit was unquenched, and she chattered cheerfully all the way along Lulling High Street, up the hill, and past Ella's cottage, the gap left by the destroyed rectory, and the grass of Thrush Green.

Winnie welcomed her with a kiss and Flossie with ecstatic barking. Harold and Isobel promised to call the next morning, and then withdrew, leaving Winnie and Dotty alone in the sitting room.

Dotty's thin hands were caressing Flossie's long ears as she gazed happily about her.

'I can't tell you how good it is to be here. They were so *very* kind to me at the hospital, but I pray that I may never need to go there again.'

'Well, I hope you will stop with me for as long as you like,' said Winnie. 'You must get your strength back, you know.'

'My strength?' exclaimed Dotty in amazement. 'But I am quite strong now, Winnie. I shall thoroughly enjoy staying overnight here, but of course I must get back to the animals tomorrow morning.'

'We'll talk about that later,' said Winnie diplomatically. 'But now I am going to ask Jenny to make the tea.'

'How is she?' asked Jenny when Winnie appeared in the kitchen.

'The same old Miss Harmer,' Winnie told her, with a smile.

'Oh dear!' cried Jenny. 'That means we might have trouble!'

Dotty's niece, Connie Harmer, had kept in touch with her aunt's Thrush Green friends throughout Dotty's illness, and had driven some fifty miles from her home at Friarscombe to see the old lady in hospital.

She was a sturdy woman in her forties, with auburn hair now streaked with grey, and a square weatherbeaten face. She was as much attached to the animals as was her aunt, and perhaps this was why she had never married, finding the human race, and particularly the male of the species, very much inferior to her own charges.

The Henstocks, Ella Bembridge and Winnie Bailey were old friends of hers, and were glad to see her when she came to see Dotty in her hospital bed. She was frank with them all.

'It's like this. I'm quite willing to have dear old Aunt Dot to live with me, but will she come? If she's too groggy to cope alone at Lulling Woods, I'd certainly consider selling up and making my home with her, if that seems the right thing to do, but I don't relish the prospect, and that's the truth. In any case, I'd need a month or two to make arrangements for some of the animals, and selling the house would take time.'

'Let's see how things go,' said Winnie, at whose house this conversation took place. 'It's best that she convalesces here, near Doctor Lovell, and we'll all keep in touch. But somehow, Connie, I can't see any of us persuading Dotty to leave that cottage of hers.'

'Nor me. Ah well, she's lucky to have such noble friends around her, and you know I'm willing to take on any permanent responsibility when the time comes. I've always been very fond of Aunt Dot, crazy though she is at times.'

'That goes for us all,' Winnie told her.

Luckily, Dotty was soon persuaded to continue to stay at Winnie's for at least another week, and appeared to have forgotten her resolve to rush back to the animals by the next morning.

It was one of the disconcerting things about the invalid at this time. She was vague about time. 'Let's say more than usually vague,' amended Charles Henstock, and although Doctor Lovell was optimistic about the full recovery of his patient, even he admitted that Dotty would be better in the permanent company of someone like her reliable niece.

It was while she was still recuperating that Lulling was agog to learn that the Misses Lovelock had been summoned to the local police station to view some pieces of silverware which had come into the hands of the police.

Full of hope, the three sisters tottered along one bright morning, stopping only by the Corn Exchange to read some extraordinary messages, written in chalk, on the walls of that building. The words were not familiar to the three ladies, but the content of the slogans was. The writer presumably did not approve of the Prime Minister nor of the country's police force.

'But, Violet,' said Ada in bewilderment, 'does one spell that word like that?'

'Ada dear,' said Violet, with some hauteur, 'it is not a word that I find myself needing to spell.'

Bertha, as usual, took charge.

'We must draw the attention of the officer on duty to this defacement, when we call in. I'm sure he will deal quite competently with the matter, correct spelling or not. It is not the sort of matter for ladies to concern themselves with.'

'Should you end your sentence with a proposition, Bertha?' asked Violet innocently.

But she was ignored, and the three mounted the steps of the police station.

Sadly, there was only one of the Lovelocks' lost objects among the display set out on a trestle table in a back room with Police Constable Darwin on guard.

'Father's rose bowl!' cried Ada.

'What a miracle!' cried Violet.

'Given to him on his retirement!' cried Bertha. 'How wonderful of you to recover it.'

They walked slowly round and round the table, gloating over the beautiful objects before them.

'And where did you find all these lovely things, officer? So clever of you.'

'Well, miss,' said Police Constable Darwin, 'I'm not at liberty to say, but it wasn't us chaps at Lulling as came across this lot. But several people, besides you ladies, have lost stuff around here, so it's our turn to show it.'

'And have the other people found theirs here?'

'You was the first to be asked,' the constable told them.

'Well, that is most gratifying. Most kind. We feel quite honoured, I assure you. Now, are we allowed to take home Father's rose bowl?'

'I'm afraid not, miss. It'll have to be exhibited in court, see, when we've picked up the thieves. There's still a lot missing. If you notice, miss, all this is the big stuff, salvers and bowls and that.'

With commendable delicacy he ignored a seventeenth century toilet set, with a pair of silver chamber pots to match, and directed the Misses Lovelock's attention to trays, teapots and other tableware, including the rose bowl, which stood at the farther end of the table.

'We reckon this is only about a quarter of what's missing. The smaller stuff's probably been passed on. Melted down already, I don't doubt.'

There were horrified gasps from the ladies, and Police Constable Darwin hastily tried to make amends for his gaffe.

'But let's hope not. After all, this lot's turned up. Keep your fingers crossed, ladies. Anyway, I'll mark this rose bowl down in the book as belonging to you. Want another look round to make sure?'

'No, thank you, officer. You have been most helpful. There was just one other little matter,' added Bertha, the natural spokesman of all three.

'Yes, miss?'

'Have you been on outside duty this morning? On your beat, I believe is the correct expression?'

'Well, no, miss. I was detailed by Sergeant Brown to stand by this lot this morning. Very valuable stuff here. But I'll pass on any message.'

Bertha wondered if this fresh-faced young man would really be experienced enough to deal with the unpleasant matter of the Corn Exchange's graffiti, but she decided swiftly that he had probably been adequately trained and was quite used to seeing — and perhaps even hearing — the phrases written on the wall.

'We just wanted to direct your attention, officer, to some quite dreadful messages written with some prominence on a public building near by.'

'Oh, them scribbles on the Corn Exchange,' replied the constable, with relief. He had begun to wonder just what else these old tabbies were going to disclose. 'Don't you worry about them. One of the Cooke boys, no doubt. Anyway, young Armstrong's been told off to clean it up, so everything's under control.'

'I'm delighted to hear it,' said Bertha graciously.

'In very bad taste to deface a building with such words,' added Ada in support.

'And not even correctly spelt,' said Violet, adding her mite.

'I think,' said Bertha ominously, 'it is time we returned home.'

17 Housing Plans

THE first two weeks of the summer holidays were spent by Miss Watson and Miss Fogerty in recuperating from the rigours of the term.

They also managed to fit in a number of personal arrangements which had been postponed during term time. Miss Watson had her hair permanently waved, one troublesome tooth extracted and two filled, and had several shopping expeditions for new corsets and other underwear.

Miss Fogerty, whose hair was straight 'as a yard of pump water', as she said, dressed it in a neat bun, and washed it herself. She did, however, need to visit the dentist who luckily only found one filling which needed attention. Her modest shopping resulted in a new flowered overall for school use, a pair of light sandals, and a petticoat. She was sorely tempted to buy a navy blue jersey suit, reduced in the summer sales, but with the possibility of helping with the purchase of a shared home she decided it would be imprudent to spend too lavishly.

The friends had reserved rooms at their favourite Barton guest house on the front for two weeks from the middle of August, and both ladies looked forward to the break eagerly. The discussion of money affairs about the buying of a permanent home there did not take place until a day or two before their departure. Dorothy Watson had obviously given the matter much thought.

'Now, I know just how independent you are, Agnes dear,

and I very much appreciate your offer to help in buying a
place to share, but I've decided against it.'

'But, Dorothy – ' protested Agnes, but was cut short.
Miss Watson was at her most decisive, a schoolteacher at her
firmest and fairest.

'It's like this. I should like to buy the house so that I can
alter my will and leave it, with any other little things of value I
might have, to be shared between my three nephews. I do not
intend to leave anything to Ray and Kathleen apart from my
mother's tea service which I know Ray would like. They have
quite enough as it is, and I consider that they have forfeited
any claim on my property after their dreadful behaviour. But
I like the three boys, and I think they are making their way in
the world quite splendidly, despite their parents.'

'Yes, I do see that, Dorothy, but nevertheless – '

Miss Watson drove on relentlessly.

'Of course, I shan't see you left without a roof over
your head, Agnes dear, should I go first. The house will
be left so that you can stay there for as long as you wish,
and when you have done with it, then the three boys shall
have it.'

'Oh, Dorothy, you are too good! But I pray that I may go
first.'

'First or second, Agnes, hear me out. I've given a great deal
of thought to this matter. Now, if you *insist* on putting
something towards this venture – '

'I do. I do indeed!'

'Then I suggest that you could contribute to the furnish-
ings which we are bound to need. No carpet or curtain ever
seems to fit a new home, and I'm sure we shall need various
extras, and possibly redecoration, although I think we should
share that expense.'

'I agree wholeheartedly with anything you suggest,

Dorothy, but it really isn't enough from me. At least I can pay rent, surely?'

'I was coming to that. If you feel that you can pay the same amount as you do here, Agnes, it would be a very great help, believe me. Now, what do you think?'

'I think you are being uncommonly generous, as always, Dorothy.'

'Well, it seems the simplest and most straightforward way of arranging things. I thought I might go and put the matter to Justin Venables. He will deal with things if we do find somewhere, and I should like him to know what we have in mind. Will you come with me? I only hope he won't retire before we've finished with his services. One wonders if those youngsters in the firm have quite the same wisdom as dear Justin.'

'Of course I will come. And I don't think we need to have any doubts about the junior partners, Dorothy. I am sure that Justin has trained them quite beautifully.'

'Let's hope so,' said Dorothy. 'And now that that's over, I think I'll go and look out some of my clothes ready for packing.'

'And so will I,' replied little Miss Fogerty.

The two ladies retired to their bedrooms, one congratulating herself on a difficult matter successfully dealt with, and the other to think, yet again, about the boundless generosity of her friend.

The abrupt conclusion of Percy Hodge's courtship of Jenny had occasioned plenty of comment at the time, but as the weeks had gone by other topics had taken its place until Percy's suit had almost been forgotten, if not by Jenny, at least by the majority of Thrush Green's inhabitants.

It was some surprise then to Harold Shoosmith when Betty

Bell, crashing about his study with the vacuum cleaner, shouted the information that Percy was looking elsewhere for a wife.

To tell the truth, Harold had not heard clearly for the racket around him, and was on the point of fleeing to more peaceful pastures.

Betty, seeing that she might be baulked of her prey, switched off the machine and began to wind up the cord.

'Percy! You know, Percy Hodge as was hanging up his hat to Jenny at Mrs Bailey's,' she explained.

'What about him?'

'I just told you. He's courting someone else now.'

'Well, good luck to him. No harm in angling elsewhere if he hasn't succeeded in landing his first fish.'

'I don't know as Jenny'd care to be called a fish,' said Betty, bending down to wind the cord carefully into figures of eight on the cleaner's handle.

Harold watched this manoeuvre with resignation. If he had asked Betty once to desist from this practice which cracked the cord's covering he had beseeched her twenty times. It made no difference. At some point in her career, Betty had decided to wind cords in a figure of eight style, and stuck to it.

'Well, who is it, Betty? Come on now. You know you're dying to tell me. Someone we know?'

'You might, and you might not. Ever been up The Drovers' Arms?'

'Beyond Lulling Woods? No, I can't say I have. Does the lady live there?'

'Works there. Name of Doris. She cleans up, and helps behind the bar of a Saturday. She's from foreign parts, they say.'

'Really? What, Spain, France, or further afield?'

Betty looked shocked.

'Oh, not *that* foreign! I mean she speaks English and goes to our church. No, she's from Devon, I think, or maybe Cornwall. A long way off, I know, but speaks very civil really.'

'And you think Percy calls there? It may be that they keep the sort of beer he prefers.'

'Percy Hodge,' said Betty, setting her arms akimbo and speaking with emphasis, 'was always content to have his half-pint at The Two Pheasants. What call has he got to traipse all the way to The Drovers' Arms, unless he's courting?

Besides, he's always carrying a great bunch of flowers, and he gives 'em to this Doris.'

'Ah!' agreed Harold, 'that certainly sounds as though he means business. I hope you all approve at Lulling Woods?'

'Well, he could do a lot worse. She's a hefty lump, ana can turn her hand to helping on the farm, I'm sure. Clean too, and cooks quite nice. Not as good as Percy's Gertie, I don't suppose. She was famous for her pastry and sponges. But still, this Doris can do a plain roast, they tell me, and is a dab hand at jam making. She should do very nicely, we reckon.'

'I'm glad she's approved,' said Harold gravely, 'and I hope that Percy will soon be made happy.'

He nodded towards the cleaner.

'Finished in here?'

'I wondered if you'd like your windows done. They look pretty grimy from your tobacco smoke.'

'Better leave them,' said Harold, deciding to ignore the side swipe at his pipe. 'No doubt Mrs Shoosmith will tell you the most urgent jobs.'

'Come to think of it,' said Betty, trundling the cleaner towards the door, 'she's waiting for me to help turn the beds. It flew right out of my head with you chatting away to me.'

She vanished before Harold could think of a suitable retort.

That same afternoon, Ella Bembridge left her cottage to post a letter at the box on the wall at the corner of Thrush Green.

It was warm and still, and she was just wondering if she would take a walk along the lane to Nidden to call on Dimity and Charles when she saw her old friend approaching along the avenue of chestnut trees.

Dimity was on the same errand with a half a dozen letters in her hand.

'Coming back with me?' enquired Ella, after their greetings.

'I mustn't, Ella. I've a nice joint of bacon simmering away, so I can't be long. Charles has gone sick visiting at Nidden.'

'Well, let's sit down for a minute or two here,' replied Ella, making her way to one of the public seats generously provided for exhausted wayfarers at Thrush Green. 'Heard any more about your housing plans?'

Dotty looked perturbed.

'Not really, but Charles had a letter this morning confirming these rumours about amalgamating the parishes.'

'First I've heard of it,' announced Ella. 'What's it all about?'

'Well, Anthony Bull's two parishes of Lulling and Lulling Woods are to be merged with Charles's Thrush Green and Nidden.'

'Good heavens! Anthony will have a massive parish to work, won't he?'

'It looks like it.'

Ella suddenly became conscious of Dimity's agitation.

'And what happens to Charles?'

'Nobody knows. All the letter gave was the news that the four parishes would be merged.'

'Do you think this is the reason for not hearing about rebuilding the rectory?'

'It looks very much like it. I simply can't get Charles to do anything about it, although I've done my best to press him to make enquiries. We really ought to know where we stand. It is all most worrying. I'm so afraid he will now be moved. If it is too far from Lulling and Thrush Green, as it might well be, I shall be so lost without all our old friends.'

Dimity sounded tearful, and Ella patted her thin hand comfortingly.

'Cheer up, Dim! Worse troubles at sea! You'll probably hear in a day or two that building's beginning on the old spot over there, and you'll have a spanking new place to live in.'

'Somehow I don't think so. I'm afraid any spanking new place we have to live in will be miles away.'

She blew her nose forcefully, and jumped to her feet.

'Well, it's been a comfort to talk to you, Ella, as always, but I must get back to the bacon. You shall be the first to know if we hear anything definite.'

She hurried away across the green, and Ella returned more slowly and thoughtfully to her own house.

As it happened, it was Edward Young, the architect, who heard more about the empty site at Thrush Green.

The rumour reached him by way of an acquaintance who was on one of the planning committees.

'About eighteenth hand,' Edward told Joan, 'so one takes it with a pinch of salt, but I think there's something brewing all right. Evidently, the Church is putting it on the market and the local council would like to buy it.'

'But what for?'

'Well, it's only a small area, but this chap seemed to think that a neat little one-storey unit of, say, four or six houses for old people might be put there. Actually, he said there were plenty of tottering old bods at Thrush Green that could do with them.'

'He's not far wrong,' commented Joan.

'Or perhaps a health clinic. I think that's a better idea myself. The one at Lulling's had its day, and it's a long way to walk there. Particularly if you are pregnant like our Molly.'

'It would certainly be useful,' said Joan. 'Which do you think it will be?'

'My dear good girl, don't ask me! You know what these

rumours are. But I'm pretty sure he's right about the site being sold. And we'll keep a sharp eye on what gets put up on it, believe me. We've had our years of penance with that eyesore of a Victorian rectory. I hope our children will see something less horrific in its place one day.'

The day of Dorothy and Agnes's departure to Barton dawned bright and clear. The taxi had been ordered for ten o'clock to take them to Lulling Station, and the pair were up early.

Harold and Isobel called to collect the key and to get last minute directions as they had offered to keep an eye on their next-door neighbours' property.

They had been told about the proposed house-hunting and were full of good advice. Both Isobel and Harold had gone through this exhausting experience within the last few years, and did not envy the two ladies. But they heartily endorsed Miss Watson's desire to retire at the age of sixty, although they wondered if her successor would be quite so good a neighbour. Time would tell.

Meanwhile, they urged them to enjoy their break, promised to look after the premises, and waved them on their way.

'I shall miss Agnes dreadfully,' said Isobel, as they returned to their garden. 'She means a lot to me.'

'It only takes an hour or so to drive to Barton,' replied Harold. 'We'll make a point of visiting them as often as you like.'

Naturally, the Shoosmiths said nothing about Miss Watson's future plans, but nevertheless it was soon common knowledge in Thrush Green that she was going to retire and planned to live elsewhere.

'We shall miss them both,' Winnie Bailey said to Frank and Phil Hurst. 'Miss Watson's been a marvellous headmistress, and dear little Agnes is a real institution. It won't be easy to replace two such dedicated women.'

'Well,' said Frank, 'they're doing the right thing to get away while they still have their health and strength.'

'And sanity!' quipped Phil. 'At times Jeremy alone drives me mad. How they can cope with dozens of them round them all day beats me.'

'They finish at four,' said Frank. 'And look at the holidays they get!'

'They certainly do not finish at four,' said Winnie firmly. 'I've often seen the light on at the school and I know those two have been getting something prepared for next day. I wouldn't want their job for all the tea in China.'

Comment at The Two Pheasants was less complimentary.

'Time old Aggie packed it in,' said one. 'Why, she taught my mum as well as me! Must be nearly seventy.'

'But Miss Watson don't look that age! Mind you, she's no beauty, but she've kept the colour of her hair, and still hobbles about quite brisk with that bad leg of hers.'

'Living at Bournemouth, I hear.'

'I heard it was Barton.'

'Well, somewhere where all the old dears go. Bet that'll cost 'em something to find a house in those parts.'

And this gloomy prognosis gave them a pleasurable topic for the rest of the evening.

Meanwhile, the two holiday-makers were finding the property was indeed expensive, especially of the type they had in mind.

The house agents who attended to them all pointed out, with depressing unanimity, the fact that most retiring people wanted just such a place as they were seeking, small, easily-run, with a view, but not too much garden.

'Of course, people come from all over England, and particularly from the north, to enjoy our milder climate,' said one exquisitely dressed young man. 'There are always plenty of clients — usually elderly — who are waiting for something suitable. It won't be easy to find you exactly what you want.'

This was the fifth estate agent's they had visited that day. Dorothy's feet hurt, and her temper was getting short.

'I imagine that these elderly clients of yours die fairly frequently,' she said tartly.

The young man looked startled.

'Well, of course, in the fullness of time they er — pass on.'

'In which case there must be vacancies cropping up,' pointed out Miss Watson. 'You know what we are seeking. Please keep us informed.'

She swept out before the young man could reply, followed by her equally exhausted friend.

'No more today, Agnes,' she said. 'Let's go back to the hotel for a cup of tea, and I will write a few postcards when we've had a rest. Isobel and Harold were absolutely right. House-hunting needs a great deal of stamina.'

After tea, the two sat on the veranda with their tired legs resting on footstools. Agnes was busy knitting a frock for Molly Curdle's expected baby and Dorothy busily filled in her postcards.

'I shall send one to Ray and Kathleen,' she said, sorting through half a dozen on her lap. 'So much easier than writing them a letter which, in any case, they don't deserve. Still, I should like them to know our plans. What about this one of the sunset? Or do you think they would like this clump of pine trees?'

Agnes, sucking the end of her knitting needle, gave both pictures her earnest attention.

'I think the sunset,' she decided.

Dorothy nodded, and set to work, as Agnes re[turned to] counting her stitches. She wrote:

'Very much enjoying a few days here. Good [and] comfortable hotel.

'Also looking for a house, as I am planning to retire next year. Agnes joins me in sending

   Love,

   Dorothy'

'There,' said she, thumping on a stamp, 'that should give them something to think about. I've two more to do, and then perhaps we might walk along to the pillar box if you are not too tired.'

'I should like to,' said Agnes, obliging as ever. 'I have only to finish my decreasing and I shall be ready.'

The two ladies bent again to their tasks, while overhead the gulls wheeled and cried, and a refreshing breeze from the sea lifted their spirits.

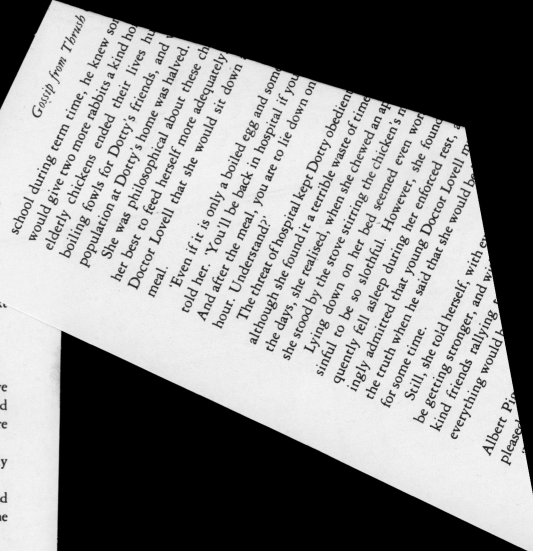

school during term time, he knew so[me]
would give two more rabbits a kind ho[use]
elderly chickens ended their lives hu[ng]
boiling fowls for Dotty's friends, and [the]
population at Dotty's home was halved.

She was philosophical about these ch[ickens]
her best to feed herself more adequately
Doctor Lovell that she would sit down
meal.

'Even if it is only a boiled egg and som[ething]
told her. 'You'll be back in hospital if you
And after the meal, you are to lie down on
hour. Understand?'

The threat of hospital kept Dotty obedien[t]
although she found it a terrible waste of tim[e]
the days, she realised, when she chewed an a[pple]
she stood by the stove stirring the chicken's m[eal]

Lying down on her bed seemed even wor[se]
sinful to be so slothful. However, she found
quently fell asleep during her enforced rest, a[nd]
ingly admitted that young Doctor Lovell m[ight]
the truth when he said that she would be[come]
for some time.

Still, she told herself, with e[very]
be getting stronger, and wi[th]
kind friends rallying r[ound]
everything would b[e]

Albert Pi[ggott]
pleased [...]

before evening and I haven't found anyone to do it. I'm darned if I'm going to. Any ideas?'

Arms clutching sheets, Dimity turned her mind to Ella's problem.

'Percy Hodge might do it, I suppose, but he's pretty busy. Let's ring Charles. He might know of someone. He comes across all sorts of interesting bits of knowledge on his parish visiting.'

'And tell him to come down to tea,' said Ella, as her friend dialled. 'You'll need the car to get the sheets home, let alone the blackcurrants.'

Dimity relayed the message and then broached the subject of Dulcie.

'But Albert Piggott once had goats,' said Charles immediately. 'I'm sure I could persuade him to take on a little task like that. He would be delighted to help Dotty. I'm sure.'

Dimity could not feel quite as positive about Albert's delight as her warm-hearted husband, but passed on the good news to Ella.

'God bless Charles!' cried Ella. 'If anyone can persuade Albert to take on extra work then he's the man to do it.'

Charles was as good as his word. He left the car outside Ella's house and walked by the church to Albert's cottage.

He found his sexton standing at the sink, washing up some crockery in water so murky and afloat with unsavoury flotsam that Charles wondered if it would really be more sanitary to leave the china unwashed.

Charles explained the purpose of his visit while Albert prodded morosely at the congealed food in a pie dish. His expression brightened considerably when goats were mentioned.

'Now, they're animals with a bit of character,' said Albert.
'It was my dad, not me, sir, as kept goats. We had two
nannies and a billy. We was brought up on goats' milk, all
the lot of us. My old mum swore you could get the tubercular
from cows' milk. Lor' bless you, I can milk old Dotty's — I
mean Miss Harmer's — Dulcie, with one hand tied behind
me.'

He waved the dripping dish mop confidently.

'It's uncommonly good of you, Albert,' said the rector. 'I
shall pay you myself while the arrangements last, of course.
And I'm quite sure that Miss Harmer would want you to have
any surplus milk. It would do your indigestion good, I'm
sure.'

'I always enjoyed a mug of goats' milk,' said Albert. 'And
my cat'd help out.'

'Then that's settled then,' said Charles, getting to his feet.
He gazed thoughtfully at the bowl of filthy water in the sink.

'Is there any hot water in the kettle?' he asked.

'Plenty. Want a cup of tea?'

'No, thank you, Albert. I'm having tea with Miss
Bembridge who will be so grateful to you for coping night
and morning with Dulcie's bounty. No, I just thought that
some fresh hot water might make your present task easier. I
fear I interrupted your work.'

'They're clean enough by now, I reckon,' said Albert,
casting a perfunctory glance at his handiwork. 'They'll soon
be dirty again time I've used 'em. Housework's a thankless job at the best of times. Fit only for women, I always
say.'

Charles, thankful that no woman was present to take up
the cudgels, hastened out into the fresh air of Thrush Green.

The summer term proceeded with increasing activity, as

18   Help Needed

DOTTY Harmer returned to her cottage after ten days with Winnie Bailey. To everyone's relief, Connie came to Lulling Woods each week, staying overnight and seeing that the larder was stocked, the laundry done and that Dotty was taking her pills.

Albert Piggott, of his own volition, offered to continue to milk Dulcie. The two had become very fond of each other, and whether the free milk, enjoyed by Albert and his fast-fattening cat, had anything to do with the arrangement, no one could say, but everything worked out well for everybody.

Betty Bell called in each morning on her way to work, and often on her return, and Ella and the Henstocks called frequently.

It was not the ideal arrangement, for it was quite apparent that Dotty needed a constant companion, but it was the best that the community could devise for someone as independent and headstrong as Dotty. They were aware that Connie was keeping a sharp eye on things, and knew that she would come to the rescue if need be.

Meanwhile, Dotty began to put into practice some of the good resolutions she had made in the hospital. Within a month of her return, the ducks had been dispatched and their remains rested in the deep freezer of the Lulling butcher. Jeremy was the doting owner of two rabbits: ('Of the same sex, *please*' Phyllida had begged), and although Paul Young could not take on any more pets as he was now away at school during term time, he knew someone in Lulling who would give two more rabbits a kind home. Some of the more elderly chickens ended their lives humanely and became boiling fowls for Dotty's friends, and very soon the animal population at Dotty's home was halved.

She was philosophical about these changes, and also did her best to feed herself more adequately. She had promised Doctor Lovell that she would sit down at midday to eat a meal.

'Even if it is only a boiled egg and some milky coffee,' he told her. 'You'll be back in hospital if you neglect yourself. And after the meal, you are to lie down on the bed for a full hour. Understand?'

The threat of hospital kept Dotty obedient to his demands, although she found it a terrible waste of time. But gone were the days, she realised, when she chewed an apple for lunch as she stood by the stove stirring the chicken's mash.

Lying down on her bed seemed even worse – positively sinful to be so slothful. However, she found that she frequently fell asleep during her enforced rest, and so grudgingly admitted that young Doctor Lovell must be speaking the truth when he said that she would be bound to tire easily for some time.

Still, she told herself, with every day that passed she must be getting stronger, and with Albert to manage Dulcie, and kind friends rallying to her support, she told herself that everything would be back to normal in no time.

Albert Piggott's daughter, Molly Curdle, was particularly pleased to see the improvement in her father's health.

'You know,' she said to Ben one evening, 'it's not just the milk that's setting him up. It's having a job that he likes.'

'Well, it certainly seems to suit the old boy,' agreed Ben.

'And I've a feeling he'd be better off helping out with animals round here somewhere, than trying to keep the church going.'

'It'd be ideal. I know he don't really pull his weight as sexton, and never has, to tell the truth. But these days some of the work's too heavy for the old chap. I wondered if we might have a word about it with Mr Henstock. What d'you think?'

Ben looked thoughtful.

'Best have a talk to your Dad first in case he cuts up rough. Might think you're interfering. But if he don't mind, I'll speak to the rector. I reckon he might be pleased to get someone to take proper care of the church and graveyard. At the moment they're both a shocking sight. Coke crunching underfoot whenever you walk in church, and weeds up to your knees round the graves. It must vex the rector, and plenty'd complain, but you know Mr Henstock! Too good by half!'

'I'll speak to Dad this week,' promised Molly.

To her relief, Albert agreed with uncommon docility that the work was too much for him, and that he would welcome some help. He was not quite so keen to accede to Molly's suggestion that more work with animals might be found, if he liked the idea.

'Depends what sort of animals,' he said. 'I ain't going to Percy Hodge's, for instance, to muck out his cow shed. That'd be jumpin' from the frying pan into the fire. But I don't mind helping out with pets like Miss Harmer's.'

'Well, I'm sure Mr Henstock will have some ideas,' said Molly hastily. 'Ben might mention it when he sees him.'

Charles Henstock was as pleased as Molly at the turn of events. For a long time he had realised that his curmudgeonly sexton and caretaker was not doing the job satisfactorily. He had hesitated to call him to account for two reasons. First, was there anyone else willing to take on the work, and second, would Albert be hurt to be thought incapable of carrying on?

With Ben's disclosures it was plain that the second difficulty was overcome. If Albert were given the lighter duties, such as sweeping, dusting and cleaning the silver and brasswork, then the outside duties in the graveyard, and the heavy work of keeping the boiler filled with coke, could be offered to a younger and more energetic man.

'The snag is,' said Ben, voicing the rector's fears, 'there don't seem to be many suitable chaps available. Of course, Bobby Cooke has given our Dad a hand now and again in the past — but them Cookes — ' His voice trailed away.

The rector replied cheerfully.

'Well, I know that the Cookes as a family do tend to be a little *feckless*, but Bobby as the eldest child was always more *reliable*. Poor Mrs Cooke had so many children, and so fast, you know, that I think the later arrivals were somewhat neglected.'

No one, thought Ben, could have put the Cookes' case so kindly as the rector. On the whole, the tribe was dismissed as dirty, dishonest and a disgrace to Nidden and Thrush Green.

'And I happen to know,' went on the good rector, 'that poor Bobby Cooke was made redundant — if that is the correct expression — last week, from the corn merchant's. He may be glad to take on some of Albert's duties. I could certainly find out.'

'I'm sure you'll do what's right, sir,' said Ben. 'It would be a great weight off our shoulders if we could see the old man settled.'

'I shall do my best,' said Charles. 'And how is Molly keeping? When is the baby due?'

'Around Christmas,' Ben said.

'Ah! Then I shall look forward to a christening in the New Year. Another little Curdle to greet! We still remember your wonderful grandmother here, Ben.'

'I never forget her. Never for a day,' replied Ben soberly.

And Charles Henstock knew that this serious young fellow was speaking the truth.

After a remarkably dry summer, the latter part of August turned cold and wet.

Luckily, the bulk of the corn crop was gathered in, and although strongly denied by the local farmers it had been a good year.

Not, of course, that this made the farmers happy. A good harvest meant that prices would be low, and that ruin faced them. A poor harvest meant that they had little to sell and so, equally, ruin faced them. Farmers have always had hard lives.

'No good trying to please 'em,' declared Albert in The Two Pheasants. 'If the weather's right for the turnips, it's all wrong for the wheat. And if the sun shines for hay-making, it's too dry for the kale to grow. Farmers is kittle-cattle, to my way of thinking. Always on the moan.'

'He can talk,' observed one to his neighbour, but he said it behind his hand. 'Is that what Percy Hodge does?' he enquired more loudly. 'Moan, I mean?'

There was general laughter.

'Percy's too taken up with that Doris up The Drovers' Arms to worry over much about harvest this year. Come October I'll bet he's getting wed, with all the other young farming chaps.'

'But his Gertie's not cold in her grave,' cried one.

'She's been gone over a year,' said his drinking companion. 'I bet that house of Percy's could do with a spring clean by now.'

'His sister, Mrs Jenner, goes in now and again, they tell me. She'll see him right. Pity Jenny wouldn't take him on, but then why should she?'

'If you ask me,' said Albert, although nobody had, 'girls is too choosy by half these days. Comes of learning 'em the same as boys. They wants a good wage, see, and forgets they ought to be glad to look after a good husband for the love of it.'

There was a short silence after Albert's little speech. Most of them were thinking privately of Albert's wife Nelly. She certainly hadn't had a good husband, and one could hardly blame her for leaving Albert's abode to take up residence with that oil man chap who, though markedly unpopular with the males in Thrush Green, seemed to have had a way with the women.

And that, both sexes would agree, was a quality singularly lacking in Albert Piggott.

'Well,' said one at last, putting his tankard down, 'I'd best get back to work.'

He opened the door, and a squall of wind and rain blew in.

'Looks like summer's gone,' he commented, as he went out into the wet.

Rain streamed down the windows of the local school house as Miss Watson and Miss Fogerty unpacked after their holiday.

They had returned much refreshed, although little progress had been made with their plans for buying a house. However, they had met several house agents who promised to keep them informed about suitable properties as they became available, and from what the two ladies had seen they were even more sure that Barton and its immediate neighbourhood would suit them both very well. Their efforts had not been wasted.

'How lucky we were to have such a fine spell,' remarked Agnes, gazing out at the driving rain veiling the houses on the farther side of Thrush Green. 'Somehow I don't mind a bit if we get rain now. It's quite restful, isn't it?'

'It is while we're still on holiday, Agnes dear. But quite a different kettle of fish if it continues into the beginning of term next week. You know how fractious infants get if they are cooped up indoors.'

'I do indeed,' said little Miss Fogerty, with feeling. 'By the way, I've sorted out the post, and your letters are on the dresser. Not much for me, I'm thankful to say, but a pretty card from Isobel's daughter on holiday in Ceylon. Always so thoughtful.'

'You mean Sri Lanka,' corrected Dorothy, turning her attention to the pile of letters.

'I shall always think of it as Ceylon,' said Agnes, with gentle dignity. 'Fancy asking one's friends if they would like China or Sri Lanka tea!'

It was an hour or so later, when the two ladies were enjoying a cup of the latter, that Dorothy opened the letter from her brother Ray.

'Well!' she exclaimed, putting down her cup with a crash. 'Of all the effrontery! Really, Agnes, Ray and Kathleen would try the patience of a saint! Do you know what Ray is asking?'

She tapped the letter with her teaspoon.

'Listen to this: "If you are getting rid of any of your furniture when you move, would you please let us have first refusal of the following." And then, my dear, he gives a list of about *twenty* of my best pieces of furniture! What a cheek! What a nerve! I've a good mind to ring him — after six, of course – and tell him what I think of his grasping ways.'

Agnes, recognising the flushed cheeks and heaving cardigan as danger signals, assumed her most soothing air.

'Don't upset yourself over such a thing. I should ignore the letter, and if he writes again, or telephones, you can answer him then.'

'I expect you are right,' conceded Miss Watson, stuffing the objectionable message into the envelope. 'And in any case, now that the telephone charges have gone up again, it would be a most expensive call.'

'Have another cup of tea,' said Miss Fogerty diplomatically, and refilled the cup.

Across the green, Phyllida Hurst was also drinking tea, with Winnie Bailey. She had called to deliver the parish magazine, and had been divested of her dripping mackintosh and persuaded to stop for a while.

'Have you heard this rumour about Albert getting some help with the church?' asked Phil.

'Dimity said it's pretty certain that Bobby Cooke is going to do the heavy stuff. Albert seems to be past digging graves and humping coke about.'

'Wasn't he always?'

Winnie laughed.

'Well, he hasn't exactly strained himself over any of his duties, all the time I've known him, but I think he really does need some help now. The Cooke boy is as strong as an ox.'

'And about as bright, I'm told.'

'At least he's honest,' responded Winnie, 'and you can't say that about the rest of the family.'

'And speaking of church matters, is there anything in this tale about Anthony Bull leaving St John's?'

'I've heard nothing except from Bertha Lovelock, and it's

my belief she's got hold of the wrong end of the stick. Not that one would be surprised to hear of his advancement. He's much too decorative and ambitious to stay long here, I fear. He always reminds me of dear Owen Nares.'

'I never came across him,' confessed Phil.

Winnie sighed.

'It's at times like this that I realise how old I'm getting,' she said. 'But what's your news? Any more lecture tours?'

'Yes indeed. They want us to go again next year. I'm not sure if I shall accompany Frank though. In any case, we don't intend to let the house again. That was rather a disaster I feel.'

'No harm done,' Winnie assured her. 'And don't forget, I will caretake very willingly. And Jenny will help too. It's a great relief to me that she is still with me.'

'And likely to remain here, I imagine,' said Phil, getting

up. 'I must be on my way, rain or no rain. We see Percy sometimes ploughing along with a nice bunch of roses for Jenny's successor. Does she mind, do you think?'

'Frankly, I believe she's relieved. It was an embarrassment to her to have the poor fellow calling here so often, and she's quite sincere, I'm sure, in saying that she's happier as she is.'

'It's all worked out well then,' replied Phil. 'Better to be single than unhappily married,' she added as she went into the porch.

Winnie watched her splash down the path.

'Poor Phil,' she thought. 'She knows all about an unhappy marriage. Thank goodness this second one has turned out so satisfactorily.'

The rain grew heavier as darkness fell, and by ten o'clock a strong wind added to the unpleasantness of the night.

It tore the leaves from the horsechestnut trees on Thrush Green, and buffeted Nathaniel Patten as he stood on his plinth, gazing with sightless eyes upon his windswept birthplace. It howled round the grave-stones in St Andrew's churchyard and screamed down the alleyway by Albert Piggott's cottage.

The signboard at The Two Pheasants creaked as it swung, and very few inhabitants of Thrush Green dared to open a window more than a slit in the face of such violence.

Charles Henstock, lying awake at Nidden, listened to the tapping of the plum tree's branches against the window pane. The old house creaked now and again, and occasionally gave a shudder as the full force of the gale caught it, but it stood as sturdily four-square as it had done for centuries, and it was a comfort to be in such a solidly constructed building.

There was no doubt about it, Charles told himself, he had grown uncommonly fond of this ancient farmhouse and would miss its mellow beauty when they had to leave. Of course, a new house would have advantages, but there was something about an old loved house, where generations had lived, which gave one a comforting sense of continuity.

He realised now that his old rectory had never provided such a consolation to the spirit. It was not only the bleakness of its position and its poorly planned interior. This earlier house, where now he awaited sleep beside his slumbering wife, had an indefinable feeling of happiness. Perhaps builders in Georgian times enjoyed their work more than their Victorian successors? Perhaps the families who had lived here were contented with their lot, and their happiness had left its mark? Whatever the cause, Charles thanked God for giving him this pleasant place in which to recover from the shock of that disastrous fire.

He hoped for, but was too modest to pray for, as pleasant a home in the future, but was confident that by putting his fate in God's hands all would be for the best. He was sorry that Dimity worried about the delay. He knew that most men in his position would press for information about any proposed plans, and would make demands about their rights.

Charles knew, as Dimity knew, that he was incapable of behaving in such a way. Before long, he would hear something. God would never desert him.

He remembered the story of the falling sparrow, turned his face into the pillow and, ignoring the storm raging outside, was comforted.

The next morning, the garden was littered with wet leaves and twigs.

Willie Marchant splashed up Mrs Jenner's path, and put a letter through the box.

The rector opened it carefully at the breakfast table. It was a beautiful thick cream-coloured envelope and bore a crest on the back.

The letter was short, and Dimity, watching its effect on her husband, felt some alarm.

'My dear,' said Charles, 'the Bishop wants to see me next Thursday afternoon. He doesn't say much, but I expect it is to do with the rearrangement of the parishes.'

'What time?' asked Dimity.

'Two-thirty, he says.'

'Well, I'll come too and you can drop me in the market square. I've so much shopping to do it will keep me busy while you are gallivanting with the Bishop.'

'I don't suppose we'll be *gallivanting*,' said Charles, smiling. 'But I've no doubt you will be able to get in two hours' shopping quite comfortably.'

And so the matter was left.

THE start of the new school year fell on the following Tuesday and, as the two friends feared, the wet weather still shrouded Thrush Green with veils of windswept rain.

Miss Fogerty's new arrivals were unusually tearful, and there were one or two trying mothers who wanted to stay with their offspring until they had cheered up. Little Miss Fogerty, who had been coping with the reception class for more years than she cared to remember, had great difficulty in shooing them away. She knew perfectly well that once their mothers had vanished the howlers would desist from their lamenting and would resign themselves, after vigorous nose-blowing organised by Miss Fogerty, to threading beads, making plasticine crumpets, or having a ride on the rocking horse.

But within an hour, peace reigned in the infants' room and Miss Fogerty had pinned up the weather chart, found two clean Virol jars to receive the bunches of asters and marigolds brought by the children, and decided to appoint George Curdle as blackboard monitor.

Dear George, for whom Miss Fogerty had a very soft spot, was becoming rather boastful about the new sister he was hoping for at the end of term, and a little energetic board cleaning might channel his energies usefully, thought his teacher. Besides, he would have the inestimable privilege of going outside with the board rubber now and again to free it

of excessive chalk dust by banging it briskly against the
school wall. To be appointed board monitor was recognised
as an honour. George Curdle, she felt sure, would perform his
duties with proper zeal.

Next door, Miss Watson's older children were busy writing their names on the covers of their new exercise books,
exhorted by their teacher to be neat and clear in their
calligraphy.

While they were thus seriously engaged, Miss Watson
surveyed the rain-drenched view through the window and
wondered if she would write or telephone to the office when
informing them of her decision to retire. Of course, the
formal resignation would be written, well in advance of the
specified three months' notice required, but as her mind was
now made up it would be helpful, no doubt, to the office to
know her plans well ahead.

She turned to look at the bent hands, the carefully guided
pens and the odd tongue protruding with the effort involved.
Her last class! After all these years, her very last class!

Well, they looked a nice little lot, and she would do her
level best by them. But a warm glow suffused her when she
thought that this time next year she would probably be
looking through the window of some charming little place at
Barton, and admiring the sea in the distance.

Thrush Green had been a happy place to work in, and had
brought her the ineffable good fortune of meeting dear
Agnes, but she would not be sorry to go. A complete change
of scene would do them both good, and Thrush Green, after
all, would still be waiting for them whenever they wished to
pay a visit to their old friends.

'I can see some *beautiful* writing,' said Miss Watson,
limping down the aisle towards her desk. 'I think we are
going to do some good work in here this year.'

*

Molly Curdle, dusting her flat at the top of the Youngs' lovely house, wondered if the rain would stop in time for George and the other children to have their break in the playground.

He had run off on his own to school this morning, looking forward to seeing his friends and Miss Fogerty again. No doubt, he'd be blabbing to all and sundry about the new baby, thought Molly resignedly. Not that she worried unduly. Most people knew now, anyway, that a second child was coming. She only hoped that it would be as amenable and happy as George.

Strange to think that in five years' time another little Curdle would be running to Thrush Green School! Who would be there to teach them then? Not Miss Watson and Miss Fogerty from all she had heard.

But of one thing she felt certain. She and Ben would still be at Thrush Green whatever occurred. In all his years of wandering with his grandmother's fair, this place was the nearest he had had as a settled home. Now old Mrs Curdle lay in the churchyard, and her grandson and great-grandson lived close by. Molly prayed that they might never have to move again.

She stooped, with some difficulty now that her pregnancy was advancing, and attended to the legs of the chairs. This afternoon, rain or no rain, she must go across to see her father and collect his washing, and hear his news.

Sometimes she wished that Nelly, trollop though she was, would return to look after her husband, but there was small chance of that, thought Molly, and one could hardly expect it.

Well, things could be a lot worse. She had her health and strength, and Ben was happy in his work.

If this new baby was a boy she was determined to call him

Benjamin after his father. Ben had said it would be muddling to have two of the same name, but Molly was adamant.

'You can't have too much of a good thing,' she had told him. 'He'll be Ben – another Ben.'

'With any luck,' he had replied, 'it'll be a girl.'

Albert was newly returned from The Two Pheasants when his daughter called early that afternoon.

'Was just about to have a nap,' he grumbled. 'Come for the washin'?'

'That's right, dad. How's the job? Seen young Cooke yet?'

Albert grunted.

'Ah! He's coming down one evenin' this week, so he says, to see what needs doing. Rector's coming too, and we're goin' to sort things out then.'

'What about wages? Will you have to share now with Bob Cooke?'

'Seems I'll be havin' a bit less, but that's only fair if I'm not doin' the work. Anyway, old Dotty's paying me well for the milking, and the rector wanted to know if I'd take on odd jobs like feeding people's hens and cats and that when they're on holiday. I've said I'll see to young Jeremy's rabbits when they go to Wales at Christmas – that sort of thing. Suit me fine, that will. Probably make as much like that as digging the dratted graves in this 'ere clay.'

Molly doubted it but kept her counsel. In any case, the old man's temper was better than it had been for many a long year which was all that really mattered.

'And Jones next door said he could always do with a hand with the empty beer crates at closing time, so I shall have plenty to do.'

'Will you get paid for that?' asked Molly suspiciously.

'Well, not in hard cash, like,' admitted Albert. 'More in kind.'

'I was afraid of that,' said Molly, picking up the bundle of washing.

After tea, the rain ceased. The clouds scudded from the west, leaving a strip of clear sky on the horizon. Lulling Woods stood out clearly, navy blue against the golden strip, and Jenny, looking from her window, guessed that tomorrow would bring a fine day. Perhaps she could take down the landing curtains? It would soon be the end of summer, she thought sadly, and time to put up the velvet curtains again to keep out the bitter winds of a Cotswold winter.

As she stood surveying the scene, a well-known figure trudged into sight from the lane to Nidden.

In earlier times, Jenny's heart would have sunk, for without doubt the man would have turned left along the chestnut avenue to approach her house.

Now, to her relief, she saw that Percy Hodge was plodding straight ahead, past The Two Pheasants, no doubt on his way to see his new love, Doris.

He was carrying a basket this evening. What delectable present was in it this time, Jenny wondered. A chicken, perhaps? A dozen pearly eggs? Some early plums? Whatever it was, Doris was more than welcome, thought Jenny cheerfully. She only hoped that Percy's second attempt at wooing would end successfully.

She remembered with amusement what Bessie had forecast. 'He'll soon find someone else,' she had said, 'if he's as nice a man as you say he is.'

Well, thank goodness he had found someone, decided Jenny. Whether he would be married again before the year was out, as her old friend had surmised, was in the lap of the gods, but at least she would be relieved to know that dear old Percy was settled.

She watched him turn down the lane by Albert Piggott's on his way to Lulling Woods and Doris.

And with a sigh of relief, and no regrets at all, Jenny turned back to her happy solitude.

Jenny's weather forecast was correct. The rain had gone, leaving a sodden countryside and dripping trees and gutters, but above the sky was clear and blue and there was a freshness in the air that made one think of autumn.

'Bit parky coming along,' cried Betty Bell, bursting in upon Harold and Isobel Shoosmith still at the kitchen breakfast table. 'Are you late or am I?'

'We've been taking our time,' replied Isobel. 'Lots of letters this morning. But we've finished now, and we'll get out of your way.'

'No hurry,' said Betty. 'I called to see Miss Harmer as I came by. Actually, I popped in last night after I'd done the school. She don't look right to me.'

'Oh dear! Is she eating properly?'

'Seems to be. I mean, she'd got a bowl of cornflakes this morning with some brown sugar on it, and Dulcie's milk. Nourishing, I should think, if you can face goat's milk and brown sugar. Which I can't, and that's a fact.'

'Shall I go down there, Betty?'

'I don't think I would today. She'd think I'd been telling tales, see? Anyway, Miss Connie comes this afternoon, and stays there tonight, so she'll have company.'

Betty tugged off her coat and hung it on a peg on the back of the kitchen door.

'If you haven't got any particular plans for me,' she said, 'I thought I'd have a bash at the china ornaments in the drawing room. They look a bit grubby.'

As the china ornaments were Chinese porcelain, very old, beautiful and valuable, it was hardly surprising that Harold winced. 'Having a bash' was exactly how Betty attacked her work.

Isobel, with habitual aplomb, coped beautifully with this kind offer.

'I'd rather hoped to turn out the spare room today, Betty. I'll come up and help you turn the mattress and we'll make up the bed.'

'Right,' said Betty, rummaging in the cupboard for the carpet sweeper, handbrush, dustpan, polish, dusters and other equipment for the onslaught. 'See you pronto.'

She lugged the paraphernalia into the hall, and then returned.

'You know them two next door are going to leave next year?'

'Yes,' said Harold, folding his newspaper.

'And Albert Piggott's givin' up half his job?'

'Yes,' said Harold.

'And the Hursts are going to America again?'

Harold nodded.

'And they're not going to put up another house for poor Mr Henstock? Ain't it *mean*? There's going to be an ugly great clinic place there. Heard anything about that?'

'Not a word,' said Harold, rising from the breakfast table. 'And you don't want to believe all you hear, Betty.'

'Sorry I spoke!' said Betty, flouncing from the room.

Husband and wife exchanged rueful glances.

Charles Henstock polished his old car during the morning, ready to visit the Bishop promptly at two-thirty.

The Bishop detested unpunctuality and was not above saying so. Charles respected the great man's principles, and was determined not to offend.

'Let me just see how you look, dear,' Dimity said, before they set off.

She scrutinised her husband from his pink and shiny bald head to his old but gleaming shoes.

'Very nice, Charles, but do remember to pull up your socks before you go in. The Bishop is always so beautifully turned out. He's as immaculate as Anthony Bull, and that's saying something.'

'Anthony has a great advantage. He is a fine-looking fellow. Anything would look well on him. The last time I saw him he was tending his bonfire, and he still looked as though he had just emerged from a band box.'

Dimity privately thought that Anthony Bull's stipend allowed him to buy expensive suits made by his tailor, while dear Charles was obliged to purchase his off the peg. However, she did not voice this unworthy thought.

'Well, you look very well yourself,' she told Charles comfortingly, 'and now we must be off.'

The rain had freshened the countryside, and the shabby hedgerows of late summer were now sparkling with moisture. Already the ploughs were out, turning over the bright stubble into long wet chocolate furrows.

Dimity noted the yellowing leaves already showing on the beech and wild plum trees. Soon autumn would be upon them, and although she loved the mellowness, the rich colouring and the joys of bringing in the harvest fruit and vegetables, she felt a little shiver of apprehension about the cold weather to come.

The rectory had always been so bleak. Surely, wherever they went would be more comfortable than their last domain!

Perhaps the Bishop would give Charles some firm idea of his plans for their new home. It was certainly most disconcerting to be kept in such suspense.

However, Charles knew her views well enough on this matter, and it was useless to try to make him assert himself. Charles was Charles – sweet, far too humble and a living saint. She would not have him changed one iota!

'If you drop me at the back of Debenham's,' she said, 'I can go through their bed-linen department, and you won't hold up the traffic by trying to stop at their main entrance.'

Charles did as he was told, promised to pick her up again at four o'clock, and set off, feeling a little nervous, to his appointment.

The Bishop lived in a fine red-brick house at the end of a long drive bordered with lime trees.

Charles parked his car in as unobtrusive spot as possible beside a flourishing prunus tree, and tugged at the wrought-iron bell pull by the white front door.

A very spruce maid welcomed him and showed him into the Bishop's drawing room.

'I'll tell the Bishop you are here,' said the girl. 'At the moment he is telephoning.'

She departed, leaving Charles to admire the silver cups on a side table, and the oar hanging above the fireplace. The Bishop was a great oarsman, Charles remembered, a true muscular Christian. Perhaps that contributed to his good looks, thought Charles, and bent to pull up his wrinkled socks as Dimity had told him.

The solemnly ticking grandfather clock by the door said two minutes to the half hour when Charles heard the Bishop approaching.

He stood up as the door swung open.

'My dear fellow! I hope I haven't kept you waiting. You are wonderfully punctual. Come into my study. We'll be unmolested there.'

He strode through the hall, followed by the good rector who admired the clerical grey suit which clothed those broad shoulders and neat waist.

He certainly was a handsome fellow.

But at least, thought Charles, I remembered to pull up my socks.

Connie Harmer arrived at much the same time as the Bishop invited Charles to take a seat in the study.

She found her aunt resting obediently on her bed, kissed her affectionately and enquired after her progress.

Connie's expression was as calm and competent as ever, but inwardly she was much alarmed. Dotty looked old and haggard. Her lips and cheeks wore a purplish tinge. She was definitely vaguer in manner than at her last visit.

'I'm dying for a cup of coffee,' said Connie, pulling off her driving gloves. 'I'll bring you one too.'

Dotty nodded dreamily in agreement, and Connie went downstairs.

Her first job was to ring Doctor Lovell. His receptionist promised to tell him the minute he returned from his rounds. Then she put on the kettle, and thought hard while it came to the boil.

Well, the time had come. She had made her plans, and friends had offered a good price for her house and land. Aunt Dot had always been good to her, and she could live very happily here in her cottage, bringing only a few of her most cherished animals to share the rest of their lives with Dotty's.

She carried the tray upstairs and put it down on the bedside table.

'There we are, Aunt Dot. And when you've finished it, we're going to have a little talk about the future.'

At four o'clock Dimity waited in the vestibule at the rear entrance of Debenham's, surrounded by parcels.

Charles arrived soon after and they piled everything into the back of the car in great haste, as a van man drew up, practically touching Charles's back bumper with his own, and putting his head out of the window to address the rector.

From his accent he would appear to be a Glaswegian, thought Charles, and so — perhaps fortunately — his message was entirely incomprehensible to southern-English ears. His demeanour, however, was threatening and abusive, and Charles and Dimity were relieved to drive off.

'I was going to suggest that we had a cup of tea at Debenham's,' said Charles, 'but it wasn't a good place to park evidently. We'll stop at the Oak Tearooms instead. Anyway, they have quite the best toasted tea cake in the district.'

Dimity knew better than to question her husband while he was driving in traffic, and it was not until they were safely ensconced among the oak panelling and chintz curtaining of the renowned tea rooms that she began.

'And how did you find the dear Bishop?'

'As upstanding as ever. He enquired most kindly after you. Ah! Here comes the girl!'

The girl was approximately the same age as the rector, must have weighed thirteen stone, and was dressed in a rather tight flowered coat overall.

'Could we have some of your delicious toasted tea cake? And a pot of China tea for two?'

The waitress wrote busily on a little pad.

'Any jam, honey or other preserve? We have our home-made apricot, mulberry and quince.

'How lovely that sounds!' cried Dimity. 'Like a list of jams from Culpeper!'

'We only keep our own, madam,' said the girl with some hauteur.

'Then shall we try mulberry, dear?' asked Dimity. 'I don't think I've ever had it.'

The waitress added MJ to her pad and departed.

'And now tell me, what happened, Charles?'

The rector began to look quite shy.

'Did you know that Anthony Bull is leaving Lulling?'

'Really? Now you come to mention it, I believe Bertha Lovelock said something about it.'

The rector's look of shyness was replaced by one of startled exasperation.

'But how on earth could she know? It isn't general knowledge yet!'

'Well, you know how things get about in a small community,' said Dimity soothingly. 'Anyway, where's he going? Not retiring surely?'

'Far from it. He's been appointed to a splendid living in one of the Kensington parishes. Rather High Church, I gather, and a most beautiful building. Anthony will be just the man for it, the Bishop said. I'm so glad he has got preferment. I always felt that Lulling was only a stepping stone to greater things for Anthony.'

The waitress reappeared with the tray and set out the teapot, milk jug, hot water container and a large dish covered with a silver lid.

A small bowl containing a wine-coloured confection aroused Dimity's interest.

'And this is the mulberry jam? What a beautiful colour.'

'We make it on the premises,' replied the waitress, thawing in the face of Dimity's enthusiasm. 'We have a tree in the garden. It is reputed to be a hundred and fifty years old.'

'How wonderful!'

The waitress made off again, and Dimity applied herself to pouring out the tea.

'But what about us, darling? Did he mention anything about our new house?'

'He did indeed. I think two of those sugar lumps. They seem rather small.'

'They're called *fairy* lumps, I believe,' said Dimity. 'Well, go on.'

'I'm afraid there won't be a new house, my dear.'

Dimity dropped the sugar tongs in her dismay.

'Not a new house? Then where on earth are we to go?'

Her husband had now bent down to retrieve the tongs from beneath the table. When he reappeared his face was very pink.

'To an old one, Dimity. I have been offered the living of
the four merged parishes, and we should live at Lulling
Vicarage.'

Dimity gazed at him open-mouthed.

'Charles!' she croaked at last. 'I can't believe it! That
lovely, lovely house!'

'Don't cry, Dimity! Please don't cry,' begged Charles.
'Aren't you pleased?'

Dimity unfolded a snowy handkerchief and wiped her
eyes.

'Of course I'm pleased. I'm just completely overwhelmed,
that's all. Oh, Charles dear, this is an honour you so richly
deserve. Won't it be wonderful to have our own home at
last?'

'I'm glad you are pleased. It means we shall still be among
our friends, and I shall still be able to take services at St
Andrew's.'

'And when do you take over?'

'Probably before Christmas. Anthony expects to be in-
ducted in October or November.'

'And then we shall be able to move in,' said Dimity
happily. She spread mulberry jam in reckless bounty upon a
slice of tea cake. 'What a blessing I didn't fall for some
curtaining remnants this afternoon. They would never have
done for the vicarage windows.'

She looked with surprise at the jam dish.

'Oh dear, Charles! I seem to have taken all the mulberry
preserve.'

'I think we might be able to afford some quince as well,'
said Charles. 'By way of celebration, you know.'

And he raised a plump hand to summon the girl.

AFTER the long dry summer, autumn came early to Thrush Green.

The great leaves of the chestnut avenue turned golden and soon the boys from the village school would be collecting conkers.

In the cottage gardens, Michaelmas daisies and goldenrod flourished, and Mr Jones began to wonder if his hanging baskets would last out their time before the first frosts came.

Ploughing and sowing was done, and the fields lay brown and bare. Busy housewives bottled the last of the fruit, the blackberries, the bramley apple slices, and the quartered pears, and added them to the richness of the earlier summer fruits in their store cupboards.

Ella Bembridge added two more handwoven scarves to her Christmas collection, and decided that she must buy a replacement for the tweed suit she had had for ten years, not to mention a stout pair of brogues ready for the winter.

Miss Fogerty and Miss Watson decided to go to their favourite guest house at Barton for half term at the end of October. At least three houses sounded hopeful, judging from the estate agents' information. Naturally, one expected them to over-egg the pudding a little, as Dorothy pointed out to her more trusting partner, but even so, things looked promising. It would be lovely to clinch a deal, and thank heaven they had no house of their own to dispose of, added Dorothy. With any luck, they should have a place of their own before the winter had passed.

The news of Charles's new appointment gave enormous pleasure to everyone.

'The ideal man!' said Harold. 'The Bishop's done the right thing.'

'And we shan't really lose you,' as Ella said to them both. 'I mean, you'll be nipping up to take early service just as usual, and Dimity can still get the crib ready for Christmas at St Andrew's.'

Connie Harmer arrived to take up residence with her aunt during November. The old lady appeared to be delighted at the arrangement, and her doctor and friends who had feared that she might suddenly dig in her heels and refuse to countenance any change in her way of life, breathed sighs of relief and welcomed Connie in their midst. Dotty herself was so absorbed in the half a dozen new animals of Connie's that her health seemed to be much improved, though, no doubt, as Betty Bell pointed out, Connie's cooking, which was first-class, had a hand in the old lady's improvement.

Doris, at The Drovers' Arms, displayed a pretty engagement ring, and Percy Hodge put up the banns at the end of November.

'And thank heaven for that!' said Jenny to Winnie. 'I must write and tell Bessie she was dead right!'

Albert Piggott continued to help at Dotty's and elsewhere when needed, and also found time to supervise Bobby Cooke's church duties. The young man received rather more kicks than ha'pence, but his upbringing had inured him to such discomforts and he seemed happy enough.

The most encouraging news for Thrush Green and Lulling came one afternoon at the beginning of December when a notice appeared on the door of The Fuchsia Bush in Lulling High Street.

'*This establishment will be open from* 9.30 *a.m. until* 6.00 *p.m. in future*' read the astonished passers-by.

'I hear they hope to get the Christmas shoppers in,' said Miss Bertha.

'And I heard that those evening meals never really caught on,' added Miss Violet.

'About time they realised that it is *tea* people want,' said Miss Ada, voicing the view of all.

It was during the last few frenzied days of Christmas shopping, when The Fuchsia Bush was certainly doing a roaring trade from four o'clock onwards, that Molly Curdle's baby was born.

'Just think,' said Winnie Bailey to Jenny. 'It weighed nine pounds!'

'Poor thing!' said Jenny. 'But at least it's a girl. I know Ben hoped it would be. I wonder what they'll call it? It was going to be another Ben, if it had been a boy.'

'I have a shrewd idea that it will be "Anne" after Ben's dear old grandma,' said Winnie. 'If she grows up as splendid as her namesake she won't hurt.'

One mild January afternoon a small entourage walked out from the Youngs' gate.

Skipping ahead was young George Curdle, unnaturally clean and tidy, from his watered-down hair to his well-polished shoes.

Behind him walked his mother, holding the new baby well-wrapped in the beautiful old shawl which had first enveloped Ben himself. Beyond his parents came Joan and Edward Young and Mrs Bassett, Joan's mother. Her father had promised to come to the christening tea, but did not feel equal to standing at the ceremony.

The air was soft and mild. It had a hint of springtime in it, and some early snowdrops and aconites, near the churchyard gate, made an encouraging sight. Against the church wall a shower of winter flowering jasmine spilled its yellow flowers.

As Ben passed his grandmother's tombstone he patted it approvingly, noting the name and date anew.

'Pity she can't be here to see this one named for her,' he said to his wife.

'Maybe she knows anyway,' was her reply, as they passed into the church porch.

CHRISTIAN HERALD ASSOCIATION AND ITS MINISTRIES

CHRISTIAN HERALD ASSOCIATION, founded in 1878, publishes The Christian Herald Magazine, one of the leading interdenominational religious monthlies in America. Through its wide circulation, it brings inspiring articles and the latest news of religious developments to many families. From the magazine's pages came the initiative for CHRISTIAN HERALD CHILDREN'S HOME and THE BOWERY MISSION, two individually supported not-for-profit corporations.

CHRISTIAN HERALD CHILDREN'S HOME, established in 1894, is the name for a unique and dynamic ministry to disadvantaged children, offering hope and opportunities which would not otherwise be available for reasons of poverty and neglect. The goal is to develop each child's potential and to demonstrate Christian compassion and understanding to children in need.

Mont Lawn is a permanent camp located in Bushkill, Pennsylvania. It is the focal point of a ministry which provides a healthful "vacation with a purpose" to children who without it would be confined to the streets of the city. Up to 1000 children between the ages of 7 and 11 come to Mont Lawn each year.

Christian Herald Children's Home maintains year-round contact with children by means of an *In-City Youth Ministry*. Central to its philosophy is the belief that only through sustained relationships and demonstrated concern can individual lives be truly enriched. Special emphasis is on individual guidance, spiritual and family counseling and tutoring. This follow-up ministry to inner-city children culminates for many in financial assistance toward higher education and career counseling.

THE BOWERY MISSION, located at 227 Bowery, New York City, has since 1879 been reaching out to the lost men on the Bowery, offering them what could be their last chance to rebuild their lives. Every man is fed, clothed and ministered to. Countless numbers have entered the 90-day residential rehabilitation program at the Bowery Mission. A concentrated ministry of counseling, medical care, nutrition therapy, Bible study and Gospel services awakens a man to spiritual renewal within himself.

These ministries are supported solely by the voluntary contributions of individuals and by legacies and bequests. Contributions are tax deductible. Checks should be made out either to CHRISTIAN HERALD CHILDREN'S HOME or to THE BOWERY MISSION.

Administrative Office: 40 Overlook Drive, Chappaqua, New York 10514
Telephone: (914) 769-9000